The Roosevelt Rescue

Restoring Dutch America

The Roosevelt Rescue

Restoring Dutch America

Zachary Finch

This book is a work of fiction. All characters, locations, and events are the product of the author's imagination or used fictitiously.

All descriptions of historical situations are based on facts. Any inaccuracies are solely attributable to the author, who thanks readers for comments that lead to the improvement of this book. zacharyfinchlit@gmail.com

ISBN-13: 9782955610206
ISBN-10: 2955610208

For my love, Natercia

Time Line (AD)

500–1000	Anglo-Saxons settle in England
1568	Start of the Dutch Revolt—fight for independence from Spain
1579	Union of Utrecht—cooperation of northern Dutch provinces
1581	Act of Abjuration—Dutch declaration of independence from Spain
1588	The Republic of the Seven United Netherlands is founded
1609	Henry Hudson discovers Manhattan
1652–1654	First Anglo-Dutch War
1653–1658	Cromwell reigns over England
1660	English Restoration—Charles II king of England
1664	King Charles II grants American territories to his brother James, the Duke of York
1664	Colonel Richard Nicolls captures New Amsterdam, which is renamed New York
1665–1667	Second Anglo-Dutch War
1667	Treaty of Breda—England keeps New York
1673–1674	Third Anglo-Dutch War—New York is recaptured by Holland and renamed "New Orange"

1674	Treaty of Westminster—New York is transferred to England
1685	King Charles II dies; Duke of York becomes King James II
1688	Glorious Revolution begins—William III of Orange becomes King of England (1689)
1747	Dutch position of *stadtholder* becomes hereditary
1776	American Declaration of Independence
1777	American Articles of Confederation
1780	GDP of Britain surpasses the Netherlands'
1780–1784	Fourth Anglo-Dutch War
1782	John Adams ambassador to the Netherlands—Treaty of Amity and Commerce between the United States and the Netherlands
1789	French Revolution
1795	End of the Dutch Republic; founding of Batavian Republic
1797	John Adams becomes President of the United States
1806–1813	The Netherlands under French rule
1815	The Netherlands becomes a kingdom under King William I
1837	Martin Van Buren becomes President of the United States
1933	Franklin Delano Roosevelt becomes President of the United States
1945	FDR dies
1948	Juliana becomes queen of the Netherlands
1962	Eleanor Roosevelt dies
1980	Beatrix becomes queen of the Netherlands

Prologue

Gloved hands put the heavy paper letter in an envelope, which was subsequently wax sealed with crafty gestures, ready to start its long journey by diplomatic mail. Centuries of innovation had not changed much about the way nations exchanged top-secret correspondence.

The letter traveled the same route as its equally explosive predecessors: from the city of The Hague in the Netherlands, across the Atlantic, to the capital of the United States of America. That destination had changed slightly over time: in colonial times, America's first de facto capital was still using its original Dutch name, New Amsterdam. That name had long since been changed into New York City, while Washington, DC, had replaced that city as the capital. And the wooden sailing ships that had once maintained a regular connection between Holland and America had, of course, been replaced by airplanes.

After the letter had reached the Dutch embassy in Washington, DC, it was picked up for hand delivery by a diplomatic courier, immune from arrest and detention. Under normal circumstances, the courier would have delivered it to the State Department, responsible for the international relations of the United States. But there was a particularity to this letter, so the courier had instructions to deliver it directly to the White House instead.

The White House's Mail Support and Operations Division performed the compulsory security checks, scanned the letter, and logged it into the database. Without much hesitation it was identified as important enough to be read by the President personally, and together with only a handful of other documents, it was placed on the trolley for this purpose.

At the habitual hour, the trolley was rolled over the thick carpet in the direction of the world's most important office. Inside the Oval Office, awaiting final delivery to the President, the trolley with the letter was placed in front of a bust ornamenting a corner of the office—the bust with the very concerned face of Franklin D. Roosevelt.

Part I

1

Attorney Daniel Van Wart had just committed the most terrible of all crimes. Even if the act had lasted only ten minutes, it was the last thing someone in his position was supposed to do. He had slept.

He looked hazily in the mirror and saw his tired face staring back at him. The same confident, small blue eyes as always, but this time they were blood laced and had large grayish rings around them. He splashed some cold water on his face to accelerate the process of waking up.

He had done it before: lock himself up inside a restroom stall, lean against the wall, close his eyelids, and let himself be carried away on a roller coaster of sleep. The waking up was always a somewhat-scary moment: so intense was the sleep that afterward, his mental computer had to "reboot," taking some time to remember who and where he was. But as always, the tiny nap had done wonders. *Thank you, Grandmother,* he thought. It was she who had taught him the secret of the power nap.

Although mentally he had renewed energy, physically he was still completely exhausted. It was no surprise, after three short nights in a row. Very short nights.

From the restrooms, he walked back along the shining corridor to the reception desk and hoped that the receptionists in front of the discrete letters GOLDMAN SACHS had not become suspicious of his prolonged stay in the washroom. And he hoped even more that he would not come across one of the men from the meeting upstairs. During that meeting, which had taken all night, they had put him in an extremely awkward position. He shivered when he thought of the consequences it could have for the entire project. And for him personally. The stakes were tremendous. One thing was sure: for the men in the meeting room, sleeping was intolerable now.

Daniel walked out of the building through the automatic doors and stood still for a moment, blinded by the sunlight. It was just after eight in the morning, and the first beams of sunlight found their way between the Manhattan skyscrapers that surrounded him.

He didn't remember exactly which of the men in the room had raised the point, but it had hit him right between the eyes. It concerned his part of the deal, so everyone present at the large wooden table had turned to face him—the team of his client Goldman Sachs, the bankers of the consortium, and the team of his own law firm, Stiglitz & Arrowsmith. He had realized immediately that he had never thought of the issue, and couldn't answer the quick "affirmative" that all participants had cried out when they collectively ran down the interminable Excel spreadsheet that represented the deal's checklist.

"Still under verification," he had stammered. But at this stage of the deal it was clearly the wrong answer. He wasn't used to these situations, as he kept up a reputation of impeccable preparation and research. Utter reliability and the absence of surprises was exactly why he was with the firm Stiglitz & Arrowsmith, and it was why the firm was retained by the prestigious Goldman Sachs to do most of their legal real estate deals. And in the current deal, the largest ever in the history of New York City, there was no room for error: literally the whole world was following the redevelopment of Ground Zero after the devastating 9/11 events.

"You better have that confirmed straight away!" the huge man in the corner chair had barked at him in reply.

"Of course, sir, don't worry," he had replied, begging there would be no further questions. During the next ten minutes, with a red face and temples throbbing nervously, he had thought furiously how he could ever solve this problem in such a short time. It would be impossible to check the entire history of Manhattan's ownership! Of course, it was standard practice to check a seller's legal title of ownership to the real estate the deal was about. It was the essence of his firm's involvement in the deal: giving a legal opinion on the validity of the real estate transaction. But in all the real estate deals he had worked on over the years, no one had ever really investigated the *full* historical chain of title of previous ownership. And certainly not back to colonial times! It would mean checking consecutive transactions of over more than four centuries...

While the people at the table around him had continued the deal checklist, his panic had slowly ebbed, and he got his thoughts back together. He agreed that in theory, there was an unquestionable logic to the question. Any third-party claim on the property, however unfounded, could cause a delay worth millions of dollars. That risk had to be assessed and excluded.

Daniel stepped aside to let some freshly shaven office workers enter the building. In their slipstream, he smelled the crisp odor from the coffee cups they were carrying, which electrified his tired brain.

The problem, he mused, would be to find a reliable starting point for the historical verifications. What were the first property transactions on Manhattan? He immediately realized that his family's descent gave him a lucky break here: the *Van Wart* family. The name contained the typically Dutch adjective *Van*, meaning "from," which denoted so many other Americans of Dutch descent: Vanderbilt, Van Halen, Van Dyke, and countless others. Contrary to most other Americans, Daniel had learned at least something of New York City's early history. He knew that New Amsterdam, as New York City was named initially by its Dutch founders in the seventeenth century, had been the subject of at least two major historical transactions: the first by which the Dutch governor Peter Minuit purchased the island of Manhattan for the equivalent of sixty guilders from the native Indians; and the second by which the Dutch colony was surrendered by governor Peter Stuyvesant to the English. Those deals would have to be the starting point, Daniel decided.

The next question was *where*, for heaven's sake, he could find information on those events. Because the United States didn't exist yet at that time as a nation, the agreements probably involved the Dutch authorities. It would be sheer impossible to research that part.

Unless…

A possible solution came to Daniel's mind. He quickly typed a short message labeled URGENT on his Blackberry and sent it to his colleague Evelyn at his firm's Dutch branch in Amsterdam, the Netherlands.

If only she would answer quickly!

2

Daniel left Goldman Sachs's Manhattan headquarters at 85 Broad Street and slowly walked around the corner of the building. He hesitated about what to do now. While sleeping was not an option, he could still go home and take a shower. After all, he had just finished an *all-nighter*, a term often and proudly used by his colleagues from Mergers and Acquisitions.

Indecisive, he followed the arcades of the building and stood still for a moment at the oval brass fence at the southern side. He stared down at the glass floor panels inside the fence. Noticing a curious jumble of old stones and objects visible under the glass, he wondered what it was. He looked up when an early group of obvious tourists approached the fence from the other side. Daniel quietly laughed at their outfits: a carnivalesque parade of flashy colors, some of them gift wrapped in transparent foil. While the guide waited to start his monologue, the group busily prepared their cameras for a new attack.

"Here we have arrived at the point in Manhattan where the remains of some colonial buildings are still visible," the guide explained while pointing downward. "Down here, excavations revealed the foundations of an area called Stadt Huys block, after the Dutch word for town hall. The stones you can see through the glass panels were the foundations of a tavern; the town hall itself was a couple of meters to your right, at the corner of Pearl Street."

Heads turned.

"The building became the first town hall when New Amsterdam formally obtained certain city rights in 1653. It was the place where the governors had their seat and where all official documents, land titles, and so on were kept."

Daniel couldn't believe his ears. The guide mentioned the very documents he was looking for: the land titles of early New York City!

"In fact," the guide continued, "you could say that it was from this very location that the extraordinary ascent from a tiny, far-off Dutch trading post named New Amsterdam to the mightiest city in the world, New York City, started."

Daniel, seized by the story, read the back of the guide's windbreaker: NEW YORK DUTCH HISTORICAL TOURS. He'd never heard of the existence of such tours and wondered what else was left of New York's Dutch past. He decided to continue eavesdropping some more.

"New Amsterdam closely resembled a typical village in Holland, with canals, windmills, and all. It may surprise you, but the location of the canals—or *slips*, as they were called—can still be seen in Manhattan's street plan today, where the slightly wider streets of Old Slip and Coenties Slip—the one we see in front of us—betray their previous function as waterways. The peculiar name *Coenties* is derived from Coentje Ten Eyck, a prominent merchant who had his house at this spot back in Dutch days. Not only the slips but important parts of the entire current street plan of southern Manhattan have remained unchanged; when you walk on Broadway or Wall Street, you are in fact walking on old Dutch streets, in Dutch footsteps. By the way, the name of the world's most famous street, Wall Street, refers to the defense dike—or *wal*—that the Dutch constructed at the town's limits."

Daniel was surprised; he'd never heard of this. And he noticed how the information also provoked an excited buzz among the group.

"Across the street, at the corner, you can see Fraunces Tavern. It was constructed in 1719, and its yellow bricks were all imported from Holland."

The crowd turned again, and cameras clicked. Some seconds later, one of the tourists raised his hand.

"When you say *Holland*, does that include the Netherlands?"

"Good question, but in fact it's the other way around: the Netherlands is the name of the country, and it includes Holland, its most important province. In the seventeenth century, Holland was still independent, but later on, it become synonymous with the entire country of the Netherlands. Follow me please."

Daniel waited patiently until the group had started to move. Then he slowly walked around the fence and quietly mingled with the tail of the group. He realized that with his suit, tie, and briefcase, he was the ugly duckling among them; it surely wouldn't take long before the guide would spot him and kick him out of the nest. But the story was too interesting not to try.

While walking in a westward direction, he looked back at the building he had left ten minutes ago. It was more than symbolic, he thought, that at the exact location where the Dutch traders founded America as a trading nation, Goldman Sachs, the pinnacle of capitalism, had established its head office.

Daniel regretted he'd never really studied the Dutch past of America, despite his family's Dutch roots. The only thing he knew was that Henry Hudson, an English captain in Dutch service, discovered Manhattan and explored the river that would take his name: the Hudson River. The Dutch established a small trading post on Manhattan, which would transform into New York City.

"You may never have realized it," the guide continued, "but New York City's main neighborhoods still carry Dutch names. Some were called after towns in the Netherlands: Harlem after the city of Haarlem; Flushing after Vlissingen and Brooklyn after Breukelen. Others were called after Dutch settlers: the Bronx after Jonas Bronck and Yonkers after Jonkheer Van Der Donck, America's first lawyer. The same for the city's main islands: Coney Island stems from Conijnen Eylant, meaning "rabbit island"; Long Island comes from Lange Eylant, which means the same; and when you look down south from here in the direction of the harbor, you can see the biggest Dutch name in the city—in size, I mean."

Curious heads turned and saw the giant letters on the ferry terminal in the distance: STATEN ISLAND.

"The name *Staten* refers to the Staten Generaal, the highest body of state in the Netherlands."

Daniel was utterly surprised. He never knew there were still so many tangible elements left of the city's Dutch past. New York's main neighborhoods!

The group continued, and when they had come to a halt at the corner of Bowling Green and Battery Park, the guide stretched out his arm in the direction of the lush space.

"Here in front of us, a fortification named Fort Amsterdam was constructed, to defend the settlement on Manhattan and other Dutch operations in the Hudson Valley. The location is now occupied by the US Custom House, and among the sculptures on its front is Maarten Tromp, the Dutch navy commander who defeated the Spanish fleet during the struggle for independence of the Dutch Republic."

Another tourist raised his hand.

"Why do you say Dutch *Republic*? I thought Holland had a queen."

"Very good question! In fact, during most of its history, the Netherlands was a republic. It was even one of the earliest republics in the world, way before famous republics like the United States or France. It changed to a monarchy only several centuries later, in the nineteenth century, marking the decline of the country as a world power."

The tourist nodded appreciatively.

"Inside Fort Amsterdam," the guide continued, "stood a church and a house. The house formed the office of the Director General of New Netherland. You may remember that the last Director General was Peter Stuyvesant, the man with the wooden leg. He didn't have the long commute of many New Yorkers today, as his house was close by: just behind this Customs House building. It was a scenic house at the waterfront, made of white bricks—hence, today's street name Whitehall. Stuyvesant finally retired to his large farm more to the north, at the current location of St. Mark's Church in-the-Bowery, where you also find his tomb. In fact, *bouwerie* means 'farm' in old Dutch, so the name actually refers to Stuyvesant's farm."

The group entered Battery Park and reshuffled beneath the tall flagpole in the middle of the lane.

"This flagpole was donated by the Netherlands in 1926 to commemorate the city's Dutch origin. The stone pedestal shows the famous scene of Peter Minuit purchasing Manhattan from the Indians, which I told you about earlier. Now when you look up the flagpole, you'll notice the original Dutch flag, with the colors orange, white, and blue, rotated sideways. And would you believe me if I tell you that this is still the official flag of New York City?"

Tourists looked at each other questioningly. "Are you saying that New York still has an old Dutch flag, even today?" one of them asked.

"Yep. And in the white part of the flag, you can also see the official seal of the city, in which you'll recognize a Dutchman and an Indian with a windmill between them. The year 1625 indicates the year the Dutch founded the city."

Together with the rest of the group, Daniel looked at the logo on the flag and was astounded by what he saw.

"The flagpole also symbolizes something else, folks—namely, the end of our tour. I hope you've seen that below the surface of New York City, if you look closely, you can still find lots of references to the Dutch past of the city. And now that the story has been shared with you, I'm sure that you'll discover many other examples yourself. Just to arouse your interest a bit more: do you know what a *doughnut* is?"

One of the tourists looked at the half-eaten object in his hand.

"We consider it a typically American delicacy, but in fact, it has a purely Dutch origin. The cakes of sweet dough were called *olykoecks*, and in the Netherlands today, people still eat the original version at New Year's Eve.

"And what do we call a typical New Yorker?" the guide asked quizzically. "Let me help you: New York City's main baseball team also carries this name."

"The Yankees!" the orange poncho in the front screamed proudly.

"Exactly! Nothing more American than a Yankee, right? But do you know where the word comes from? From the common Dutch first name Jan-Kees. In other words, your typical American is in fact a Dutchman!"

The tourists applauded enthusiastically.

"Oh, one final thing. If you promise to give me one of those things called dollars, I'll tell you the origin of our currency!"

With a large smile, one of the tourists put a bill in the guide's cap.

"Thanks, buddy! The dollar, another symbol of the United States, took its name from a coin the Dutch brought with them to America, the *daalder*."

While the group thanked the guide, Daniel stretched out his hand and touched the base of the flagpole, amazed by what he had just heard. He never realized the Dutch influence on the United States was so pervasive. The dollar, the donut, the Yankees—some very symbols of the country were all Dutch! How come he'd never heard of this before?

He looked at the inscription on the pedestal of the flagpole and was even more intrigued when he read:

IN TESTIMONY OF AN ANCIENT AND UNBROKEN FRIENDSHIP.

3

Kate Bates stretched out her left arm to indicate to the traffic around her she was about to turn left. It was a simple and efficient gesture, and she recalled it had taken her some time to master the Dutch art of cycling with only one hand on the handlebar. She followed the large stream of Amsterdam's cyclists that also pedaled northward onto the Nieuwe Spiegelstraat in the city's gallery district, leaving the silhouette of the famous Rijksmuseum directly behind her.

As always after stressful pleadings in the badly ventilated court rooms, she enjoyed the fresh air and gentle physical exercise of the ride back to her firm's office. But this time, she was not heading for the office. Immediately after having said good-bye to her client in front of the Court of Appeal building on the Prinsengracht, her thoughts had turned back to the call she had received just before the hearing from her friend Evelyn. A somewhat disturbing call. Not only because it broke her concentration just before the pleadings but also because the unusual character of her friend's request intrigued her.

It was certainly not the first time Evelyn had consulted her on legal matters, and from time to time Kate asked Evelyn for similar favors or simply for her feeling on a particular situation. But it was especially Evelyn's view as a friend—and perhaps also as a woman, in a world dominated by often not-too-sympathetic men—that she valued most.

Their feeling of mutual understanding had been there from the first day they met, at the bar classes in their first year of their new lives as young professionals. Kate inadvertently smiled as she thought of the fun they had had together, in spite of—or perhaps thanks to?—the discouragingly boring courses. While Evelyn had subsequently chosen a more conservative and economically oriented path as a commercial lawyer with an international "magic circle" firm of British origin, Kate had remained loyal to the ideals she had already had as a young girl, and after an internship at the International Court of Justice, she had chosen a small firm that focused on cases with a social and political character, often human rights issues. Her clients consisted of refused immigrants, unfairly convicted suspects, journalists on trial to divulge their sources, and so on. And all had one thing in common: little money to pay their lawyer. Although she was certainly not in it for the money, sometimes she did think there was a certain unfairness to the fact that society rewards lawyers who defend the most valuable principles of modern society, such as freedom of expression or fair trial, in a lesser way than those handling banal commercial conflicts.

Over the years, Kate had concluded that her strong interest in social justice originated in the fact that as a girl, she had always been an outsider. Her parents had emigrated from Britain to the Netherlands in the late 1970s, during the hard years of restructuring under Thatcher, and Kate was forced to find her way at school without speaking Dutch properly. Although her intelligence enabled her to learn quickly and effortlessly, during her school years, her Dutch remained laced with an English accent—the kind of accent that makes one an easy victim of bullying.

Kate's university years in Amsterdam had been a liberation. Historically one of the most internationally oriented cities of the world, her English background didn't matter there and faded so much that most of the time it even escaped her mind. She had freedom, confidence, and friends.

After her studies, which she finished cum laude with a thesis on the role of treaties in international public law, she became an attorney, and immediately grabbed public attention when she defended several activists accused of obstructing the construction of a nuclear power plant.

Kate halted her bicycle at Dam Square to let some of Amsterdam's ever-impressive number of cyclists pass. The tunes of a typical street organ resonated against the walls of the monumental Royal Palace. After all those years in Amsterdam, she knew enough of the city's history to be aware that the imposing gray building, which seemed one size too large for the mostly narrow streets and houses of Amsterdam, had in fact been built as a city hall. It had become a royal palace only relatively recently in its history. She knew that the city hall formed the culmination of Holland's power and splendor in its famous Golden Age, reflecting its success and glory. At the time of its construction in the 1660s, the monumental building was the largest of its kind in the world. Its only rivals in splendor were St. Peter's Basilica in Rome, the Escorial in Madrid, and the Palazzo Ducale in Venice. But there was one striking and revolutionary difference: the Amsterdam building was a city hall, entirely for public use, and not a palace of a ruler or holy seat. Amsterdam's city hall symbolized of supremacy of the civil society, and proof that the republican state form, uniquely modern at that time in a world still dominated by monarchs, was feasible. To complete the symbolism of the awakening of new times and express the hope that one day progress, freedom, and prosperity would become global goods, the floor of the building's main hall—aptly called the Burgher Hall—was inlaid with a giant map of the world. In a way, with Amsterdam's domination of the globe-spanning Dutch empire, that floor map itself formed the center of the world.

Back then, Kate thought, hoping the old ideals would someday come true again. *If only...* She realized how the thought frustrated her, so she mounted the bike again and continued to her destination.

Kate pondered Evelyn's request and concluded it was especially peculiar because she mentioned it was for a colleague in her firm's New York office. Why would someone over there be interested in old documents on the history of the Netherlands? She knew that New York City was founded by the Dutch and had even been called New Amsterdam in the beginning. But that was in colonial times, and she couldn't see the relevance of it to a commercial conflict today. And above all, how could such centuries-old information be so urgent?

4

The President of the United States walked toward Roosevelt's bust in the corner of his office and pulled the cart with the day's personal mail toward him. At his desk, he sifted through the mostly kind messages and invitations from other heads of state and wrote quick instructions to his staff on some of them.

The pile contained one letter of a different nature. It was addressed to him personally through diplomatic mail, with wax seals and all. It always amused him when countries still used such medieval adornments—it was if they had to compensate for something or justify a lack of authority. He briefly touched the seals and noticed that they depicted the same lion as in the logo at the top of the letter: a lion holding in its paw what looked like arrows.

The contents of the letter were less amusing though. They referred to an issue that his predecessor had already once mentioned, going back to the same man of the bust in the corner: former President Roosevelt. It was part of the list of top-sensitive issues transferred from president to president, together with the nuclear football, the famous briefcase allowing the authorization of nuclear attacks. Not that the issue was of military nature—it was more foreign-policy related and without imminent threat to the country's security. But while for an outsider the contents of the letter in front of him could seem farfetched, the President knew that the claim contained in it touched the heart and soul of his country.

5

While pedaling frantically on her classic Dutch bicycle, Kate sighed. She knew it was both a strength and a weakness of her character: once a question occupied her mind, she couldn't switch off her brain until she had the answer. And the curious request from Evelyn was such a question.

The writing of the legal conclusions scheduled for that afternoon would have to wait until tonight, she concluded.

At Amsterdam's Herenmarkt, Kate looked up at the building that formed her destination. The sober red-brick facade didn't betray anything of the world-changing decisions that had been made inside—decisions that had shaped large parts of the world as it was known today. Above the door she read in stylish letters:

WEST INDIA HOUSE

She knew the building had been the headquarters of the Dutch West India Company, the association of investors in the early seventeenth century to explore and develop the American continent. The West India Company was a pendant to its older sister, the famous East India Company, which had explored Asia and stood at the basis of the vast and powerful Dutch Empire.

The building's link to America seemed confirmed when Kate read the metal plaque at the entrance door: JOHN ADAMS INSTITUTE. John Adams, one of the early Presidents of the United States. She entered through the heavy wooden door, which gave access to a dark and narrow corridor. Intuitively, she walked to the source of light at the end.

A beautiful courtyard appeared in front of her. In its middle was a small fountain with a statue. She slowly walked toward it and sat down at the fountain's stone rim to look around. There was a mysterious atmosphere, provoked by the utter silence, and pitch-black walls that surrounded the courtyard. Kate contemplated the location's importance in Dutch history. The remarkable history.

She recalled how Mum, when she was still well during Kate's school period, had been keen on teaching her the history of their new host country. She said it was a form of respect. They had read Dutch historical books and articles together, while looking up new Dutch words in the dictionary and writing them down in a notebook for later rehearsal. Kate guessed that her choice of studying law may have been influenced by those intimate childhood experiences of analysis and memorization.

She had learned of the country's continuous fight against the water. Located on the North Sea coast and consisting almost entirely of the low river delta formed by the mouths of the major European rivers the Rhine and the Maas, the Dutch territory was under constant threat of floods and inundations. Over the centuries, the techniques for the construction of dikes and dams had been perfected, boosting education and engineering skills among relatively large parts of the population. Due to their geographical situation, the Dutch were forced to be constructive. This resulted in a culture with an emphasis on ingenuity and more respect for individual character than for outer appearances or sheer authority.

The fight against the water was financed through taxes directly spent on public works, and not on the personal wants and needs of some ruler. Such civil initiative developed the notion of "power to the people," permanently blocking central, absolute power. It became a principle that would become and remain a cornerstone of Dutch politics, centuries before most other countries.

The traits of social coherence, perseverance, and practical ingenuity of the small Dutch society were violently put to the test during the second half of the sixteenth century. The Spanish king Philip II sent a well-equipped army to the Netherlands and started an extremely bloody and violent campaign of persecutions by the Inquisition. The Dutch, not willing to give up their precious freedom, took up arms, and a long period of resistance against Spanish domination ensued, called the Eighty Years' War. Kate recalled how at school this topic had been studied endlessly, especially the role of one of the emblematic leaders of the Dutch revolt, William of Orange, founder of the Orange-Nassau family branch that would centuries later become the royal family. The color orange would from then on symbolize the country.

It was the fight against Spanish domination that made some Low Countries decide to join forces through the foundation of the famous Republic of the Seven United Provinces, the state that would exist for more than two centuries. The republican state form was highly exceptional and very advanced at that time, in a Europe dominated by kings, queens, princes, emperors, and other absolutist regimes. In most countries, it would take another two hundred years before democratic principles became generally accepted.

When Spain was finally forced to sign a truce ending the conflict, it marked the beginning of the period in Dutch history for which the country is best known: the Golden Age. This was the period between roughly 1600 and 1700, when the country witnessed a tremendous growth of economic power and dominated large parts of the world. High-tech industries of that time, such as weaving, pottery, and brewing, flourished—the famous delft blue tiles and Heineken beer company still testify to this today. And the invention of the wind-driven water-pumping mill, now the classic symbol of Holland, vastly accelerated the creation of so-called polders by emptying entire lakes, yielding extremely fertile soils. The arts were pushed to new heights with famous Dutch masters as Rembrandt, Vermeer, and Hals, whose works still draw large crowds to museums around the world today.

But it was especially the spice trade that accelerated the huge economic boom that lifted the Netherlands to levels of richness and development never witnessed before in the history of the world. In a period where the choice of food was still extremely limited and largely subject to climate and season, and the preservation of food was difficult, the availability of spices did wonders for old and tasteless food and made a huge difference in terms of quality of life for large parts of the population. It was no surprise that the public was willing to pay very high prices for these exotic flavorings.

As the journeys to spice-rich Asia were risky and required huge upfront investment, the Dutch invented the company owned by shareholders in order to pool the risks. In fact, the famous Dutch East India Company, founded in 1602, was the first joint-stock company in the world. Its shares could be traded at another Dutch invention of that year: the world's first stock exchange, located in Holland's capital, Amsterdam. Amsterdam subsequently became the undisputed financial center of the world.

The Dutch Republic's prospering economy, combined with the religious and social liberty, acted as a magnet for people from all over Europe. Many came to find work or to trade, but many also came to find shelter from persecutions in their country of origin. Protestants, Huguenots, Jews, and Catholics from everywhere made Holland a uniquely multicultural, multiethnic, and multireligious place on earth. Travelers of that time were astonished by the number of languages they heard in the streets, the diversity of dress they saw, and the variety of exotic products they smelled. Amsterdam in particular was—and would remain—one of the most internationally oriented cities in the world. It was the world's first true melting pot.

The roots of the Golden Age lay in that unique form of civil society, with self-government and free enterprise, not hindered by absolute rulers. In essence, the Dutch Republic marked the very beginning of liberalism, democracy, and capitalism. The combination of these elements proved to be an explosive cocktail of progress and would become the ideal of most countries in the world.

"Do you know who that is?"

The sudden voice from the other side of the fountain abruptly startled Kate awake from her thoughts.

6

Kate looked up and saw a friendly face with funny eyes above small reading glasses. The man saw the surprised look in Kate's eyes and pointed to the statue on top of the fountain.

"Do you know who that man is?" he repeated.

Kate looked at the figure and shook her head. "Eh...no, not really."

"It's Peter Stuyvesant. The last Director-General of New York, when it was still Dutch."

Kate had heard of the name Stuyvesant before and recalled it was also a cigarette brand.

"By the way, my name is Hendrik, and I'm the concierge of the building. Are you here for the first time?"

Kate nodded.

"Are you aware of the building's historical function?"

"The former headquarters of the Dutch West India Company, I believe."

"Correct. And inside this very building, the company's directors ordered the construction of a village on an island—a faraway island on the other side of the Atlantic. The directors had decided the island would keep its original name as used by the local Indian tribes: Manahatta."

Kate thought for a second. "Manhattan?"

"Indeed. The village they ordered, named New Amsterdam, was the very beginning of the United States of America."

Kate looked up at the facade of the building and marveled at the historical significance. "Actually, I came to look for some historical documents on the West India Company."

The concierge shrugged. "Well, I'm afraid I have to disappoint you then. We don't keep any such documents. In fact, there's nothing here about the company or the colonial history in the Americas."

Kate lifted an eyebrow. "What about John Adams? I saw the plaque outside."

"The institute you mean? They maintain the special relationship between the Netherlands and the United States. But no documents there either."

Kate was curious what the man meant with this "special relationship." But when she wanted to ask a further question, the concierge gently touched her elbow and pushed her in the direction of the door.

"I'm sorry, miss, but I'm afraid I have to let you out now. You should know that we're preparing for a wedding here tonight. We're closing."

"A wedding?"

The concierge nodded. "We need the rental income to cover the maintenance. Unfortunately not enough people know about the New York story to make us self-funding. Maybe one day..."

Kate pulled an apologetic face. "Any idea where I can find sources on the West India Company's American operations, especially any links with the situation today?"

Kate noted the concierge froze.

"Is there something the matter with that?" she asked.

"Eh...no," the man stammered. "It's just that, as said, nowadays, not many people are interested in the situation. Are you a journalist?"

"No, I'm an attorney. But actually, I'm helping a friend."

The concierge gently pushed Kate toward the small office next to the exit, took a pen and a piece of paper and scribbled something down.

"Now this should help you further." He handed her the paper. "And if you leave your contact details, we can add you to our mailing list." The funny eyes squeezed in something of a smile.

Taking the note, Kate hesitated briefly and then opened her handbag and gave the concierge a business card. The concierge took the small card without studying it, thanked her, and let her out.

When the heavy wooden door locked behind her, Kate found herself standing on the street again. Despite being disappointed that the location had not yielded more, for some reason, she had the feeling there was more to this story.

Kate took her cell phone and retyped the concierge's note in a message to her friend Evelyn.

7

"Daniel, it's Evelyn from the Amsterdam office."

Daniel felt relieved she had called back so quickly and thanked her for it. "How are things over there?" he added politely, aware that unbillable chitchat wasn't commonplace at the firm.

"Not too bad. Quite some deals going on. I think we'll have a good year. How about you? Judging from your message, you've also got work to do."

"You can say that," Daniel said and grinned. "We're working on a huge real estate deal in Manhattan. Just had another all-nighter—that kind of stuff."

"Well, you still sound okay then."

"Had a shower before going back to the office."

"Ah, so nothing to complain about then!"

"Apart from my Dutch research questions, no."

Evelyn laughed. "Okay, then I've good news for you. I think I found some of the possible sources you're looking for. But tell me, what is the deal about that this all is of interest to you?"

"Ground Zero."

"Ground Zero?" Evelyn asked, surprised. "You mean the place of the 9/11 terrorist attacks?"

"Yep. The city of New York is redeveloping the entire area, and our client is involved in the financing of the commercial real estate.

It's a huge deal—the largest project in the history of New York. It's worth tens of billions of dollars."

"Wow, sounds exciting. But what's the link with Dutch history?"

"Well, I'm not sure yet whether it's relevant or not, but it may be a starting point for further research. In short, we need to guarantee the current ownership of the ground, so we have to check the chain of previous owners. And as the Dutch were the first in Manhattan, we will make a start from there."

"I see," Evelyn said hesitatingly. Like most Dutch people she only vaguely knew about the Dutch origin of New York. She recalled something about New York having been exchanged for Surinam.

"Daniel, as you mentioned *treaties* in your request, I thought I'd ask a friend of mine, Kate. She's also a lawyer, more or less specialized in international law. We did our bar exams together, and she's really bright. She mentioned some sources. Do you have a pen?"

"Hit me."

"The first one is the National Archives of the Netherlands. And the second one is the Royal Library, called the Koninklijke Bibliotheek." She doubted Daniel would even try to write down the Dutch name.

"Okay, great. I'll check both of them. Many thanks again Evelyn for your quick response—also to your friend. It's all kinda urgent."

"Sure, no problem. By the way, my friend said that if you have any questions on the sources, you should feel free to call her. Her name is Kate Bates. I'll e-mail you her telephone number."

Immediately after terminating the call with Evelyn, Daniel pressed the red button for his assistant and started talking instantly.

"Please look up the contact details of the following institutions in the Netherlands: the National Archives and the Royal Library. It's urgent."

Daniel leaned back in his chair. It would be a hell of a job. The area of Ground Zero was vast; it may have contained hundreds of plots and buildings in the past, each of which could have been transferred dozens of times over the centuries. He wasn't even sure all the materials to expose the chains of title even existed.

He knew that in other countries, such problems were less likely to arise, as most countries had a land registration system in which the data in the register on land titles are guaranteed by law, and anyone can rely on its accuracy and truthfulness. The United States, on the contrary, had a "recordal" system, which meant that only the *date* of the recordal could be relied upon and not the transfer itself; it was up to the parties of the transaction to verify the validity of previous transfers and, thus, the current owner of a title; in case of conflict, this would ultimately have to be determined in court.

In a flash, Daniel thought that perhaps the whole thing was a nonissue, and they should simply be able to rely on the ownership information provided by the Lower Manhattan Development Corporation, or LMDC, the joint city-state body charged with the redevelopment of the Ground Zero area. According to LMDC's information, the Ground Zero site was the property of the Port Authority of New York and New Jersey, a public body. But on some parts of the site rested a long-term lease by Silverstein Properties, the investment firm of businessman Larry Silverstein, which owned the former World Trade Center complex. However, since the decision had been made not to rebuild the Twin Towers and instead to create a memorial at the exact spots where the towers stood, Silverstein, in return for renouncing his existing rights on Ground Zero, logically demanded the right to construct elsewhere in the area. This "swap" had a value of billions of dollars, and in his entire career, Daniel had never seen a property transaction of such size and complexity.

Intuitively, Daniel's brain pushed the issue to its legal limit. What would happen if LMDC's title information proved wrong? Could a claimant force a halt of the project? Would his client be liable? If yes, could they subsequently sue the LMDC and claim compensation? One of his associates was already checking whether such recourse was excluded in the contracts.

His assistant entered his office with the swift and confident stride that was compulsory at the firm.

"I'm sorry Mr. Van Wart, but for the moment I couldn't find any of the two institutions in Amsterdam. I'll continue searching but thought that maybe you have other information that may help in locating them."

Daniel thought for a second, turned to his computer, and opened his inbox. It was there, as promised: the confirmation message from Evelyn. It read only "Telephone number Kate Bates," followed by a number.

Daniel didn't hesitate and typed the number on his telephone and waited. He wondered what time it was in the Netherlands—much later, for sure. He heard the metallic voice of an answering machine and slammed the phone down. *Damn, too late!* Defeated, he stared at his assistant in front of him.

"I did come across an address in a place called The Hague but assumed it was wrong as the institutions would probably be located in the capital."

Daniel's eyes widened. "It's correct. The Hague is where the Dutch government is." He didn't blame her for her ignorance and admitted it was weird that the government didn't have its seat in the capital; he wondered what the reason was.

When the assistant let, Daniel's thoughts immediately returned to Ground Zero. In some of the materials of the development plan he had read that the site was the exact spot where in 1613 Dutch explorer Adriaen Block's ship named *Tyger* had accidentally burned. It forced Block and his crew to spend the winter on the island and subsequently build the very first structures of what would become New York City. In 1916, during excavation work for a subway line, the remains of the ship were discovered. Block had been the first to explore the area after its discovery by Henry Hudson in 1609, and Block Island was named after him.

And then there was of course the other dramatic link between Ground Zero and the city's Dutch origin. The development team had stumbled on it accidentally, but after an informal verification, the official 9/11 Investigation Commission affirmed, to their astonishment, that the fact that the Dutch convoy under Henry Hudson had first discovered Manhattan on September 11 of the year 1609 was one of the few viable explanations why the terrorists had chosen that date; it would symbolize an attack on the very start of the United States.

Daniel's assistant entered his office again, this time with a sheet of paper.

"I found both institutions in The Hague. Here you have all contact details. I called them to check the telephone numbers, but due to the hour, they're all closed now. I wrote down the e-mail addresses of their information desks. There's a six-hour time difference with the Netherlands. The country has only one time zone."

"Okay, thanks. Good work." Daniel took the sheet and gently nodded her away. He typed a message and sent an identical version to both e-mail addresses indicated on the sheet. He knew it was a long shot.

Part II

8

As soon as the driver had put the car in motion, Oscar Smeenk opened the small compartment between the two front seats. In the darkness of the car, the white light from inside the fridge lit up his heavy, spectacled face from underneath and played with the escaping cloud of ice-cold air, swirling slowly until it evaporated. It had always been the best moment of his day. After a busy day, alone in the dark silence of the comfortable service car, he enjoyed a frozen glass of *jenever.* He took out the small bottle, opened it, and poured the thick, transparent liquid into the small glass until it reached the rim. It was a habit he had copied from a former prime minister of the Netherlands and his onetime boss.

The car stopped slowly for the first traffic lights just behind the office. Smeenk kept the glass in front of his eyes and let the orange streetlights twinkle in the rounded head of liquid above the rim of the glass. A green light appeared among the orange, and the driver accelerated abruptly.

"Dammit, Albert!" Smeenk shouted while his hips shot up to avoid further liquid spilling onto his crotch. He hastily took a sip from the glass to prevent further spilling. When he had swallowed, he drew an ugly grimace. "Ahh! Not only do you drive uncomfortably but you also bought the wrong bottle again!"

The driver turned his head sideways. "Apologies, sir," he said in a low voice.

Annoyed, Smeenk moved to the dry seat behind the driver. Was it so difficult, the choice between old and young jenever? He admitted that the brown pottery bottles all looked somewhat old. But any adult man should know there is no age difference at all between *old* and *young* jenever. Only the recipe is different—the young could even be made from sugar, like the inferior gin the Brits love so much. They probably didn't even realize that the word *gin* came from the Dutch *jenever.*

The word immediately made him think of his daughter, Jennifer. It was only a few years ago, when she was fourteen, that he realized her name shared the same root: juniper. He emptied the rest of the small glass in one draught and leaned back against the leather headrest.

Jennifer. Would she give the same dry, juniper taste in her boyfriend, Patrick's, mouth when he licked her body?

Smeenk abruptly came forward to dismiss the thought. What a disaster this boy was. He still didn't understand how she could have fallen for him. The arrogance! Okay, maybe it hadn't been a good idea for him to tell the boy he lacked character because he'd dropped some subjects right before the school's exams. At least, not during their first dinner together. The discussion had turned into an embarrassing scene, with Jennifer and Patrick leaving the table shouting ugly things. When they had left, his wife, Hedwig, had cried softly, and it had taken two days before she had talked to him again. Jennifer still didn't talk to him and was now with Patrick most of the time.

Smeenk sighed and poured another glass, this time less full out of precaution. He looked out of the window into the early darkness of the Dutch fall. The same drizzle as in the morning. The wet gabled roofs of another social-housing project glittered in the lights of the provincial road, leading the stream of commuters out of The Hague. *Next year, after her exams, she would have left the house anyway,* he thought, trying to comfort himself. But the last few months had given him the feeling he had already lost her. His little Jenny, their only child. Hedwig and he had had her relatively late, mainly due to the constantly changing missions he was on at the beginning of his career. It had not mattered to him. As often with daughters, she had clung to her father more than to her mother. He had always had a natural authority over her. But

Patrick had changed it all by a stroke of lightning. He felt he'd lost a duel against a nineteen-year-old boy.

The tensions of the latest months had also had their effect on his work. He had realized that at sixty-two, one's mind is not as flexible anymore as at the beginning of a career. Although he had always lived for his work, for the first time, he had caught himself thinking of his retirement a few years from now, doing some home repair at their holiday cottage in the French countryside. Maybe it could even be in a year from now, if the mission were concluded successfully.

No time to get sentimental now, he reminded himself. There was work to do. He finished the glass and stored it with the bottle in the fridge. He already felt the warmth of the liquid activating him, his mind becoming relaxed and confident again. He smiled. He knew the English also called it "Dutch courage", an expression dating back to the time when English mercenaries were hired by the Dutch to liberate their country from Spanish occupation. A few glasses before a battle rendered a soldier much more confident and combative.

Smeenk opened his attaché case and took out the file with the remaining documents for the day. With a little luck, he could finish them before he arrived home. When he looked past the driver and saw the endless rows of red taillights in front of them, he was sure the work would be finished.

He placed the pile of documents on his lap, started to read them one by one and scribble instructions on them if necessary. There were some press clippings of statements he had validated the previous week; they didn't require further action and would be filed automatically by the Rijks Voorlichtingsdienst, the communications department of the Dutch government. There was an invitation from the financiers, but as always, he would decline cordially; it was much too sensitive for him to be seen with them. And there was the weekly report from the Internal Information Branch. He flipped open the slim report and noted nothing special on the first pages. Then his eyes fell on Paragraph 6, entitled KEYWORD SCREENING REPORT. To his surprise, the paragraph contained some text this time:

A regular information report was received from the authorities concerned from data center DH-PWA-20. A request was received involving several of the event-triggering terms: see attached Annex A. Recommended action: investigation level 1.

Even after having circled around the Dutch intelligence agency for more than thirty years, he still marveled at the suffocatingly implicit speak. *Regular information report* stood for "alert message," and *the authorities concerned*, for "secret informant." He also knew instantly what DH-PWA-20 meant; all addresses were abbreviated in a similar way, just in case a message was intercepted. It was simple and efficient: this time the abbreviation took the capitals of Den Haag, Prins Willem Alexanderhof number 20. The address of the National Archives of the Netherlands.

Smeenk frowned quickly to squeeze his glasses higher up his nose without using his hands. Although similar messages were not uncommon and came in several times a year, this time it gave Smeenk a slightly uncomfortable feeling. Apparently *several* terms had been consulted at the same time. Of course it did not necessarily mean anything; it could simply concern the habitual scholar or university research assistant doing research on a related topic. But with the event approaching, he could not be careful enough.

He flipped the page to look at the Annex with the reported combination of terms. It read as follows:

1. *New Amsterdam*
2. *Transfer of New York*
3. *Chain of title*

Good God! Smeenk thought. *The third term was disquieting!*

He took his pen and underlined the recommendation, which was the sign that he agreed, and they should proceed with the investigation.

9

The transaction was so important for the firm that the team had been given the top floor for their meetings. It was a rare occasion for the real estate team, as the floor was mostly occupied by large M&A deals, which could last for months. It was equipped with a large meeting room with breathtaking views over Manhattan, a sort of sitting room corner with large chairs, a small kitchen, and a large bathroom with even a shower.

As a senior associate, Daniel had a team of three junior associates, three paralegals, two interns, and two assistants working for him full time. The same applied to the other two senior associates that reported to partner Ben DiAngelo. It had been more than two months now that the entire team had spent day and night at the top floor. It had become their camping ground—quite literally, in view of the used mugs, empty takeaway boxes of Lebanese meze, and the field bed in the corner. Dozens of paper piles were stacked on the floor, and enlarged city plans were taped to the walls. On one of the tables at the far end of the room stood several scale models of the designs for the new towers that could possibly be erected around Ground Zero.

As Daniel had been the only one of the team present at the meeting at Goldman, he briefed DiAngelo on the chain-of-title question.

"Intelligent nonsense." DiAngelo qualified the issue. "Interesting only in theory."

"But do you agree with me," Daniel asked, "that in the absence of any precise information on the subject, it needs exploring, if only to avoid surprises later on?"

DiAngelo nodded.

"And besides, it's knowledge that'll keep its value and can come in handy in future Manhattan real estate deals."

Both men knew there were two practical obstacles: time and money. The time issue would be solved by working even harder, as usual at Stiglitz & Arrowsmith.

"What about our fees for the research? It'll be huge! Do we bill the client for it even if it becomes firm know-how?"

DiAngelo moved up his chin. "It's billable, no doubt about that. After all, they came up with the question themselves."

"Okay, so we'll do it this way." Daniel turned to his team, which had been following the conversation from a corner of the room. "First, check the deal documentation to see if the city can be held liable for providing us with incorrect ownership information."

Hands scribbled on yellow legal pads.

"Second, work down the recorded transfer deeds of the Ground Zero lots, starting with the most recent ones. Third, for you, Billy, with your BA in history, prepare a short memorandum on New Amsterdam to better understand the historical situation. From my side, I'll work on the sources in the Netherlands."

When the team had left, Daniel leaned against the window and gazed over southern Manhattan. From the top floor, the view was even more spectacular than seen from lower floors. Below him sprawled the large collection of lean skyscrapers, bound together by a ribbon of glistering waters surrounding the island. Daniel imagined what it must have looked like during the times the city guide had told about. The small Dutch town, with its rows of narrow houses, its canal, some wooden vessels anchored at the shore, Fort Amsterdam at the southern tip, and the windmill on its right. It was an incredible story, and he imagined what it would look like in a film in fast-forward: the rough woodlands with the small settlement evolving into the capital of the world.

He lowered his eyes and looked straight down the building. Below him he saw the gaping hole of Ground Zero. He found it difficult to recall the situation when the Twin Towers of the World Trade Center had still been there. They had disappeared from one day to the next. Like many New Yorkers, he had felt it as an attack aimed at him personally. Was he as an American citizen co-responsible for the conflicts America was involved in? Through the simple fact that the American public had voted for the politicians in charge? In essence, that was true, of course, but it would be a very democratic thought for terrorists.

Daniel turned back to the huge, shining conference table. He opened his computer and screened the long list of new messages.

It was there! The answer from one of the Dutch institutes. He scrolled farther down the list. And the other one too!

The message from the Royal Library simply reported that their collection concerned books and writings, not official documents. They recommended consulting the Dutch National Archives.

Damn, nothing concrete, Daniel thought.

The National Archives reported they were indeed in possession of original documents. In relation to the transfer of New York from Holland to England, they mentioned one document in particular: the *Treaty of Westminster.* It could be consulted, and copies of digital versions could be made. Unfortunately, the digital versions were not yet available online; such a tool was still under construction.

Daniel leaned back in his chair, gazing at the ceiling.

This wasn't moving fast enough.

He concluded he needed serious help in the Netherlands and looked up the number he had tried earlier.

10

"Please contact me in the usual way," read the first message that Kate found on her desk when she entered her office. She sighed, took off her coat, and hung it over the chair in front of the high window overlooking Amsterdam's majestic Keizersgracht canal. The cryptic message came from a client hiding abroad—she didn't know where, and she didn't want to know either—who feared discovery by the authorities. She'd been working on his case for almost two years, and it was now pending before the European Court of Justice, the highest court in Europe. The man was sought after internationally and risked imprisonment, as he refused to pay taxes as long as he didn't have the right to vote in his host country. When taking on the case, Kate had immediately seen the strength of her client's argument: a modern variant of "No taxation without representation," the famous slogan of the Boston Tea Party, which had led to the American independence. In the twenty-first century, Europe still had a long way to go.

Even after so many years of legal practice, Kate still didn't feel she could rely on routine; her cases were never ordinary. In the beginning of her career, she had been fascinated by the purely legal questions and dug into them until she had found the right solution. The winning solution. But over time, she had come to realize that it was the people involved in the cases—her clients—that made them interesting. That didn't mean, of course, that she sympathized with all her clients.

Some of them had scared her. And some had even threatened her. But she had become convinced that under the right—and especially the *wrong*—circumstances, anybody could eventually find himself or herself in a similar position and commit the same acts. What would then be the fair solution?

The key, as devised by many philosophers over the centuries, lay in the assumption that every person on earth is born equal, in the sense that one cannot choose one's parents nor the place and time of one's birth. That meant that if one had to devise a legal and social system that would be acceptable for oneself without knowing where and when one would be born, one had better find a fair and balanced system that allowed one to have the same opportunities, irrespective of one's situation of birth. It wasn't an issue of redistributing food or money but of having equal, fair chances to make the best of it.

This philosophy—although Kate believed it was simply common sense—could be applied to almost anything. It explained why discrimination shouldn't be tolerated: one cannot choose the color of one's skin, one's origin, one's age, or one's gender, so one's life shouldn't be negatively impacted by it. Although in many countries, religion is also recognized as a source of discrimination, Kate had received the top note of her class for her thesis arguing that religion should *not* be put in the same category of prohibited discrimination grounds, since people can choose religion themselves. It had created quite a stir; the university dean had even been summoned by the minister of education!

Kate knew she had a strongly developed sense of justice. It made her tick. It was what allowed her to defend any case of injustice, irrespective of whether the people involved were sympathetic or not. Flavored with a hint of rebelliousness in her character, it was what made her one of the sharpest lawyers around.

The second message Kate found on her desk was a telephone note from Evelyn's American colleague. His name was Daniel Van

Wart. *Funny Dutch name for an American,* she thought. He had called to follow up on the sources she had sent and now asked for a copy of the Treaty of Westminster.

The Treaty of Westminster!

Incidentally she knew what the treaty was about: a peace treaty ending a sea war between England and the Dutch Republic in the seventeenth century. The treaty was had contained a secret protocol, the Act of Seclusion, in which England promised never to accept a member of the family of Orange-Nassau as head of state in Holland. She had learned this from a journalist she had defended some years earlier in a press case against the Dutch royal family, the same family of Orange-Nassau. It had been quite a case, and the fact that Kate had been illegally wiretapped, shadowed, and summoned by the president of the bar had left a bitter taste when it came to the Dutch democratic principles in relation to their royalty.

But why should the treaty be of interest to an American lawyer? He had asked for sources on the transfer of New York to England, but as far as she recalled the Treaty of Westminster had nothing to do with New York. Now she was even more curious about what this Van Wart was working on.

11

Some forty miles southwest of Amsterdam, in The Hague, Oscar Smeenk served himself an espresso from the machine on the drawer cabinet. His secretary entered his office with a discreet knock and laid the file containing the day's mail on the corner of his desk. It was the habitual hour, just after lunch. Smeenk preferred reserving the mornings to study longer documents or handle difficult issues that needed full concentration. After lunch, when the body diverted the energy from the brain to the digestion system, he preferred more diverse tasks, such as handling correspondence and making necessary calls.

Smeenk took the file and opened it. As in recent months, most of the documents concerned the thrilling event that would take place very soon now. Reports on the countless preparatory meetings for the secret operation and brief transcripts of the direct meetings with his employer.

That day's mail also contained a report on the financial transactions that would still have to be completed before the event. With his employer's financiers, he had studied the options for more than a year, and they were now reasonably sure that the funds—all of them—could be handled and eventually transferred without a trace. He admired the skills of the financiers, who managed to shelter the assets, worth many billions, from preying eyes, even in times with tighter controls and transparency requirements. They were the very best one could get. According to their report, which didn't contain any factual information of course, all was going according to schedule, so Smeenk concluded it wouldn't take much time before they would all receive the final go-ahead for the action. *The action that would change the course of the Dutch history.*

The next document on the pile was the phase-one investigation report concerning the surprising keyword request. Smeenk instantly recalled the term "chain of title" that had been submitted to the National Archives. The report was a one-page memo, in the usual format for phase-one investigations. It contained mainly the rough data, which had for sure been checked by his team with the National Archives.

Smeenk had devised the keyword system himself and was very proud of its simplicity and effectiveness. Sometimes he could hardly resist boasting about it to his international colleagues, but he knew that could be fatal. After all, the digital keyword filtering system was completely illegal, and as it involved government agencies—such as the National Archives—the divulgation of the system would certainly have catastrophic political consequences. The issue was a potential Dutch Watergate, especially in view of his employer's identity.

He frowned to mount his glasses and read the information in the report. Apparently the three keyword terms had been found in a short e-mail containing a rather general request for information on the transfer of New York from the Dutch to the English. The e-mail had been in English. The e-mail address through which the message had been sent contained the name of a law firm in New York City in the United States. The person who had made the request was a certain Daniel Van Wart, Esq. The firm's website had been checked and seemed to confirm that Daniel Van Wart was indeed employed by the firm. The name of the law firm was Stiglitz & Arrowsmith.

"Stiglitz & Arrowsmith!" Smeenk yelped in amazement. The same law firm used by his employer!

He thought of the implications. It seemed almost contradictory: the very firm that protected his employer popping up in the security filter!

He wondered whether there could be any link at all with his employer. After all, this Van Wart was with the firm's New York office, while his employer's counsel was in the firm's Amsterdam office. It could be a simple coincidence.

Coincidence or not, the peculiar situation made further investigation necessary. Fortunately that would be relatively easy: he would simply ask Hein Van Olden, his employer's legal counsel at Stiglitz & Arrowsmith's Amsterdam office, to make some internal inquiries at his firm.

12

The New York City subway in the direction of Van Cortlandt Park was packed, despite the fact that it was almost midnight. Daniel was exhausted, and he had difficulty keeping his balance. The daily meeting of the transaction team had taken hours, as they waded through the endless details and additional clauses that had to be taken into account. On top of that, his client had come up with a major new project that had to be integrated into the deal: the development of the new Goldman Sachs headquarters, right next door to Ground Zero.

His firm's chairman, Lee Sutherland, had been invited to the meeting, and he had stressed the importance of the transaction for the firm. He had demanded full dedication from everyone. It was the dreaded word he had used: dedication. Everyone in the firm knew what was meant by it: success would be rewarded generously at the end of the year; mistakes would mean the continuation of one's career outside Stiglitz & Arrowsmith.

While trying not to nudge his fellow commuters, Daniel fished the short memo from his briefcase that the intern had prepared on the development of the city under the Dutch. He saw that the memo started with the discovery of Manhattan in 1609 by Henry Hudson, followed by the first settlement, and so on. He already knew that part, so he moved on several pages and started reading.

The Dutch presence in New Netherland got off to a difficult start. The Dutch West India Company (WIC), which had obtained the government charter to develop the American colony, realized that the exploitation of the area would require enormous investments. After lengthy debates in the West-India House, its Amsterdam headquarters, the governing board of the WIC finally decided the only solution would be to allow private investors to participate in the development. A new system of land distribution was introduced called patroonship, after the Dutch word for "patron." A person wishing to become a patroon could apply for ownership of very large tracts of land, with the obligation to cultivate it and to have at least fifty families settle on it. In essence, the patroonship system entailed the privatization of the colonization process. One of the first and foremost patroons was Kiliaen van Rensselaer. Another influential patroon would be Van Cortlandt, the later burgomaster of New York City.

Daniel looked up in surprise. *Cortlandt!* The name of the subway line he was on. Intrigued, he read on.

The colony of "New Netherland" comprised most of the present-day states of New York, New Jersey, and Delaware. Another American state even carries a Dutch name today: Rhode Island. It stems from Roodt Eyland, *meaning "red island," a name the Dutch explorers probably gave due to its red earth.*

In 1640 the Dutch West India Company gave up its monopoly on the trade with New Netherland, allowing any ship to freely travel to and from the colony. It marked the beginning of the development of New Amsterdam as an important commercial hub, and it was from this moment on that the colony experienced an era of economic progress and prosperity. Trade became the most important activity and involved the majority of the population, now free to trade for their own account. Together with another unique trait of the Dutch society, namely the absence of feudal class structures, this resulted in a remarkably large upward social mobility, essentially forming the first sprouts of the famous "American dream."

In 1653, the principle of municipal government was recognized in New Netherland. This meant that the colony did not fall under the authority of the WIC anymore. The towns could grant land patents and thus allow citizens to become private landowners, which triggered a wave of new immigrants.

Among these immigrants were many Jews, especially after the fall of Dutch Brazil in 1654. As in Holland, the Dutch colony in Brazil had a large Jewish population due to its religious tolerance. When Dutch Brazil fell into the hands of the Portuguese, many fled to New Amsterdam. The community survived, grew, and even prospered. While over the centuries that followed the city would attract Jewish immigrants from all over the world, the core of the community remained Dutch: in 1830 still more than half of the Jewish population in New York was of Dutch origin, shaping the strong Jewish influence on New York that lasts until today.

Local governing rights did not automatically mean more freedom rights, and further civil initiatives were necessary to transform the relatively rigid and traditional stance of Director General Stuyvesant. In 1657, a group of citizens of Flushing—then still spelt "Vlissingen," after the capital of the Dutch province of Zeeland—requested an exemption to the director general's ban on Quaker worship. This petition, named the Flushing Remonstrance, is by some considered a precursor to the recognition of freedom of religion in the famous Bill of Rights.

Over the years, the small town of New Amsterdam developed and attracted ever more settlers. They were not only Dutch but also of other origins. New Amsterdam was an attractive destination, not in the last place because of the freedom and religious tolerance. It were the Dutch characteristics of New Amsterdam—liberty, diversity, and commerce—that would forever mark the culture of the city of New York and the United States of America, at that.

Daniel was forced to stop reading when he reached his station and had to get out. He realized that the tiredness was completely gone; his brain was still working on the story in full gear. The feeling of pleasant surprise when he had followed the city tour had turned into burning curiosity. He *had* to know the story: it was about his family's roots! And something told him he had only scratched the surface of something much bigger.

13

"Albert, pick me up here in an hour from now," Smeenk ordered his driver as he stepped out of the car just in front of the entrance. He had to admit that the American Hotel on Amsterdam's Leidse Square was not a bad choice—that is, for a location in Amsterdam, of course, as he largely preferred The Hague. It had something to do with the mentality of the people. For some reason, the Amsterdammers always had something boastful about them, as if they ruled the world. Perhaps that had been the case in the past, but nowadays, the country's decision center was without any doubt The Hague. He knew that better than anyone else, as that city was not only the government seat but also the residence of his employer.

He briefly looked up to the yellow brick facade of the stylish Jugendstil building before he entered through the revolving door. He had no idea why it was called the American Hotel, but it surely was an appropriate name for the purpose of the meeting!

In the entrance hall, he turned right to the impressive restaurant area. Although the place was known for its famous reading table, Smeenk chose one of the secluded corners; he didn't want to be overheard and was sure that Hein Van Olden would appreciate his choice.

They had met each other on a regular basis over the last two years, mostly in The Hague. He knew that Van Olden had spent a lot of time with his employer. The event meant a lot of preparation for him also, and there were still lots of issues to be solved, even in such an advanced stage. In the beginning of their cooperation, there had been some friction, largely due to the way his employer had arranged things. Van Olden was supposed to work under Smeenk's instructions, but later, it was decided that Van Olden would report directly to their employer. This created a competition of egos that could have been avoided. Sometimes he couldn't suppress the thought that this had been on purpose, a Machiavellian move to make it very clear to both who was calling the shots.

Later on, Smeenk and Van Olden developed a mutual respect. Both had been used to dealing with large responsibilities and pressure before they had accepted the job, but they had largely underestimated the terrible weight that was now on their shoulders. It had forged some sort of bond. Smeenk agreed that his employer's choice of Van Olden as principal legal counsel had been an excellent one. With his sixty-two years, he was very experienced, and as former president of the Dutch bar and part-time judge in the Court of Appeal of The Hague, he was both well connected and respected, which were necessary conditions to enable him to defend the sometimes-arbitrary position his clients were in. These qualities had without any doubt also been the reason that Van Olden had been retained by the firm Stiglitz & Arrowsmith to establish their Dutch office from scratch. In the competitive but notoriously archaic Dutch bar, only the best could pull off a feat like that.

Smeenk was reading the *Trouw* newspaper and had already sipped from the small glass of jenever that was standing on the low table in front of him when he felt a hand on his shoulder.

"Hello, Hein. Good to see you," Smeenk said while rising slightly from the club chair.

Without a word, Van Olden gave his coat to the servant standing next to him to take the additional order. The servant looked at the coat in bewilderment.

"I see you already ordered a *borrel*," Van Olden said to Smeenk as he took a place in the chair opposite him. "In that case, I will immediately order a *biertje*," he said in the direction of the servant without looking at him.

The boy nodded and left with the coat.

In accordance with Dutch tradition, the two men didn't exchange pleasantries but went straight to the point. Smeenk told Van Olden about the keyword request and the remarkable fact that it was an associate of Van Olden's firm based in New York that had come up. Van Olden was also surprised. He confirmed he had heard of the name Daniel Van Wart but knew nothing of him.

Van Olden was less amused by the request subsequently made by Smeenk.

"Screening correspondence of an associate? I'm sorry, Oscar, but that's not a common thing to do." He knew the firm could do it—and had done it—in cases of reported insider trading or in case of employment conflicts. But neither situation seemed to be the case here. And communicating such information to someone *outside* the firm was unheard of.

"You should know," Van Olden continued, "as a lawyer, it's even an offence to divulge information on cases and clients."

"Don't understand me wrongly, Hein," Smeenk retorted. "We don't need such information, and it can all be left out. The only thing we need to know is why that fellow made that search and if he's been in touch with other people in the Netherlands. I don't have to tell you about the importance of security measures, especially now."

Van Olden knew this was a subtle threat. If he declined the request, Smeenk would have to report it. The whole thing would come back as a boomerang, in the form of an order from above. Van Olden's mouth was dry. He drank half of the small beer in one quaff and then savored the remaining froth on his upper lip.

"Of course I understand. I'm not saying it can't be done, but I'd have to pull some strings first. I'll see what I can do for you."

Ten minutes later, the two men shook hands and said good-bye in front of the small fountain outside the American Hotel.

Van Olden had tried to make the commitment sound if he was in charge at his firm, but he knew perfectly well that in the firm's pecking order, he was not in a position to give such instructions easily. His practice was far less profitable than those of his American partners, and in the United States, the level of profitability was always decisive. The fact that his client was the Dutch royal family wouldn't change the slightest bit to that.

Part III

14

Too excited about his discovery of the Dutch history of the United States, Daniel found it impossible to sleep. He switched on the bed light again, projecting a soft glow on the high ceiling of his Upper West Side apartment. He reached for the intern's memo and started flipping through it in search of clues for his case. A question that slowly started to bother him was, what had happened to the Dutch property later on in history? After all, at a certain point, the Dutch had lost New York to the English. If the English had confiscated all property, was he maybe looking at the wrong place and should focus on English sources

When Charles II was restored to the English throne after Cromwell's death in 1658, he took in hand the mission to expand England's power. And the first step would have to be the consolidation of the American continent. Well aware of the Dutch presence in New Netherland and the conflicting Anglo-Dutch territorial claims in North America, Charles was not too keen on provoking new conflicts with the Dutch Republic in view of its military power. The king's brother, however, the Duke of York, was less opposed to a conflict. Incidentally, he was also a director of the Royal African Company, which had the monopoly on the English slave trade. He had his eyes on the Dutch territories on the African West coast, and a war would be the perfect opportunity to bring these territories within reach.

Together with the English envoy to The Hague, George Downing (after whom Downing Street is named and who despised the Dutch), he persuaded Charles to take steps in North America that would risk a war with Holland but potentially bring the two men great personal gain.

In 1664, King Charles II divided his North American territorial claims in two and granted the territory between the Delaware and Connecticut Rivers to his brother, the Duke of York, in a transaction known as the "Duke's Grant." This territory included New Netherland, despite its discovery and occupation by the Dutch.

Following the land grant, the Duke of York, who was conveniently also Lord High Admiral of the Navy, *instructed a colonel named Richard Nicolls to take possession of his freshly acquired American lands. In May 1664, Nicolls left with a fleet of four ships bearing 450 armed men and arrived in New Amsterdam at the end of August.*

The Dutch colony was not prepared for a military fight to defend itself. In fact, in the preceding years, Governor General Peter Stuyvesant had made numerous requests to the West India Company in Amsterdam to send more soldiers and weapons. In vain.

But Stuyvesant, a native of the Dutch province of Friesland that was reputed for its stern defense of liberty and independence throughout the ages, did not cede easily, and he proved both courageous and a skillful negotiator. He managed to forestall English action several times. Knowing that his adversaries had nothing to win either from the colony if it were *destroyed or forever rancorous, he forced the English to accept the setting up of a council with representatives from both sides to negotiate the conditions of surrender. The negotiations resulted in a set of "Articles of Capitulation," which guaranteed the rights and property of the Dutch.*

That's it! Daniel exclaimed while putting down the memo. *He needed the Articles of Capitulation.* They expressly mentioned property rights: it was the research lead he needed.

He looked at the alarm clock and saw it was just past 2:00 a.m. He typed in a last message marked URGENT on his Blackberry and knew the intern would add the term *all-nighter* to his vocabulary that night.

15

As usual, the revelation came to Kate's mind at the most banal of moments. It often happened during her morning shower or when she did her exercises—apparently, the ritual stretched not only her muscles but also her brain. This time, it was when she was sitting on the office toilet. She was looking at the toilet calendar, a typically Dutch decoration, which hung on the door in front of her and contained the birthdays of colleagues, friends, and relatives. It had been offered to her by her staff as a joke for her fortieth birthday a few months ago. The theme of the calendar was London, and each month showed a picture of one of the city's attractions.

First the calendar had made her think about her trip to London scheduled for the next day. She had been asked to join discussions on a defense strategy for Greenpeace in a case of alleged damage caused by blocking a nuclear-waste transport from France to Germany. Although Greenpeace had its worldwide headquarters in Amsterdam, the action had been coordinated from Greenpeace's London branch office.

She'd been a member of the International Advisory Board of the environmental organization for the past three years. When she had been approached for the function, "in view of her commitment to honorable causes and her experience and reputation in the field of complex international legal matters," as the official letter had stated, she had been surprised but profoundly honored. She had always admired the organization for its noble motives and courageous actions and had accepted the invitation without hesitation. At that time, before their recent move, Greenpeace's Amsterdam headquarters were still located at Keizersgracht 174, just across from her office. As the very same quarter also contained the Anne Frank House, the offices of Amnesty International, and the world's first monument to gay victims of persecution, the quarter was referred to as the Justice Quarter, and Kate was proud to have her office right in the heart of it.

Apart from the Greenpeace case, she was also looking forward to her trip to London for another reason. It felt as if she hadn't seen Dad for ages, despite the fact that the frequency they saw each other had not changed since he had decided to move back to England. Somehow the physical distance between them affected her perception.

Making the decision to move had been difficult but understandable. Dad wanted to spend the last years of his life in his country of origin, England. The decision had taken some years to ripen, despite the fact that he did not have to worry anymore about Mum's well-being after she had passed away. He had regained a certain freedom after so many years attending the sickbed of his wife.

The revelation came after Kate briefly peeked at the following month's picture on the toilet calendar: Westminster Palace.

How stupid! The Treaty of Westminster!

She suddenly realized that the name of the treaty probably referred to the name of place where it was signed: at Westminster Palace in London, the houses of parliament. Dozens of treaties must have been signed there, the one ending the Anglo-Dutch War just one of them. Maybe there was another Treaty of Westminster the American lawyer was looking for—one that *did* have something to do with New York.

She hastily walked back to her desk, typed "treaty of Westminster" in the search engine, and scrolled down the results. When she was halfway down the list, she instantly knew which treaty Daniel Van Wart was interested in:

> *Treaty of Westminster 1674; ending the third Anglo-Dutch War; transfer of New York to England.*

Kate's mind was racing now. Should she visit the National Archives in The Hague to look up the treaty? She looked at her watch and realized she didn't have enough time before closure. And with her imminent departure to London Daniel Van Wart would need to be patient a couple of days more.

Unless...

She slowly whispered the name again: *The National Archives.*

An idea came to her mind, and she smiled.

16

Oscar Smeenk knew that they knew. They probably didn't know who he was, but they knew that he was someone important. He could see it in the way the staff looked at him when he entered the brasserie for his habitual lunch and the overpolite—in his eyes, exaggerated—treatment they gave him. His employer's security team had probably instructed the place's owner. The precaution was especially likely since it was the only moment during the day he was left alone, without a driver or security guard close by.

He ordered his customary sandwich with *Filet Americain*, the Dutch version of what the French call tartare, accompanied by a glass of buttermilk. The usual lunch crowd, mostly civil servants of various ministries in the center of The Hague, gathered at the tables around him. He recognized them immediately by the way they dressed and the way they talked. It was no surprise; he had been one of them for a good many years.

Too many years, he thought.

But now he was different from them. Their situations were light-years away from his. Now he was a man of means, of real power. Gone were the badly ventilated offices with uncomfortable chairs and bad coffee. Gone was the waiting in the rain for the overcrowded trains in the morning. The pitiful lunch boxes prepared at home.

He admitted he'd been lucky. He was not at all a brilliant technician like the financiers, the lawyer Van Olden, or the security people generally hired by his employer for the management of the business.

And a business it was, managing of one of the largest fortunes in the world. And certainly one of the best-protected ones—or rather, best hidden. No, his task was not one of a specialist but expressly a generalist—creating the right conditions for things to happen. Or *not* let them happen. He was a strategist.

His talent had been spotted when he was a young campaign manager for Ruud Lubbers, who would have a stellar political career and become prime minister in three consecutive cabinets. Lubbers had been a sort of Dutch Margaret Thatcher, turning around the unproductive, aid-addicted Dutch economy. Lubbers had been Smeenk's luck. During many years he managed the crises, the controversies, and especially what he called the "neutralization of risks." It was this experience and his fabulous knowledge of the Dutch and international political scene that had earned him his current job.

He chewed and swallowed the pickle on the side of his plate. He always started a plate with the trimmings; someone had once remarked that it resembled an act of strategic reconnaissance before the real attack. He was about to take the first bite of his sandwich when his telephone rang. Annoyed, he put the sandwich down, some fillet still on his thumb.

"Smeenk," he said in a low voice, following the Dutch habit of saying one's name first when receiving a call. It was one of his team members. "I'm having lunch."

"I know, sorry about that. I thought you'd want to know anyway."

"Keep it short."

"Of course. Remember the report we received yesterday from Van Olden?"

"Yes, with the telephone numbers dialed by that American lawyer."

"Exactly, Daniel Van Wart. We checked the telephone numbers—at least, the foreign ones—and I think we may have a problem."

There was a short silence before Smeenk reacted.

"What problem?" he asked in a low voice.

"Well, among the foreign numbers was one Dutch number he dialed recently. With an Amsterdam prefix. We checked whom it belonged to, and it's the firm of Kate Bates."

Smeenk almost choked.

"Kate Bates? Bloody hell!"

Both men were silent for a few seconds. Smeenk's brain boiled with thoughts and questions. He tried to get ahold of himself the usual way in case of panic, by switching to cool facts.

"How often? How long?"

"Two times in total. The first call was just a few seconds, so he probably reached voice mail. The second call was somewhat longer. A few minutes. We don't know whether they actually talked. I mean, Van Wart and Kate Bates. He could also have reached someone else at Bates's office. Or he could simply have left a message."

Smeenk was already two steps further, assessing the possibility to obtain other information on the call. There were probably no recordings, unless Bates's lines were tapped by the Justice Department, but that was unlikely. And even *if*, he knew it would be difficult to obtain a copy, as lawyers' conversations enjoyed a special protection. Troubled, he leaned back in the chair. He ran his hand slowly through his remaining hair, now containing some fillet.

"I think you agree this is very serious," his assistant said calmly.

Smeenk nodded. "Yes. This is top priority indeed. What puzzles me is that I can't see the link between Kate Bates and the case Van Olden said his American colleagues are working on. A real estate deal in Manhattan!"

Smeenk knew very well what the link was about, but he had to keep his colleague in the dark about it. No one knew about the real causes, except for the tiny group of insiders. He was not even entirely sure Van Olden knew. He probably did, as he would be the one taking care of the legal consequences of the operation. But for security reasons, it was of course impossible to ask questions about it.

"I propose that we inform Van Olden," the assistant suggested. "Maybe he could take some measures against this Van Wart."

Smeenk thought about it. Van Olden would certainly understand the seriousness of the fact that Van Wart had contacted Bates. After all, Van Olden had personally handled the previous cases Bates had initiated against his employer in the past. Awkward cases, which had generated very unwelcome media attention. Bates had proven very smart and had handled the cases with surprising ferociousness, more as an activist than a lawyer. Since then, Bates had become a known figure in the Dutch political landscape, and her cases always went beyond the legal contents and had clear political dimensions to them, sometimes even on international level. Bates was a serious threat to his employer—that much was sure. And a threat that had come to the surface again at the worst possible moment.

"No," Smeenk said decisively. "We should focus on Bates first and deal with Van Olden later. We must find out what she's working on and why she was contacted by the American lawyer."

And whether she's found out, he thought.

"Do you want me to start a phase two on her?"

"Yes. Right now."

17

The intern entered Daniel's office with an obedient posture that would certainly have to change if he wanted to get hired. Maybe it was just the fatigue. Daniel noticed that the intern looked exhausted, which was no surprise after being awake for at least forty-eight hours.

More important was the quality of the work, of course. And Daniel had greatly appreciated the intern's memo on the history of New Netherland. He was looking forward to the fresh report that the intern now handed to him.

"Did you find the Articles of Surrender?"

"Yes, sir. But the difficult part was finding a translation."

"Why? Were they not in English?"

"They were, but in seventeenth-century English. And the document was handwritten, so quite difficult to decipher. I found some modern transcripts, but I didn't always agree with them, so I made some corrections myself. All should be quite clear now; I marked the important points in yellow."

Daniel read the title page of the document.

ARTICLES OF SURRENDER OF NEW NETHERLAND
August 27, Old Style, 1664.

The intern quietly left the office, and when Daniel tuned the page he started reading the parts marked in yellow:

1. *We consent that the States-General or West India Company shall freely enjoy all farms and houses.*
3. *All people shall still continue free denizens and enjoy their lands, houses, goods, and ships, wheresoever they are within this country, and dispose of them as they please.*

That's it! Daniel thought. It couldn't be written in clearer language: the transfer of New Amsterdam to the English respected the existing property rights. It was surprising, as Colonel Nicolls could simply have seized all property in name of the Duke of York. The articles seemed indeed remarkably generous to the Dutch!

He continued reading the other highlighted articles.

6. *It is consented to that any people may freely come from the Netherlands and plant in this country and that Dutch vessels may freely come hither, and any of the Dutch may freely return home or send any sort of merchandise home in vessels of their own country.*
8. *The Dutch here shall enjoy the liberty of their consciences in divine worship and church discipline.*
9. *No Dutchman here, or Dutch ship here shall, upon any occasion, be pressed to serve in war against any nation whatsoever.*
21. *That the town of Manhattans shall choose Deputies, and those Deputies shall have free voices in all public affairs, as much as any other Deputies.*

Daniel sat back in confusion. Had the intern found a wrong document? He checked the title again: "Articles of Surrender." The conditions laid down in the articles could hardly be called a surrender, and they were a far cry from what could be expected from a military annexation by foreign troops. On the contrary: the document seemed to *guarantee* rights instead of imposing new rules. And they were extremely far-reaching rights for the seventeenth century:

property rights, freedom of movement, freedom of religion and conscience, and even the right to vote!

His hands behind his head, Daniel stared out of the window over the New York skyline. If it was all true, the early history of the United States was different from what he'd learned in school. Apparently there were already foundations of a modern society before the American Revolution, buttressed with written documents confirming citizens' rights dating way before the Declaration of Independence and the Constitution. And the Dutch, his own ancestors, had apparently not been expelled or overthrown by the English. Either he was missing something, or Peter Stuyvesant had really performed a masterpiece.

Again he wondered how much more there was to this story. He'd seen snippets of it by pure coincidence, but the latest ones had confirmed his feeling there was much more to it.

Somewhat frustrated he concluded that he could do only two things—for the moment, at least. One was informing his team that 1664, the year of the English "take-over" of New York, was *not* a correct starting point for their research, as earlier property rights had remained unchanged. Their research should go beyond the English times and start at the Dutch period immediately. The second thing was simply waiting for that Dutch lawyer Kate Bates to get back to him on the Treaty of Westminster, the only other potential source. Although with every hour that passed it became less likely that would yield something.

Part IV

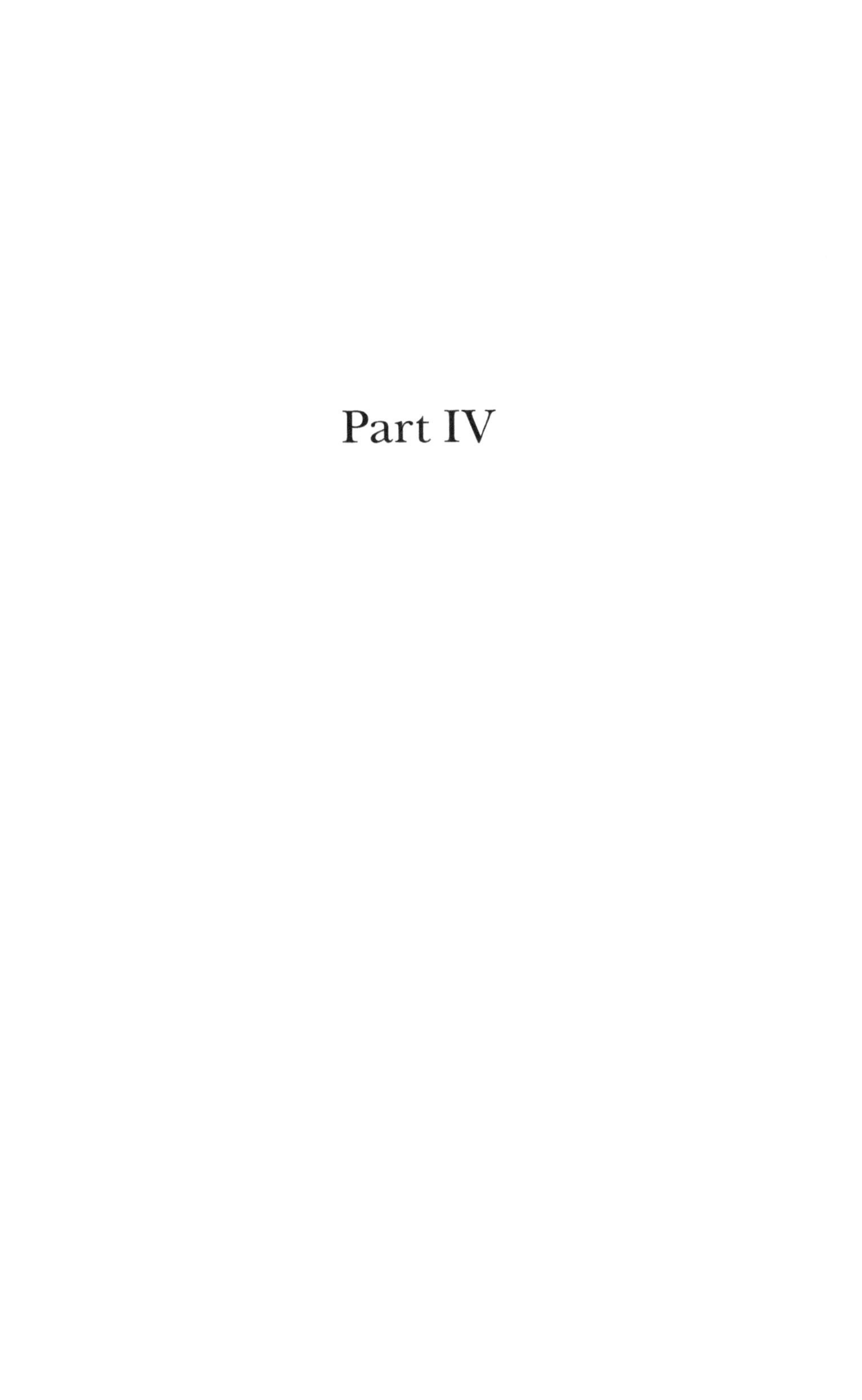

18

It had been a long tube ride from the Greenpeace offices in Canonbury in London's north to Gloucester Road in South Kensington. Standing under the glass overhang outside the tube station, Kate let her lungs fill up with fresh air and observed the busy London street scene for a moment. Then she started to walk in the direction of Hyde Park.

She had made the walk several times, and each time she was filled with joy. In a strange way, it felt a bit like home, though she'd never really frequented the area before Dad had moved there. She was also happy for Dad himself, as it was a nice area. It had all the shops he needed, excellent transport links, and, above all, Hyde Park. He could go out any time, sit in the sun on the benches, and watch the people.

She had nevertheless become a bit worried about him. Last time, he hadn't radiated the same energy as before. He didn't have the same temper in their conversations. But the sharpness of his analysis remained unchanged. She doubted that would ever fade.

The black cab coming from the right surprised her: she wasn't used to cars driving on the wrong side of the street. It also reminded her that she temporarily had to abandon her Amsterdam attitude with eternal priority for pedestrians and cyclists. Obediently she waited for the green light and then continued along Gloucester Road. She glanced at her watch and knew she would arrive in less than ten minutes.

Kate and Dad ate sandwiches together for lunch in the kitchenette and discussed the usual things. It was only after they had seated themselves in the small but cozy living room that Kate asked him about the Treaty of Westminster. As a result of his emigration Dad's knowledge of English and Dutch history was far above average, so perhaps he could tell her something about the treaty.

"You can probably tell more about it yourself than anyone else," Dad answered.

"What do you mean?"

"You mention that treaty, so you must know something about it, don't you?"

It was Dad all over, Kate thought. "Actually, I found out there were two of them. One in 1654 that ended the First Anglo-Dutch War and excluded the Orange family from being head of state. The second one in 1674, which ended the Third Anglo-Dutch War and confirmed that Dutch New York from then on belonged to England."

"Exactly, my dear."

"Now, I was wondering what consequences this treaty had for New York."

Dad lifted his eyebrows. "Well, in essence, your question is probably to what extent the English differ from the Dutch!"

Kate nodded, although she wasn't sure the American lawyer was looking for this. But it could be a start.

"Dad, I know the Dutch and English have a lot in common today, but what about *then,* a few centuries ago? It must have been a huge difference for the population of New York to live under Dutch rule or English rule."

She looked into Dad's eyes and noticed that smile. The smile that betrayed he knew something and was about to let her discover it.

"Would you believe me if I told you the two countries were almost one at a certain time?"

Puzzled, Kate shook her head.

"Well, still, it's true. In fact, England has been greatly influenced by Holland in roughly four historical periods."

Kate was all ears.

"You know that the population of England found its origin for a large part in the people that migrated from the European mainland, starting in the fifth century after the breakdown of the Roman Empire. Many of these migrants came from a region named Angeln, in present-day Denmark, and from a region comprising Lower Saxony, in the north of the present-day countries of Germany and the Netherlands."

"Hence the Anglo-Saxons." This much she knew.

"Indeed. Now, you should know that the Anglo-Saxons that settled in England consisted for a large part of Frisians."

Kate recalled what she'd learned in high school about the Frisians, the name givers of Holland's northern province Friesland. "Fiercely independent people," she stated. "Even Charlemagne had to accept Frisian rules, while as king of the Franks and emperor of the Romans he dominated most of Europe."

"Exactly, my dear. To the extent that the word 'free' itself stems from the *Fri*-sians."

While Dad slowly got up and walked to the kitchen, Kate wondered how many people in the world knew this.

"The second wave of Dutch influence," Dad continued when he returned with the tea and milk, "was at the time the Spanish Inquisition ravaged the Low Countries, halfway through the sixteenth century. It triggered a massive exodus of Dutchmen to England, and more in particular, East Anglia. Their number was estimated at one hundred thousand—roughly the number of London's inhabitants at that time. Being much more advanced, the Netherlanders brought progress in many domains."

"Colchester?" Kate asked.

Dad nodded and was happy she understood. Colchester in Essex, his town of origin. A large number of Dutch fugitives settled there, which the Dutch Quarter still testified to that day.

"But also in Canterbury and Norwich. They mechanized agriculture, drained swamps, and built dikes. They introduced the use of glass and steel. One could say that the Dutch immigrants of that time laid the foundations for England becoming a superpower later on."

After tea, Kate and Dad decided to go out and take a stroll in Hyde Park. From Dad's apartment, it was just a matter of crossing Kensington Road, and they entered the park at Palace Gate, past the guard standing bolt upright, his large, protruding chin in the air.

"Dad, you mentioned that the two countries almost became one," Kate said while strolling up the main alley, arm in arm with her father.

"Indeed my dear, that was a few decades later. The growing competition between Holland and England and their East India companies became so intense, and the costs of defending their faraway trading posts became so unsustainable that they discussed a merger. First between the companies and later even between the countries."

"A merger between countries?" Kate had never heard of that before. "So why didn't it work out?"

"In short because England proposed a combined Dutch-English conquest of the world, whereby England would take the American continent, and the Dutch Republic the whole of Africa and Asia. But the Dutch had already taken over most of Asia by themselves, so they saw little advantage in the proposal."

While they sat down at one of the benches around Hyde Park's Round Pond, Kate thought about the consequences the deal would have had. *An Anglo-Dutch world!*

"So when the deal failed," Dad continued, "the confrontations continued by force: the famous Anglo-Dutch Wars. They mostly took place at sea to claim trade routes. And an increasingly important route between Europe and the city of New York was finally secured by England in the Treaty of Westminster of 1674."

It reminded Kate of her other planned visit for that day, so she nervously looked at her watch.

"The episode coincided with the third wave of Dutch influence, during Holland's Golden Age. England did everything to copy the success of its neighbor, to such an extent that historians now refer to the period as "Going Dutch." It touched every aspect of society, culturally and economically. For example, England copied the Dutch system of private lending to finance its fleet. They hired Dutch scientists in many domains. The nobility was attracted by Dutch art and architecture. It's no coincidence that the Royal Palace in Kew Gardens is called 'the Dutch House.'"

Kate looked up again. *Kew Gardens*! Another hint at her afternoon visit. In a hurry now, she took Dad by the arm and started the stroll back to Dad's apartment.

"Dad, you mentioned there were *four* waves of influence."

The grin appeared again.

"Don't tell me you saved the best for last."

19

The wailing sirens disturbed the serene calmness of The Hague's city center as the convoy of service cars raced along the Hofvijver, the small lake in front of the Dutch parliament. Guided by two motorcyclists, the convoy left the Kneuterdijk boulevard a few hundred yards farther, entered a narrow side street, and finally came to a halt in front of a stylish red-brick building on Noordeinde Street.

The doors of the service cars swung open, and Smeenk stepped out of the first car. He looked around him for a few seconds and took a deep, nervous breath. At the far end of the street, he noticed a police car temporarily blocking the access for all other traffic. Just right of the brick building, he saw Noordeinde Palace, the Dutch queen's working palace. But the building they were about to enter was the private residence of the crown prince, the queen's eldest son and heir to the throne.

The small group of men quickly entered the building. The heavy wooden door shut behind them, and they walked through the marble corridor to the large reception room on the ground floor.

Smeenk took a glass of Champagne from the waiter and looked around at the other guests that had already gathered in the room. He immediately noticed Van Olden. They exchanged polite nods. Smeenk decided not to approach him; there was too much tension and excitement in the room for chitchat. And above all, he needed to avoid giving any hints to the others about their recent private meeting.

The other guests were the rest of the event committee: the financiers, and a small circle of the prince's other direct advisors. All knew exactly why they had been summoned: it was the moment. The time for the announcement they had planned for for months—some of them even years.

A sudden silence fell over the crowd when the prince slowly descended the stairway. He wore his dark-blue navy uniform with golden decorations and a black tie. Smeenk knew the black tie was standard for navy uniforms throughout the world, a custom started in 1676 to mourn the death of the Dutch naval hero Michiel de Ruyter, the main figure in the Anglo-Dutch wars.

The thought sent a shiver down his spine: it reminded him of the Treaty of Westminster.

The prince stopped his descent at the third step from the bottom, providing him with a natural elevation to address the men below him. When he started his word of welcome, Smeenk noticed how the prince's left hand kept caressing the decorative crystal ball at the end of the stairway's handrail. The boy had never been a natural speaker, but it was a clear sign that he was just as nervous as the other people in the room. And not without reason: the operation would also have vast consequences for the prince himself; so much was sure.

The speech didn't last long, as most other instructions had already been shared during the countless previous meetings. Smeenk recalled that some of the meetings had been difficult, also for the boy personally. They concerned the conditions he would have to accept should all go according to plan. Far-reaching conditions. Like most of the group, Smeenk didn't have a high opinion of the prince's vision and political instincts, but the boy surely had to realize the consequences of the operation. Anyway, now he'd given the green light for the operation a minute ago, there was no way back anymore.

After the speech, another round of drinks loosened the atmosphere somewhat, and the men congratulated each other on the prince's decision. The financiers seemed the most in their element, but that was no surprise. For them, the operation had hardly any downsides, while the upside was difficult to fathom, so colossal would be the financial windfall that could result from the operation. In fact, all of them knew that the financiers were behind the whole operation, and the prince had little choice but to obey.

Smeenk observed the group while sipping from his glass. A boyish fever had filled the air, in a way that reminded him of his fraternity days at the University of Leiden. *It was their finest hour,* he mused. The decision had been made: the operation would take place.

It meant that until the date of the event, all his attention and energy would be required. His wife, Hedwig, would have to be patient once more, and his Jennifer would surely finally be proud of him once in power. There was no room for failure; all elements that could pose even the slightest threat to the operation would have to be eliminated at once. It was what all the men in the room expected from him. The event would take place exactly two weeks from now.

20

When the District Line tube came above the ground, Kate was wakened by the blinding daylight. She realized she had dozed off briefly—no surprise, given the early hour of her flight to London that morning. It had been fantastic to see Dad again, and she was very happy to see him so energetic. Her question about the Treaty of Westminster had visibly inspired him. She wished she could have stayed longer, but she didn't want to miss the opportunity of being in London for where she was heading now.

She got off at Kew Gardens and walked out of the station. They had told her it was only a ten-minute walk. When she didn't see any signs, she turned back at the ticket counter. Her sudden move made her bump against the person right behind her.

When she excused herself, the man quickly turned away. But she had briefly seen his face and instantly recognized his strange protruding chin: the man posting at Hyde Park's entrance! *He must have taken the same tube,* she thought while staring at the man's back as he returned to the train tracks at a fast pace. She shrugged her shoulders, then finally noticed the signboard of her destination. She followed the arrow and started walking.

The quiet and pleasant street was named Burlington Avenue. With its orderly features, houses with gabled roofs, and tiny gardens in the front, Kate thought it somewhat resembled a Dutch street. The resemblances between England and Holland were still on her mind after Dad's stories earlier. During their stroll back, he had concluded his story with the fourth wave of England's "Dutchification". Dad had indeed saved the best for last, and he told her how the famous "Glorious Revolution" brought William III to the English throne. The *Dutchman* William III.

Kate had been stunned when Dad told her this: King William III of England was none other than the Dutch stadtholder Willem III of Orange-Nassau. She knew vaguely that the royal families were in some way related—as most were—but she didn't know the Dutch influence had gone that far.

Kate knew that William III had brought a wave of changes to the English society. Protestantism became firmly established. Public finances were modernized. And the famous Bill of Rights was passed, confirming certain civil rights. Apparently all after Dutch example.

The picture was complete now: the Anglo-Saxon settlers, the Protestant refugees in East Anglia, England's "Going Dutch," and William III's Glorious Revolution had made England resemble the Netherlands profoundly. It answered her question about the effects of the transfer of New York from Dutch to English hands. The answer was simple and followed logically from Dad's story: the transfer couldn't have triggered major social or cultural changes in view of the similarities between England and Holland.

When the contours of her destination became visible at the end of the street, her mind was immediately thrown back to the purpose of her current mission: the Treaty of Westminster. She followed the footpath over the large water basin in front of the imposing, spaceship-like building. It was gigantic and stood in stark contrast with its surroundings. She walked to the entrance, and high above the rotating doors she read the in large, static letters:

THE NATIONAL ARCHIVES

21

At the top floor of Stiglitz & Arrowsmith in Manhattan the tension was palpable.

"Everybody leave the room except Daniel!" partner Ben DiAngelo cried out loud, visibly furious.

Without saying a word, the team rose and headed for the elevator. Throughout the night, they had been analyzing the historical real estate transactions of the Ground Zero area, to which the dozens of empty coffee cups and Chinese takeaway boxes testified.

"What do you mean, 'impossible to give an opinion'?" DiAngelo shot at Daniel.

"Ben, we've come to the conclusion that it's simply impossible to give a full guarantee of the legal validity of the actual situation. We did everything to obtain the chain of documentation, but the time span is simply too large. Most deeds are non-existent or missing, others are impossible to read, pages are missing, etcetera."

"Do you realize what you're saying? Now a carve-out has to be made in the legal opinion! It will vastly reduce its value."

Daniel knew what it meant. Limitations in the *Representations and Warranties* of a legal opinion often triggered intense negotiations between the parties. Moreover, they required time.

"Why not simply *insure* the financial risk of defaults in the chain of title?" Daniel suggested. "After all, what are the chances that someone suddenly comes up with a legitimate ownership title dating back so long?"

DiAngelo thought for a moment. Due to the absence of a registration system that determined ownership with legal certainty, subscribing a so-called *Title Insurance* was common practice.

"In the end, it all comes down to quantifying the premium," Daniel said.

"And who will pay for it?" DiAngelo asked.

Both men already knew the answer: it would be difficult to hold the Lower Manhattan Development Corporation liable in case of problems, so the risk premium would have to be carried in full by their client.

"Anyway," DiAngelo continued, "as a starting point for any calculation an insurer will take the value of the ground. So the question is this: what's the value of Ground Zero?"

"We already did the maths, Ben."

"Something tangible. Not like that Dutch clown some centuries ago who bought Manhattan for two peanuts!"

The team had talked about it before: the twenty-four dollars' worth of merchandise that the Dutchman Peter Minuit had paid the Indians for Manhattan was often regarded as abusive. But the intern had calculated that with 6 percent compounded annually, the twenty-four dollars would today be in excess of one hundred billion dollars. A tantalizing amount, that made Minuit's deal look far less ridiculous.

"We made alternative calculations," Daniel said and placed a file before DiAngelo, who now seemed to have lost some of his initial temper. "You take the current average purchase price in Manhattan of $1,000 per square foot. When multiplied by the surface of Ground Zero of 65,000 square feet, that gives $700 million. Assuming the area can be constructed with 30 floors on average, the total value would be around $21 billion. If you estimate the chances at 1 percent that a breach in the chain of title would cause a problem, this represents a value of $210 million. Spread over an assumed lifetime of a building of 100 years, this gives the amount of $2.1 million per year."

DiAngelo was impressed. That was a negotiable premium.

"The calculation method is far from perfect, of course, but at least it's something we can bring to the table. What do you think?"

DiAngelo was silent for a moment and then slammed his hand on his desk. "Go for it. And you'd better make it work."

When DiAngelo had left the floor, Daniel glanced down the forest of skyscrapers around him and wondered what catastrophic effects it would have if one day someone stood up with a historic ownership claim on Manhattan as a whole. Even if the chances of success in a court case were 1 percent, it would trigger revaluations worth hundreds of billions of dollars, sending a financial shockwave through the country. The claim would be a financial 9/11.

Daniel decided that this part of the transaction better remain behind closed doors. Tomorrow he would propose reinforced security measures during the transaction in order to avoid any leaks. He suddenly also regretted having contacted that Dutch lawyer Kate Bates about it. Luckily, she probably had already put the matter aside, as she hadn't come back to him on the Treaty of Westminster.

22

It didn't take Kate much time to find the treaty's reference number in the National Archives' public computer. What did take long, however, was obtaining a Reader's Ticket, required to inspect original documents. It implied dozens of questions in a test on how to treat documents, support pages, fold seals, close protecting boxes, and so on. When she finally held the plastic card, it felt as if she'd passed school exams.

"Follow me, please," the staff member said.

While crossing the huge building on their way to the document inspection desk, Kate noticed the hundreds of people poring over documents in the reading rooms. She marveled at the existence of such an institute that reunited documents from several centuries. A true temple of knowledge.

"The full archives go back to the year 1688," the staff member explained. "The year of the Glorious Revolution."

Kate thought back to Dad's story. *Apparently the changes brought by William III also applied to government archives.*

"The Treaty of Westminster of 1674 is part of a special collection. It has reference number SP 108/311. SP stands for *State Papers*. It can be consulted only in a secured room. And under surveillance."

"Under surveillance?" Kate asked, surprised, still hurrying behind the quick paces of her guide.

"As you can imagine, the document is a very valuable piece. Some special preparations are necessary."

At the inspection desk, another staff member handed her a piece of paper. "Reservation number MR009. Please wait here; you'll be called when the document and the room are ready."

When the solid gray box finally lay in front of Kate inside the secure room, she felt a certain excitement. The original Treaty of Westminster! The transfer of New York, the most important city in the world. How come so few people knew this history? It felt as if the box in front of her contained the secret answer.

She undid the linen strings of the box, carefully lifted out the large, hard-covered book, and placed it on the table. It had several wax seals, folded neatly inside and protected by foam patches. She opened the multicolored cover and noticed the beautiful, original, handwritten parchments. But to her consternation, she couldn't read them. *They were in Latin!*

She had expected it to be in either English or Dutch, the languages of the parties, and her Latin was very limited. She tried to read through the articles and found the one she thought concerned the transfer of New York.

"Do you read Latin, by any chance?" Kate asked the library supervisor standing next to her.

"The basics. This clause?"

Kate nodded, and the supervisor started scribbling down some notes on a sheet.

"It translates as follows: '*Whatsoever countries, islands, towns, ports, castles, or forts have or shall be taken on both sides, since the time the late, unhappy war broke out, either in Europe or elsewhere, shall be restored to the former lord or proprietor, in the same condition they shall be in when the peace itself shall be proclaimed.*'"

For Kate, the text was crystal clear: New York had to be handed over to England once and for all, as England was the proprietor since

1664, the year it had had captured the city for the first time. But why hand it over "in the same condition"? Why would the Dutch voluntarily agree with English rights and regulations? For Kate, the condition formed a simple confirmation of what she'd already learned that day: the city came under English administration officially, but due to the similarities between the countries, there would be hardly any changes for the population.

She restored the document in the box with the help of the supervisor and left the room. This had to be it, the final answer to the American lawyer's question. She doubted it would be useful to him.

Then in happened. In a glimpse, she saw the face of the man with the protruding chin again, just behind the second row of cabinets. They looked at each other for a split second, and then the man immediately ducked away in the aisle. She instantly knew something was wrong; it was obvious this was no coincidence anymore. First the man had been standing at the entrance of Hyde Park, then he had followed her to Kew Gardens tube station, and now he was here.

Was she being followed?

In confusion, she ran down the stairs, turned right following the restroom signs, and locked herself in the ladies' room. It took some time before she started breathing normally again and got her thoughts back. Who could this man possibly be? Was it about the Greenpeace case? It was very well possible she was being shadowed by a government agency—after all, she was in direct contact with people who had breached the law and were willing to do so again.

"Someone there?" a voice said.

Kate stiffened, terrified.

A loud bang on the door followed.

She desperately tried to peep through the narrow chink next to the door. Relieved, she noticed the blue overall of a cleaner. Still unable to speak, she knocked on the door to signal occupancy.

After the cleaner had gone, Kate cautiously opened the door and looked around if there was any sign of the Chin. When the coast seemed clear, she left the toilets and hurried to the exit. Once outside, she looked back to the building once more, then she ran back in the direction of the station.

With horror she recalled the first time she had been shadowed a few years ago. It had been a destabilizing experience; the paranoia had been overwhelming. By pure chance she had found out it was Dutch secret service, when she was defending a journalist who had written a critical history on the royal family. But currently she wasn't handling a case that involved the House of Orange.

Wait a second…

She stopped and looked up in shock. The Treaty of Westminster, at least the earlier one, *did* concern the House of Orange. It banned them from power!

It couldn't be, she tried to convince herself. They couldn't know she was researching the treaty: she had never discussed it with anyone!

It took her some seconds to realize that was not entirely true.

The American lawyer!

23

Of course it was a lie. But the bloody situation had left him no choice. He was simply too tired, and the planning had been too short. Receiving the call in the middle of the night and jumping immediately into action was not his style. *And not his client's style either.*

He was wondering what the mission was about, as normally the slightest risk had to be excluded. Now all he had received was a set of pictures and the flight schedule of his target, with the instructions to shadow and report. Such a hasty approach implied risks, which his master had to take for granted. The lie in his report was a minor one; it had only smoothed the sharp edges of the operation.

Halfway down his second pint of lager, he started to feel the effect of the alcohol, calming his nerves. He stared in front of him at the other guests of the Kew Greenhouse Café. He admitted that despite the hastiness of the operation, the mistakes had been unforgivable for someone of his experience and reputation, and he blamed himself. *Was he getting too old for the job?*

Annoyed, he stood up and walked to the restrooms at the back of the pub. A quick glance in the mirror revealed puffy eyelids. But the dark irises still looked as energetic as always, almost aggressive. He knew his stern look and protruding chin didn't make him a likeable guy, but at almost fifty, he had accepted who he was and didn't mind anymore. Besides, his success with the ladies seemed only on the rise in recent years.

From his trouser pocket, he took the piece of paper with the telephone number he had just called, tore it up into pieces, wrapped the pieces in a paper towel, and threw the whole wad in the basket in the corner. As always, it had been a one-time-use number. It was part of the rules: no mobile phones, no e-mail. Public phone booths were still the safest way of communication. The only problem nowadays was finding those bastards! It had taken him ten extra minutes, but he'd finally found one at the other side of Kew Gardens Station, in front of the bar.

Apart from the lie that he'd seen his target take the tube to Heathrow Airport, which he had not, the telephone conversation had been straightforward. He had even felt proud about the results of the day's mission, being able to report all destinations of the target, including addresses and the duration of stays. But he considered one thing in particular a stroke of genius: his decision to immediately run back to the building opposite Hyde Park when the old man and the target had passed him at the park's entrance gate. It had allowed him to quickly check the name plates of the residents inside the hall of the building without losing sight of the couple in the park. He reported that the old man was possibly the target's father, E. C. Bates.

But the most important information he'd been able to communicate was certainly the unexpected visit to the British National Archives. He'd almost lost the target when she changed tube lines at Earl's Court: he'd assumed she would change for the Piccadilly line to Heathrow Airport, back to Amsterdam. But to his surprise, she switched to the District Line to Kew. It had been a close call.

Then she had surprised him again, suddenly turning around in front of Kew Gardens station. It had been his first mistake, as she'd seen his face. As a result, she had recognized him in the library. He had quickly turned away, which was another mistake: he hadn't seen her reaction. Had it been surprise? Amusement? Or even panic? In the latter case, it meant she was possibly aware she was being followed. This was a crucial piece of information he now didn't have.

He was glad he had decided not to start looking for her right after the incident. Instead, he had found a place close to where she would have to pass anyway on the way out. In fact, he had been standing at the window several meters above her when she came through the exit and started to run in the direction of the station. Occupied by the question of whether she ran because of him or simply not to miss her flight, he headed back to the second floor to the desk where the target had made enquiries. He had asked the clerk whether the document the lady had consulted in the special room was still available.

"You mean the Treaty of Westminster?" the clerk had answered. "I'm afraid I just deposited it at the storage again."

He had thanked the clerk and left the National Archives, in search of the telephone booth.

24

Smeenk finished his weekly call with the Dutch prime minister and walked to his office window overlooking The Hague, emptying his cup of espresso in one gulp. He had never liked the man—too young and too pretentious. At the time, he'd even done some soft lobbying with his employer to prevent the man's nomination, but without success. He had accumulated a file on him containing some interesting facts about a holiday visit some years ago but had decided not to disclose it for the risk of backfiring. At least now he had something up his sleeve in case of future problems: in his line of work, survival sometimes depended on favors.

The PM was too media eager also. It made him think of Pim Fortuyn, the populist leader some years ago who was bound to become PM: he too had kicked against the Dutch political establishment. And now he was dead, the media stupidly still convinced he'd been shot by an activist.

The phone on his desk rang. It was his senior assistant.

"Sir, we have news on Kate Bates. Most disquieting I believe, so I thought you ought to hear it right away."

"Tell me."

"Two reports. The first from our informant at the West India House. She visited the place, reportedly looking for historical documents."

Smeenk felt like he had been struck by lightning. *So she's after it!* He put the phone on the speaker and walked a few steps, his right hand in a tight fist. "And the second report?"

"From the informant who followed her to London. She's on her way back to Amsterdam."

"Yes, as scheduled. Is that important?"

"The point is, sir, he reported some earlier visits that are highly suspicious. Even alarming, one could say."

"Where? With whom?"

"Just before she left for the airport, she visited the National Archives."

Smeenk thought for a moment. "Were they open that early?"

"Not in The Hague, sir—the *British* National Archives in London. In Kew, to be precise. She went there on her way back to Heathrow."

"Good God! Do we know what she was looking for?"

"Yes, we do. It seems that she saw the original Treaty of Westminster."

"Dammit, it confirms she's after it! What else did the informant say?"

"He mentioned he briefly overheard Bates when she met a person that was probably her father. Could be the case, by the way, as we know he lives in London. According to our man, her father mentioned something like 'a wave of Dutch influence on the country.'"

"On what country?"

"Not sure the informant heard that too. He didn't mention it."

"I told you this is wrong. I have no idea where she got the idea from, but she's onto it. She's searching for the pieces of the puzzle. It must have been the American lawyer, otherwise it doesn't make sense. She's looking things up for him."

"Maybe she's *his* lawyer?" the assistant suggested.

Smeenk paced up and down the room while polishing his glasses furiously.

"Could be. It all started with the American. Maybe Bates is just bad luck. Anyway, we have to stop them both while we still can. They're still searching, so they don't know the whole story yet."

"Stop them, sir?"

"Yes. Keep shadowing Bates. Find out if the American is her client officially. If not, her duty of secrecy won't apply, so we can get information out of her more easily."

"And the American? There's no official investigation running against him, so I think there's little we can do."

"There *is*," Smeenk said, nodding decidedly. "But I'll take care of that myself. "

He ended the call and immediately pressed another button on the telephone while adjusting his glasses with a frown.

"Hello, Oscar. How are things?" the loud voice of Van Olden creaked through the speaker.

"We have a slight problem. You recall what we discussed recently—about that associate at your firm?"

"Sure, Daniel Van Wart. Was the information I sent you of any help?"

"Yes, it was. But I'm afraid it only confirmed our emergency signal. You know who he's been in touch with? Kate Bates, of all people!"

It was quiet for some time on the other side of the line.

"I don't understand. What does she have to do with Van Wart?"

"I was hoping *you* could tell me, Hein. You'll understand this is more than serious. First the keyword, and now the Bates connection. Can't be a coincidence. And we've got information that Bates has been digging for information like crazy."

"What information?"

"I can't tell you exactly, but it's closely linked to the keywords Van Wart used. So he's the instigator. We think he instructed Bates. He's onto something, and it looks related to the project."

"What are you suggesting, Oscar?"

"Van Wart must be stopped—taken from the case he's working on. There must be a link between that case and our project somewhere. We can't take any risks, not at this stage."

Van Olden laughed. "That's ridiculous, Oscar! I can't just take people off cases as I please. They would never accept that in New York. Not as long as there's no concrete proof he did something wrong!"

"I don't have to tell you about the consequences, Hein. What if he *is* working on something? Do you take responsibility for that?"

"If it's so serious, you'll have to follow the normal route, Oscar. You notify the American justice department, and pending the official investigation, maybe we could take him off the case. But not just because your secret systems came up with a hunch!"

"Just send him on gardening leave or something until we're done. I know you people work long hours; he probably deserves a break anyway. I think you've got little choice, Hein."

Smeenk knew Van Olden perfectly understood the implied threat. Measures from above. The power, the connections, the immense fortune—not even the country's best lawyer could go against it.

"Hein, I interpret your silence as an agreement. Send the man away, and try to find out why in God's name he made that search!"

There was no response.

25

Kate put up the collar of her coat to protect her from the horizontal rain and looked back once more at Amsterdam's mighty Central Station, its wet roof glowing orange in the spotlights. It had been impossible to find a working phone booth inside due to construction works for a new subway line, and Kate didn't dare use her cell phone, as it was possibly also bugged. She crossed the street in the direction of the brown café opposite Karpershoek station, reputedly one of the oldest in Amsterdam. If it had a phone, it would be her first opportunity to call since her arrival from London an hour ago; the airport itself, with all its cameras, had, of course, been way too risky.

The wind and the drizzle didn't bother her, and she desperately needed some fresh air. It was back again, the anxiety of being followed. The paranoia had set in immediately, and she knew from her experience the previous time that it wouldn't be over soon. She knew the methods and the techniques, and with today's omnipresence of electronics and telecommunication, it was a sheer impossibility to escape the eavesdropping.

Unless one knew who they were. It was the first information she desperately needed to obtain. After the incident at Kew, she had acted immediately. On her way to Heathrow Airport, after having changed tubes several times to lose any other followers, she had made her request from a public phone booth. Now it was time to call back for the response.

She found a phone at the back of the bar, inserted a card, and dialed the number of her long-time contact at the Ministry of Justice.

"No pending formal investigations pending against you by any Dutch judicial agency," the contact said.

"And the others?" Kate asked impatiently. She meant the AIVD, the Dutch intelligence agency, although her contact was officially not supposed to know this, as it fell under the Interior Ministry.

"No active file either. Bye for now. Take care." The line went dead.

They were the answers she had feared the most. They ruled out the possibility that she was being followed in relation to a client of hers or due to her work for Greenpeace—such investigations would be done by a public prosecutor. She instantly understood what it meant.

The House of Orange again!

She had no doubt anymore that it was linked to the American lawyer and the research she had done for him. Apparently he was involved in something so serious that any person involved had to be checked out. Whatever it was about, her involvement had certainly made alarm bells ring: after the past incidents, her name would certainly not be cheered at in royal circles. Perhaps even feared. It was the reason they sent that protruding chin after her.

She briefly looked around the café, but no one paid attention to her. She noticed how she trembled when she put the card into the phone again, this time for a transatlantic call.

She'd thought about it long enough during the flight. If the American lawyer knew what he was working on, he had knowingly put her in difficulty. It would be unforgivable, and she would certainly let him know. If, on the other hand, he was not aware, he probably also didn't know whom he was up against. In that case, she would have to warn him. First she had considered talking to

Evelyn about it—after all, this Van Wart was her colleague. But she decided not to, in order to protect her as much as possible from the terrible adversary she now faced.

She retrieved the number of Stiglitz & Arrowsmith from her cell phone, waited some seconds until the loudly belling tram had passed the café, and then started pressing the numbers on the steel keypad.

26

The top floor of Stiglitz & Arrowsmith's posh New York office had been cleared from the takeaway boxes, and fresh flowers had taken their place. The polished shoes of the Goldman Sachs team made the first imprints on the freshly vacuumed carpet, followed by the Stiglitz & Arrowsmith team. The thirty or so people took their seats around the shiny table for a meeting they knew would be decisive.

When espressos had been served, partner Ben DiAngelo gave a short resume of the present state of the case and the work that still had to be done. Everyone sat in silence when DiAngelo announced the real topic of the day, to be presented by Daniel Van Wart. It was standard practice at the firm to let the person who had made a mistake present the solution in front of everyone involved. Daniel felt like a condemned man walking to the gallows.

Daniel immediately dropped the difficult point: it would not be possible to give a full legal opinion on the historic chain of title of Ground Zero. He tried to sound as neutral as possible, as if it was only a technicality. He quickly shifted to the proposed solution: estimating the value of the risk that had to be insured. It provoked several questions about valuation methods, but to his surprise, the expected outrage did not occur. He was relieved: it meant that his team could abandon the heavy load of historic research, however interesting he had found it personally.

Just when Ben DiAngelo had taken over again, and Daniel had taken his seat, Daniel's cell phone vibrated. His assistant.

"I'm in the meeting," he whispered.

"Got someone from Amsterdam on the line. Says it's urgent."

"The Amsterdam office? I'll call back later."

"No, not the office, someone from outside. A lady who insists it's urgent."

Daniel was surprised; he didn't know anyone in Amsterdam. "Okay, put her through," he whispered while leaving the room in silence.

"My name is Kate Bates. I'm a friend of your colleague Evelyn from Amsterdam, and we've been in touch recently on—"

"Ah, yeah, I remember! You helped me with the historical sources. I didn't have the chance yet to thank you for that personally but—"

"Mr. Van Wart, this message may come as a surprise, but I just wanted to let you know that I'm being shadowed because of the research I did on these sources."

"Eh...sorry, but I don't think I got that. You said 'being shadowed'? What do you mean?"

"I mean someone's spying on me, investigating me. Because I've been in contact with you, and apparently, the things you're working on are a great concern to someone. So much so that they're following people. Are you aware of that?"

Daniel was confused. *What was she talking about?* "Well, the case is indeed important. I'm not allowed to tell you a lot about it, but I don't think people are being followed for it. I'm not sure I understand your point."

"Daniel, if I may call you so, I know this may sound strange and unbelievable, especially from someone you don't know, but you have to believe me. Someone has been following me, probably because I've been in contact with you and was doing that research on New York. The Treaty of Westminster and so. I'm a lawyer myself with experience in this field, and I can tell you that if someone's watching me after having been in touch with you, you are certainly being watched yourself. I have no idea what you're working on and why you needed that information, but I have to warn you that these people are very serious and have virtually unlimited powers. You must be very careful what you do—and whom you involve!"

Daniel was now intrigued by the strange call. *Being watched himself?* "If you say these people are dangerous, apparently you know them."

"Not personally, but I think I know who they are."

"And who are they, if I may ask?"

"It may come as a surprise, but I have reasons to believe it might be the Dutch royal family. At least, they're involved in some way."

"The Dutch royal family?" Daniel asked in amazement. *This was getting crazy now.*

"Again, I have no idea what it's about and what you know. But you do sound surprised, so I can only tell you that you must have touched a sensitive spot somewhere with this New York case of yours. Maybe some classified information or something. Something that can potentially be harmful to their interests."

"Sorry, Miss Bates, but this all sounds a bit strange to me. I'm in a meeting now; maybe we can talk about it some other time."

"Just be warned, Daniel. Somehow you appeared on their radar, and they won't let go. Just be aware that they'll check out other people you contact, just like me. You cannot call me anymore nor send e-mails. If you want to contact me again, ask Evelyn. But keep in mind that all you say is probably being listened to. Good luck, Daniel."

With a click, the line went dead.

Daniel looked at his cell phone in disbelief. It was the weirdest call he'd ever received. *Being followed?* Because of this chain-of-title issue?

He realized that they hadn't even talked about Kate's findings in the Treat of Westminster. Although he didn't need it anymore for the case, he was suddenly very curious what it was about.

27

He walked the Leliegracht up and down twice to make sure the coast was clear, then halted before a steel porch on the canal's eastern quay. He hadn't crossed anyone, apart from a couple of blondes cycling home from what must have been a party. At just after four o'clock in the morning, Amsterdam's canals were dark and silent.

He waited for several minutes to listen if there was any activity behind the porch, but the only sound he heard was a single awake and chattering duck in the canal behind him.

From his hip pocket he took a small tool kit and started to work on the lock. During his inspection earlier that evening he had already determined that it was child's play to crack. After two minutes he was inside, and he put a piece of tape around the lock so that it wouldn't close entirely and block his escape route.

The hallway led to an inner courtyard, enclosed by the backs of the canal houses forming the same quarter. The gardens belonging to each house were entirely fenced off, so some acrobatics would be necessary. Observing the situation from the hallway, he saw his own shadow on the opposite wall: the hunchback formed by his backpack and two bulges on his head—one of his baseball cap and the other of his protruding chin. He reached to the source of the light, stuck his gloved hand in the lantern, and unscrewed the lightbulb. The courtyard was now in complete darkness.

In agile moves, he climbed two fences and then stood still for a moment to count the houses, making sure his target was the right one. After the third fence, the sudden barking of a dog stopped him. He quickly ascertained that he couldn't be seen from the windows, hidden behind a folded parasol. Judging from the sound, the dog must be in the next garden. He sat down, placed his backpack on the floor, and took out the gun with silencer. The dog barked again; he had to finish this very quickly now.

He lay down, rolled himself to the fence, and looked underneath to see if he could see the dog.

Woof! Woof!

He crawled up in terror; the animal was right next to him on the other side of the fence. He pulled the gun, put it through the fence slightly higher, pointed it downward so as not to hit the surroundings, and pulled the trigger.

The bloop was soft but still very audible.

To assess the results of his action, he didn't move for a while. There was complete silence.

He turned his head to look underneath the fence and saw the rough contours of the lap dog lying next to him, motionless.

He jumped over the fence and quickly on to the next house, his target. He knew the building was empty, as he had also checked from the front side. Not a single light was burning. The lock of the back door was slightly more difficult, but after several minutes it opened and he was inside. He felt relieved: the mission didn't allow him to leave any traces, so breaking a window was not an option.

He put on plastic shoe covers and walked cautiously through the high hallway to the front of the building. Inside the office, he judged that the streetlights of the Keizersgracht canal at the front gave enough light to do the job. He put his backpack on the floor, changed his leather gloves for a pair of thin cotton ones, and organized his equipment systematically in front of him. He looked around for a moment and decided the chimney was the ideal place. The only obstacle was the huge stack of files in front of it. At the same time, it proved the chimney wasn't in use, so the equipment wouldn't melt—or worse, be detected during cleaning.

He removed the files with care, took the small transmitter and attached the small antenna to it, and inserted the set of three flat batteries. He put a piece of double-sided tape to the back of the device and stuck the whole thing to the inside of the chimney rim, pressing firmly. He inserted a pen in the tiny hole in the device and pressed for two seconds. From the backpack, he took the headset and listened when he pronounced the letters *p*, *s*, and *h* in the direction of the chimney.

It worked.

After he had placed the files back in their exact spot, he wrapped up his gear and left the office through the backside again. When he had jumped the first fence, he knelt down beside the dead dog and maneuvered it into the backpack. He was thankful it wasn't a bigger one; otherwise it wouldn't have fit in. From the edge of a flower bed, he removed two bricks and added them to the contents of the backpack.

The backpack was surprisingly heavy, and he had difficulty climbing the other fences—he almost fell over twice. Once he reached the hallway, he removed the piece of tape from the gate lock, closed it after him, and quietly walked onto the street.

At the next bridge over the Keizersgracht, he stood still for a moment and glanced over the dark and quiet canal. There was still no one to see. He took off the backpack, knelt down at the railing of the bridge, and lowered the heavy pack while holding one strap. He looked around one more time and then let it fall with a soft splash into the dark water below him.

When the ripples in the water reached the opposite side of the canal, the lone dark figure had already vanished into the night.

28

The firm's chairman, Lee Sutherland, laid his hand on DiAngelo's shoulder and looked sternly into his eyes.

"Don't take it personal, Ben. I know it's unfair—to him and to you. But hey, see it as a consequence of being a global firm. Sometimes you're confronted with local issues that force you to change course. I mean, you have to stay flexible."

"It's a totally mad decision!"

"Ben, as I said, we'll find someone else. HR will give you the budget, and it'll be charged to Amsterdam. Even if you need two people. I know you guys have a lot of work."

DiAngelo stood up and walked to the window. "This is not about budget, Lee! It's about reputation! It simply doesn't make sense. A few days ago, you gave a speech on the importance of the deal and the client, and now, at a critical moment you take one of my senior associates off the case! For a bullshit reason! What the hell did Van Wart do? If there was a problem, it would have been revealed when we hired him, through the security screening."

"Let's not go over it again, Ben. There *is* a valid reason. Amsterdam's client is just as important as ours, so when they raise a doubt about the integrity of one of our employees, we have to respect that. That also concerns reputation."

Both men were silent for a while and stared over the Manhattan skyline, juggling the ice cubes in their tumblers.

"Okay, let's try to get back to our senses," Sutherland said after a while. "Remember the explanation we discussed? Let's ask Daniel to come up. Are you ready?"

Without waiting for an answer, Sutherland walked to his desk and pushed a button on the phone.

A few minutes later, there was a double knock the door, and Daniel entered the room.

"Hi, Daniel. Come in, please," Sutherland said jovially. "Ben and I wanted to discuss something with you."

Daniel's breath stopped for a second. Such phrases meant either heaven or hell.

Sutherland turned to DiAngelo. "Ben, do you want to start?"

"Sure. You see, Daniel, to be very short, there has been some criticism from Goldman on the way we've handled the case recently. I think you can imagine what they refer to; they were not amused by this chain-of-title issue."

Daniel knew it would be hell.

"In fact, they blame us for it and consider it a mistake. And to be honest, we agree it wasn't one of your best moves to come up with it at such a late stage."

Daniel was dumbfounded by the accusation. "But they came up with it themselves!"

"That's the point; they think it was up to us."

"Ben, you know very well the issue was farfetched, never pushed forward in any other transaction! I mean, it could have happened to anyone!"

"We're not anyone, Daniel. We're Stiglitz & Arrowsmith, and it was up to us to cover it."

"We did! We checked all available titles—a hell of a job. And the financial risks will be insured. Goldman seemed happy and confident with it. What did they tell you? That they changed their mind?"

"Well, maybe they were less pleased than you thought. The point is that we're afraid we cannot let you work on the case anymore under these circumstances. It's a question of reputation."

"What do you mean by that, Ben? That you're taking me off the case?"

"I'm afraid we have no choice, Daniel."

"But that's ridiculous, and you know it! At this stage of the case and so short before the closing? It's irresponsible! Besides, I'm not convinced Goldman seriously believes we made a mistake. I could explain things. Let's call them right now and—"

"Sit down, Daniel," Sutherland intervened, putting his hand on Daniel's shoulder. "I know the decision comes as a disappointment, and I just wanted to say you shouldn't take it personal. We all know you did a good job. But sometimes it's in the interest of the firm to show the client we take him seriously. Even if that requires making sacrifices."

"So I'm the sacrifice?"

"You see, Daniel, exactly this kind of reaction makes us believe you pushed the limits maybe a bit too far. You need some rest, buddy. The only sacrifice—if you can call it that—is taking some holidays. Paid by the firm. That's not so bad, is it?"

"Not too bad? After all the time and effort I invested in the case? That's what you call Dutch comfort!"

Sutherland and DiAngelo looked at each other in surprise: Daniel couldn't know the decision came from the Dutch office.

"You call it what you like," Sutherland said. "But I recommend that you take this chance. I'm sure that when you return, there will be lots of new cases waiting for you."

A whirlwind was blowing in Daniel's mind. *It simply didn't make sense!* What on earth explained this unexpected and illogical decision? Was it Goldman indeed? Or was there something going on within the firm he didn't know about? To avoid the looks of the two men waiting for his reaction, he gazed over the city in a northern direction, past Central Park, in the direction of Yonkers.

Yonkers.

He recalled it was another part of New York with a name of Dutch origin: *jonkheer*, a title of nobility. Was Dutch nobility now also at play? That's at least what that lawyer Bates had warned him for. He admitted he knew little about the Dutch royal house, but she had mentioned their influence. One thing was evident now: there was something about this Ground Zero case and for some reason he was in the middle of it. There was only one way to find out more about it: Kate Bates.

29

Seated at her desk overlooking Amsterdam's Keizersgracht canal, Kate tried to focus on the file in front of her. She knew it was a strength of her character to be able to canalize anger or frustration into structured action. She'd written her best legal memos when frustrated, such as the last time she was fighting the House of Orange. And the incident at the beginning of her career, when the Dutch bar refused her temporary secondment to an English firm: apparently London was too exotic for them. She tried to recall the name of the bar's president back then. Van Ouden or something. No, Van *Olden* it was. During the application procedure, he had even made sexually oriented remarks that today would undoubtedly classify as harassment. She wondered what had become of the man.

In the past hour, she'd made covert inquiries among acquaintances close to royal circles, but so far it had yielded little to nothing. The only interesting information came from a member of parliament, who mentioned that the spokesperson of the crown prince hadn't been available for the past several weeks—a curious situation in view of the imminent passage of the throne.

Her cell phone rang.

"Kate, it's Daniel Van Wart. I got your number from our mutual friend. She said it was okay. Listen, things have changed; they threw me off the case."

Kate was silent for a moment. "What do you mean, threw you off the case?"

"The case with the research on New York City. For some reason, they didn't want me to work on it anymore. I thought you'd want to know; maybe now they'll stop following you."

"I don't know, Daniel. I don't know what *you* know, and I don't know what *they* know. The only thing *I* know is that they won't stop until their interests have been satisfied. And I haven't got a clue what the issue is about. Only you can tell me that!"

"I don't know either Kate, honestly! The only thing I've been checking is the status of property claims on Manhattan, back to Dutch times. How can that be so sensitive? All I found is that America's Dutch past is not well taught, but I don't see how that can be of interest to the Dutch crown."

"What do you mean, 'not well taught'?"

"I found out that the Dutch influence on New York was much bigger than most people know."

Kate instantly thought about Dad's story. "And the influence also lasted longer," she added.

"Did it?" Daniel asked in surprise.

"Never mind; it's a long story. All we know is that we touched on something weird. The claims on Manhattan, the treaty banning the Oranges from power, me being followed, and you being fired. Is it all a coincidence?"

"I've not exactly been fired."

"They've taken you from the case. Maybe for you that's a relief, but I need to find out what this is all about!"

"Don't get me wrong, Kate, I also do. At first, I didn't take your warnings seriously, but now that they've sent me away for a bogus reason, it makes me curious as hell to know what's really going on. Besides, I have the time now; they sent me on leave!"

Kate was silent for a moment.

"Daniel, can I ask you something? Something personal."

"Eh, sure."

"Your surname, Van Wart. It's a Dutch name, isn't it?"

"Yes, incidentally it is."

"Does it have anything to do with the case? I mean, the historical research you've been doing?"

"Eh, no. Why do you ask?"

"Nothing, just a hunch. Daniel, let's do it this way. I will try to find out some more about the Dutch royalty side. At the same time, you see what you can find on the New York side. Somewhere our stories must be linked. I have no idea where it will lead, but both of us have a problem, and both of us want it solved."

"Sounds like a deal."

30

Rotterdam was another city Oscar Smeenk didn't like. He would have preferred The Hague, of course, but the financiers had chosen Rotterdam for all meetings, and they were calling the shots. He had to admit that from where he was standing, the city's waterfront skyline was impressive.

Behind him towered the proud silhouette of Hotel New York, the former headquarters of the Holland America shipping line. Next to the entrance, his chauffeur waited obediently for him, but Smeenk needed some fresh air before they would return to The Hague. He needed to think clearly now.

He listened to the loud cries of the seagulls circling around and stared at the huge set of tubular mock chimneys in front of him. It was reminiscent of the ocean liners that once left here, taking thousands of families from an impoverished Europe to the new Promised Land: America. He wondered what percentage of Americans had ancestors that once stood at that same spot.

Possibly even the family of that Van Wart.

The thought immediately made him nervous again, and he took a drag from the cigarette he had just asked from his driver. The paper message he still held in his hand was indeed terrifying. During the meeting, someone had desperately tried to reach him, and after his cell phone had rung three times he had shut it off: the crucial topics discussed had not allowed for distractions. Apparently that hadn't stopped the caller, who had sent the message to the hotel by fax. It was handed to him after the meeting.

It briefly mentioned that the security measures against Kate Bates had yielded immediate results. Only a few hours after the installation of the equipment, they had captured a telephone conversation in her office that more or less summarized the actual status of the threat. It was positive in the sense that Bates and Van Wart had not yet discovered the clue of the story. It even looked as if they were far from it.

But there was bad news to the message as well. First, apparently Bates was aware she was being followed. Surveillance was therefore much less useful, as she would surely avoid any suspicious actions. In theory, she could have even faked the conversation; after all, only her voice was captured. It wasn't probable, but with a person clever as Bates, it couldn't be excluded either.

A different question was *how* she had found out. Had the agent made mistakes and revealed himself in England? He hadn't mentioned any such incident in his report. Or did Bates somehow have inside information on the operation? That was unlikely—if that were the case, she wouldn't be asking Van Wart questions.

In any event, it was now certain that both Bates and Van Wart were actively searching for the truth. And both seemed to be on the right track. Although it was, of course, only the combination of several tracks that could reveal the truth and endanger the operation.

Smeenk smiled at the thought that Bates and Van Wart had given away the fact that apparently they had some agreed contact person, even if they hadn't mentioned who it was. It was clever of them, but his men would find out. The big question was now what Van Wart would do. Van Olden confirmed he'd been taken from the case. But the telephone conversation made clear that he was committed to finding out. And he had the time now. Maybe their action had been too rash after all.

He threw the cigarette butt over the edge of the quay and turned around. While walking to the car, he glanced up at the facade of the hotel. The last rays of sunlight illuminated the golden weather vane. In the hall of the hotel, he'd read to his astonishment that the vane represented the *Half Moon*, Hudson's ship when he had discovered New York. He wondered if the other participants were also aware of the striking link with their operation. He had not dared to mention the Bates–Van Wart issue and had given general assurances that there were no threats to the security of the event. The downside of his deliberate omission was, of course, that he had no margin of error.

While standing next to the car, the driver already at the wheel, he took his cell phone and dialed a number.

"I agree with your advice. You can take him out."

31

Daniel felt as if he'd woken up in a different world. From a coffee bar, he passively observed the shoppers' slow pace as they chatted and gazed into shop windows; it was all utterly strange to him. The last time he'd wandered around the city in the morning had been at least a decade ago. He had simply always been at work, often even on weekends.

The two black coffees had done wonders to wake him up, and the headache had become slightly more bearable. The seven or more double whiskeys the night before had hit him worse than expected. He had needed them in order to digest the frustration of having been sent *on leave.* It was a disgrace, and he imagined how the entire firm would now be gossiping about the reasons for such a sudden and highly unusual leave.

When he'd gotten home at around four in the morning, he had slipped and shattered a glass side table. He had woken up with his clothes still on and a bloody mess around him: the glass must have cut his elbow during the fall.

Well done, Daniel. It made him think of his good old fraternity days.

Or was it bachelor's behavior? It had been some time now since it was over with Melissa. Without a female presence, tiny details of style were undeniably slipping. And his single household had become fully dependent on the firm's in-house grocery and cleaning services.

He paid for his coffees and walked to the large bookstore opposite the coffee bar. Inside he followed the signs to the history section.

He tried to focus on the small lettering on the shelves, but his eyes weren't ready for it yet. And the alcohol in his system made him sweat profusely, amplified by the hot and crowded bookstore. He hung his jacket on one of the ladders and walked up to the woman at the small desk.

"Can I help you, sir?" she asked, giving Daniel an aversive look when she noticed the large sweat patches on his wrinkled shirt.

"I'm looking for a book on the Dutch history of New York."

"Okay, let me see…that would have to be the colonial period. This area over here." The woman gestured with her right arm. "We must have something on Henry Hudson. And a city guide named *Dutch New York*."

"Anything on cultural influences?"

"Anthropology, you mean. Not sure. Let me check in our database."

She returned some minutes later, shaking her head. "I'm sorry, sir, not in our collection. And to be honest, I've never heard of such a book either. In fact, little was left of the Dutch after the English took over."

Daniel was struck by the bluntness of the statement. Even in the country's best bookstore, priding itself on the academic background of its staff, the fable of the lost Dutchness had taken root!

He grabbed his jacket and left the store, disappointed. Where else could he look now?

At the subway station, he reached into his pocket for a ticket. But his hand touched on something else. It was not his cell phone. He took out the object and looked at it in astonishment.

What on earth…

In his hand he held a mat-silver plastic box, slightly thicker than a cell phone. It also had a screen but no visible buttons. Only when he turned it around and noticed a clipping system he realized what it was.

A car navigation device! But how had it gotten into his pocket?

He instinctively looked around to find the person who had lost the object, but none of the shoppers seemed to even notice him. *Someone must have mistaken jackets.* He tried to remember his goings, but his brain was slow.

The bookstore! While his jacket was hanging on the ladder.

He inspected the object more closely and saw to his surprise that something was written on the side, in black handwriting. He tried to focus, which made his brain ache. When he read the short line, his eyes widened in surprise. He immediately knew the object had not been left by mistake.

To DVW—tomorrow 8:00 a.m.—323 W. 34th Street

32

While the first rays of sunlight already illuminated Kate's apartment at Egelantiersgracht 75, in the heart of Amsterdam's Jordaan district, the bells of the Wester church tower woke her up gently, as every morning at 7:00 a.m.

She was immediately thrilled by the thought of meeting Evelyn that night. It had been ages since they'd seen each other, and there were so many things to tell. Foremost, of course, the bizarre developments that had followed Evelyn's request to look up the sources for her colleague Daniel. And that she was being followed again. As Evelyn was partly involved, she was the only person whom Kate felt she could talk to, and she desperately needed to share her emotions with someone.

After her shower, she slipped into a bathrobe and had a cappuccino at the large table in the living room. The house was so old, and Amsterdam's soil so unstable, that the floors of the apartment sloped considerably—to the extent that the cat's game consisted of running after a ball when it descended from one side of the room to the other. While sipping her cappuccino, she opened the mail of the last few days. The local newspaper reported the sad news that the dog of her neighbors at the office had disappeared; a reward was offered to the finder. Apart from that, there was a reminder letter from the Dutch bar, pressing her to obtain *Continuing Legal Education* points in order to maintain her license to practice law.

It reminded her again of that former bar president, Van Olden, who had crossed her mind yesterday. She wondered what had become of the man. She started up her laptop and found his name in the online bar register.

Mr. H.A.G. Van Olden (Hein)
Attorney at Stiglitz & Arrowsmith, Amsterdam
Secondary public functions:
1. Deputy Judge at the Court of Appeal
2. Counsel to the Royal House

"Stiglitz & Arrowsmith!" she blurted out in surprise. *The same firm as Evelyn!* Although the website didn't contain any pictures, she vaguely remembered what the man looked like and desperately hoped Evelyn didn't have to work with him.

His additional function also surprised Kate. Not that Van Olden, as an attorney, was also a deputy judge—this was common in the Netherlands, despite the obvious conflict with judicial independence. No, it was Van Olden's other function that surprised her: Counsel to the Royal House.

He was the queen's lawyer!

A thought came to her mind instantly. Now she was even more impatient to see Evelyn.

Part V

33

Daniel followed the broad stream of early morning commuters to the exit of Penn Station, one of New York City's main transport hubs. He felt somewhat naked not wearing a suit and tie, and his hands lacked the usual wide-bodied attaché case filled with bedtime literature and case law. Just outside the station, he stood still for a moment to ascertain he was on West Thirty-Fourth Street, as was written on the mysterious GPS device.

He had hardly slept, but despite the insomnia, he hadn't been able to solve the mystery of who was behind the gift. Was it someone from within the firm? Someone who wanted to reveal the real reason for his forced leave without giving himself away? He could also think of another explanation—a far more disquieting one. Kate had warned him about the House of Orange in quite dramatic terms. At first, he had taken it lightly, as the royalty story had sounded absurd to him. But since his sudden ejection from the case on a false pretext, maybe there was indeed more to it than initially imagined. Would their powers indeed wield beyond borders, as Kate suggested? One thing was sure: he would have to be careful.

When he had walked one block to the west, he started checking house numbers. Number 323, written on the GPS, could not be far anymore. What would it be? Someone's home address? But he didn't have a name or floor number. An office maybe?

Number 323 was clearly marked on what appeared to be a large garage entrance. On the right side of the entrance was a Hertz rental car office. Daniel was confused. Would someone be waiting for him inside the garage? He decided to check the Hertz office first.

"Mornin', sir, how can I help you?" the employee asked jovially.

"Quick question: Is the address here 323 West Thirty-Fourth Street?"

"Correct. What are you looking for?"

Daniel hesitated about how to explain his peculiar situation. "As a matter of fact, I was asked to go to this address, but now I see it's only a car park. I have to return this thing to someone."

He showed the GPS device to the employee.

"Ah, you must be Mr. Van Wart!"

Daniel was stunned. *How did the man know?*

The employee started shuffling some papers on the desk and then walked in the direction of the door.

"Follow me, please," the man said while holding the door for Daniel with one hand. "Everything's ready."

Perplexed, Daniel wondered whether it was this man who had put the device in his jacket. He appeared friendly, but Daniel's reflexes told him to be careful.

Their footsteps echoed deep down in the huge and pitch-dark car park. The man had a fast pace, as if he was in a hurry. Daniel looked back over his shoulder. There was no one else.

His heart skipped a beat when a sudden flash surprised him. The man had switched on the garage lights and halted next to a silver Nissan. When he unlocked its doors, it gave a soft beep and a double flash of the car's indicators.

"Like I said, Mr. Van Wart, all is ready. As requested."

As requested? Daniel wanted to object but decided not to; apparently the man was just following orders.

"And all has been settled. Full tank, unlimited mileage, open return date. If you hand me the GPS I'll install it, and off you go."

Daniel suddenly understood the GPS device. He decided to play along.

"I'm afraid I forgot to bring the directions with me. How stupid!"

"Directions? I was told the destination is preprogrammed. So you only have to follow the instructions." The man disappeared in the car with the device.

When he emerged again, he held out the key to Daniel.

"There you go; she's all yours," he said, brushing some dust off the car with his elbow. "Have a good trip, Mr. Van Wart!"

When Daniel sat behind the wheel in the dark silence of the car, he hesitated. Should he really do this? Where would he be taken? And by whom? Apparently the car was rented with an open return date; what did that mean? His guts told him he should get out of the car and walk away as quickly as possible. But his mind objected: If someone wanted to show him a lead, he should take the chance.

He started the engine and slowly put the car in motion. Just when he reached the car park's exit, a yellow arrow appeared on the screen of the GPS device.

34

The rush-hour traffic was dense, and Daniel had to concentrate on the cars around him. As a Manhattan resident, he didn't own a car, so the last time he'd driven one was quite some time ago. When exiting the car park, he narrowly avoided hitting a black Lincoln Town Car that suddenly appeared from his left. He hoped the Hertz man hadn't seen it.

From West Thirty-Fourth Street, he turned right onto Tenth Avenue in a northerly direction, obediently following the GPS indications. Tenth Avenue had now changed its name and continued as Amsterdam Avenue. When entering Harlem, he was led onto St. Nicholas Avenue. He knew the name referred to the old Dutch patron St. Nicholas, who had stood as a model for Santa Claus.

When he had left the skyscrapers behind him, the traffic became less dense. He was directed to Broadway, passing the Dutch colonial Dyckman Farmhouse. He recalled a high school excursion a long time ago where he had learned that this was Manhattan's oldest remaining farmhouse.

Amsterdam, Harlem, St. Nicholas—something started to dawn on him.

Not knowing how long drive would be, he decided to make a quick stop to grab a coffee and parked the car in front of the deli next to farm house. While sipping his coffee on the sidewalk and gazing at the wooden farmhouse, he noticed a black Lincoln Town Car across the street.

Was the driver looking at him?

The dark window slid up, and the car accelerated briskly.

Daniel stood immobilized for a while, and recalled the black Town Car he almost hit outside the car park.

The same one? Maybe it was the first sign he had made a very stupid decision.

He threw his coffee in a bin and quickly jumped into the Nissan. He had to be gone before the Town Car could turn around. The quiet car trip had suddenly lost its innocence; he had to be very cautious now. Following the directions of the GPS, he crossed Broadway Bridge over Spuyten Duyvel. He nervously looked into his rearview mirror: no trace of the Town Car yet.

A few minutes after he'd left Manhattan and entered the *Bronx,* he passed *Van Cortlandt Park.* From there he crossed the city of *Yonkers* toward the widening in the Hudson River named *Tappan Zee.* Zee was Dutch for "sea," he knew. He was now sure the names were not a coincidence anymore. He'd driven for forty minutes, and literally *every* street he'd taken carried some reference to the Dutch past. Apparently the traces were not limited to Manhattan but continued all the way up New York State. *How far would this continue?*

Just before the Tappan Zee toll bridge, he was instructed to continue in the direction of Tarrytown.

Tarrytown, another clear reference! Like many Americans, Daniel knew that name very well: it was the setting of Washington Irving's story *The Legend of Sleepy Hollow.* It mocked Americans of Dutch descent, just as in another famous Irving story, *Rip Van Winkle.*

How stupid he hadn't thought of it before! Irving had written them in the nineteenth century, well after the English take-over. So apparently the Dutch culture and customs were still very tangible at that time.

Driving on, Daniel couldn't help from feeling a certain excitement that he was now entering ancient Dutch territory. *The land of his forefathers.* Would there be anything left to see?

On the GPS screen, he noticed an icon depicting a monument or something farther up Route 9, so he decided to make a short stop there. The site turned out to be Philipsburg Manor. With a small lake, some old farm buildings, and a water mill, it breathed a rustic rural atmosphere. He parked the car, and a panel inside the reception building immediately gave the confirmation: the manor had been founded in 1693 by the Dutchman Frederick Philipse. He bought an entrance ticket and also one of the displayed historical maps called "Dutch Hudson Valley." Then he followed the indicated trail along the lake, pausing briefly when he passed the Nissan. On its hood, he spread out the map and studied it. He didn't believe what he saw.

The entire Hudson Valley region was speckled with what the map indicated as names of Dutch origin. Some of them he knew: Wyckoff, Catskill, Stuyvesant, Kinderhook, Nassau. But there were maybe a hundred more, on both sides of the Hudson River. And all the way up to Albany: Rensselaer, Voorheesville, Guilderland, Watervliet, Rotterdam...

In disbelief, he took the Hertz road map from the car. It confirmed the names were all currently existing. In fact, it seemed as if a subsequent layer of English names had been added, covering up the web of Dutch places. Staring at the two maps, he realized it was the perfect visual demonstration of the story: Dutch America continued to exist but was hidden from the eye by recent additions. But it was still there for the careful observer!

Lost in thought, Daniel followed the trail to the buildings on the other side of the lake. It felt like walking back in time, back to the days of the Dutch colony. The days his ancestors had walked the same trail and had seen the same things.

He was coming home to his motherland, Dutch America.

35

The President of the United States turned his back to his Chief of Staff and walked to one of the windows of the Oval Office. In silence, he stared over the rose garden and reflected on the situation. He agreed with the Chief of Staff that things had become somewhat critical now, and his proposal to formally request explanations seemed fully appropriate. The troop movements in the Netherlands had been picked up some days ago through the GPS system. That in itself was nothing peculiar, as most NATO vehicles were equipped with the system allowing general command to locate them. No, the particularity of the current movements lay in the fact that they hadn't been communicated to NATO in advance, as was customary.

Of course, the Pentagon had done its homework and checked for any particular events in the tiny country that could explain the activity. They concluded that the only possibility could be the imminent accession to the throne of a new king. Such a large public event required, of course, solid security measures. But the mobilization they had observed seemed largely out of proportion. And again, NATO had not been informed in advance by the Dutch.

"Any prior NATO incidents with the Netherlands?" the President inquired with the Chief of Staff.

"No. On the contrary, the country's always been a role model. Supplied three NATO secretary generals—held the position longer than any other country."

It didn't surprise the President. He knew little about the country, but the Dutch had always been very Atlanticist. Something that couldn't be said of all European countries, to his frustration.

"What else should we know about the country?"

"In fact, it's quite surprising, sir. After the Dutch had founded New Amsterdam, now called New York, economic ties continued ever since: even in the early 1980s, the two countries were the single largest investors in each other."

"And today?"

"The Netherlands is the third-largest investor in the United States, after the United Kingdom and Japan."

"What? Are you sure about that?"

"I have it here." The Chief of Staff pointed his finger to the thin file and started to read from it. "The Netherlands functioned as a bridgehead to the European market for American companies. The close cultural and economic ties between the countries have led to relatively swift acceptance in the Netherlands of new American products. For example, the first McDonald's in Europe was in the Netherlands."

"Must have liked the *cheese*burgers," the President joked. "Any incidents? I mean, political or military?"

"Several, all after Roosevelt."

"Why? Did FDR mess up relations?"

"On the contrary, seems he was quite close to the Netherlands. But after World War II the Dutch refused independence of Indonesia, their longtime colony. They sent in the army, which was condemned by the United Nations."

"I recall. The very first action of the Security Council, if I'm correct."

"Correct, sir. Then a second incident was caused by the Dutch queen in 1952."

The President froze. "What about her?"

"She made a very pacifist speech before US Congress. It was perceived as highly inappropriate, as it was the beginning of the

Cold War, and the United States was still building NATO's strength. Surprisingly, another political incident was also caused by the queen. Or her husband, I should say: Prince Bernhard."

"What about him?" the President asked impatiently.

"During the Lockheed bribery affair in the midseventies, it turned out the prince had accepted illegal payments to lobby the Dutch government to choose our Lockheed jet fighters."

The President sighed. Was another diplomatic incident awaiting them? Again caused by Dutch royalty? The unexpected letter he had received earlier was worrisome, but coupled with the troop movements, the situation had turned critical. He decided not to mention the letter to the Chief of Staff for the moment.

"Let's hope the Dutch don't cause any new trouble. You can go ahead and ask for an official explanation on their troop movements."

36

"Please come in, young man; you'll enjoy it!" the lady said at the entrance gate of Phillipsburg Manor.

She wore a historical dress, reinforcing Daniel's feeling he had traveled in time. He watched as she emptied a bucket in the huge wooden dung cart standing just outside the gate, adding its distinct smell to the countryside impression.

Daniel followed the trail until he reached the immense wooden barn, the large doors of which were half-open. He looked inside, but it was too dark to see anything. It smelled of hay and wood.

"You can go in if you like!"

The sudden voice scared him. One level above him stood a pipe-smoking farmer holding a large hayfork.

"It's a traditional Dutch barn," he said while gesturing Daniel inside.

Daniel's eye slowly grew accustomed to the darkness.

"The barns were made entirely of wood. The H frame made it possible to carry the weight of the large roof. You can climb up the ladder if you want."

Daniel hesitated but then climbed up.

"The barns were so strong that they withstood centuries. There're several left in the Hudson Valley. Do you know the region?"

"Still discovering. I'm doing research on the Dutch history of the region."

"Then you're at the right place here. There's plenty of that in this town. Starting with the street names."

"Why, are they Dutch?"

"You bet. See the entrance gate over there? Turn left and you'll reach De Vries Avenue. Then we have Holland Avenue, Beekman Avenue, DePeyster Street, Van Wart Avenue, and so on."

Daniel couldn't believe his ears. "*Van Wart*, you said?"

"Yep. Just on the other side of the toll station," the farmer replied while descending the ladder.

His ancestors? Lost in thought, he peered through a crack in the barn. He could see some goats, the lake, the dam, and—what he saw paralyzed him.

A black Lincoln Town Car. At the parking lot across the lake.

Daniel looked through the hole once more. A man was looking into the Nissan.

They were still following him!

Who the hell were they? The same who'd sent him the GPS? It didn't make sense; then they would know his destination and didn't need to follow him. Was it the firm? To make sure he wouldn't secretly remain involved in the case? Or the same people who followed Kate?

He saw the Town Car leave the parking lot and drive in the direction of the entrance gate. He hurried down the ladder and explained something to the farmer.

He noticed two men with sunglasses walking from the car to the gate, so he left the barn through the rear. He ran to a group of other visitors that was guided to the millhouse close to the lake. When among the group, he looked back: only one of the men was visible now. And coming his way.

The group entered the millhouse, which was filled with the creaking sounds of the large, rotating waterwheel. When the guide started explaining, Daniel chose a place safely in the back, overlooking the scene. He didn't hear a word of the story, too focused on the wooden doors that stood open.

Suddenly the man reappeared. He was bald with sunglasses and was now holding his jacket on his arm. He slowly entered the house and started screening the group.

Daniel lowered his body, and when the group moved farther inside the millhouse, he squeezed himself ahead of the group, down the wooden stairs. The space was filled with huge toothed wheels, and there were beams and levers in all directions. The group gathered around the millstones at the bottom, and the guide started explaining again.

Daniel immediately saw that the man had recognized him, and he was focusing on him from across the millstone. What the hell did he want? Force him to the Lincoln and kidnap him? Was he a hitman?

"Any volunteers?" the guide asked. "Really, it tastes fantastic. Real, natural flour." He dipped his finger in the white powder on the milling stone and licked it off. "You, sir, give it a try!" the guide said to the hitman standing next to him.

Daniel noticed the man's surprise. He reflexively lowered his right arm.

Was he holding something under his jacket?

With the whole group watching, the man stepped slightly forward and extended his other arm for the white powder on the stone.

In one movement, Daniel jumped up and hit the large wooden lever above him with all his force. The upper millstone immediately came down, and the mill's entire structure was set in motion. The hitman screamed violently, his arm stuck between the rotating millstones as they spun him around.

In the commotion it created, Daniel fled out of the millhouse and ran over the wooden dam across the lake, the slippery planks almost making him fall twice. When he reached the other side, he saw the second hitman was running back to the Town Car, apparently alarmed.

He jumped into the Nissan and noticed to his relief that the GPS was still there. He drove out of the parking lot, turned left with squealing tires, and continued the same route he had come from. Although he was still out of breath and his heart was pumping, his mouth produced a smile. He knew the Lincoln wouldn't come after him—at least, not immediately.

37

Daniel left Phillipsburg Manor behind him and continued on Route 9 in a northerly direction. The GPS device was still searching for the satellite signals. Daniel looked in his rearview mirror again: no sign of the Town Car. The second hitman would probably still be frantically removing the dung load that blocked its way.

It had been a stroke of luck the farmer had mentioned *Van Wart Avenue.* When Daniel had seen the two men entering the manor's gate, he'd realized he needed the farmer's help to get away. His request to the farmer to tip over the dung cart had been accepted with a smile when Daniel had showed his ID card: Van Wart.

"*Turn around where possible,*" sounded the GPS's sudden instruction.

Daniel was confused. Had he missed a turn? It meant going back in the direction of the Town Car. He made a fast U-turn and accelerated the Nissan at full throttle. After a short distance, the voice gave a new instruction.

"*Turn left!*"

Daniel quickly glanced at the small screen and saw that the highlighted route indeed turned sharp left. He braked violently and made the turn. To his surprise, he saw that it was not a normal road but a private route with an entrance gate. Behind it, he saw a tiny chapel on a sloping field.

"*You have reached your destination,*" the GPS announced.

Daniel was now even more confused. *Was the GPS in disorder after the stop?*

He decided to follow the narrow route anyway, if only to put the Nissan out of sight of the Town Car. After the slight bend, he parked the car on the grass verge and pressed the Reset button on the GPS. After two minutes, the same message appeared on the screen: "Destination reached."

So it had to be here!

He left the car and walked up the soft slope, out of sight from the main road. The tiny church was surrounded by a peaceful graveyard, with old tombstones sticking out of the ground as disorderly teeth.

What was he supposed to do here?

He looked at the inscriptions on a tombstone. Time had rendered them hardly readable, but he could make out the first numbers of a date: 16. He was perplexed. The sixteen hundreds? It meant they dated from America's earliest colonial times!

Curious now to where he was, he walked to the entrance of the church, aware he could now be spotted from the street. He looked at the metal plaque next to the door and read, to his astonishment:

OLD DUTCH CHURCH.

He pushed gently against the wooden door, which opened with a soft creak. Inside he saw neatly placed wooden benches in soft-blue tones. No one was there. A brass chandelier hung from the ceiling, and the smell of the polished wooden floor filled the air. In utter silence, he sat down on one of the benches and felt as if lost in a dream.

Suddenly the organ above him gave him a rude awakening.

Someone's here! He jumped up but couldn't see the organ player.

When the organ stopped, a figure appeared from behind it, slowly approaching the balcony.

"Welcome to the Dutch Church of Sleepy Hollow, Daniel!" the figure said.

Daniel felt as if he had been struck by lightning.

"Thank you for accepting the invitation," the figure said.

So this man had put the device in his pocket. "Thank you, sir. But now that I'm here, I think you owe me an explanation."

"I surely do. Let me come down."

The man disappeared from the balcony, and Daniel heard his footsteps on a wooden staircase. Some moments later he reappeared from the entrance hall. He estimated him to be in his mid-sixties, with a charismatic face and a ring of short silver hair. He looked tanned and in shape.

The man stretched out his hand to Daniel. "My name is William Lent, and I'm an administrator of this church."

Daniel hesitated briefly but finally accepted the handshake.

"As you know my name, I suppose you're the person who put that GPS device in my jacket to lure me to this place?"

"Your assumption is correct, Daniel. Our people did the trick, and it worked out well, I have to say." The man sat down on one of the benches.

"What do you mean, *'our people'*?"

"Let me come straight to the point. I'm a member of a historical society that is interested in the Dutch history of the United States. We've been working on a project for some time and have hit an obstacle, so to speak. We need someone to help us solve that problem, and we thought you might be the right person."

"*Me*? But how do you know me in the first place?"

The man leaned forward and looked up at Daniel sternly. "We have known you for quite some time, Daniel. To be honest, we've been keeping track of you for quite a while. That's why we're convinced you're the right person to help us. We think you may be interested in helping us, but we're not sure, of course. That's what we want to find out; that's why we let you come here."

"Why here? Why not simply send me a letter or invite me for a coffee?"

"Because you may have refused."

"I may still refuse."

"Sure, but the task can only be fulfilled with a certain level of curiosity, despite uncertainty and risk. We needed to test this. By coming here, you passed the first test."

"What do you mean *the first*? Will there be more?"

"To explain the mission, we'll need more time and a different place. For now, I propose to show you something. It will allow you to make a choice: either go home or continue. Follow me, please."

Lost in confusion, Daniel didn't respond and followed the man. Once outside the church, they slowly walked across the burial ground. The man suddenly halted in front of a reddish tombstone. On its top, Daniel noticed a sort of winged head and bent over slightly to read the inscriptions below. He immediately looked up at the man in surprise.

"My family indeed," the man nodded. "*Lent.* My Dutch forefathers. Among the first settlers buried in America."

William Lent then slowly walked on until he stopped at another old tomb. It was almost impossible to read because of the cracks and the grayish moss. But when Daniel managed to decipher the letters, he instantly knew that returning home was not an option. It read:

DANL. VAN WART.

38

Evelyn glanced at her Baume & Mercier wristwatch and noticed that her cigarette break had already lasted eight minutes. Minutes that couldn't be billed to a client. She turned back into Amsterdam's World Trade Center, where Stiglitz & Arrowsmith had moved in recently, at the heart of the modern business hub. Like everyone in the firm, she was proud that the firm's New York office was now involved in the reconstruction of the WTC in New York City.

New York City. The name made her think back to the previous night with Kate. What an incredible story it had become! The simple request for the city's historic sources had turned into a nightmare, with Kate being shadowed and Daniel Van Wart on forced leave! She still couldn't understand how things could have turned out this way. She blamed herself endlessly for having involved Kate, who was now suffering the same emotional pressure as she had a few years ago. She had to do everything she could to help her out, even if that involved obtaining information she wasn't supposed to have. Let alone divulge it to people outside the firm!

The fact that it concerned Van Olden made the mission easier to accept. He wasn't liked, but as the founding partner of the Amsterdam office, he could get away with his behavior—*all* behavior. It was a public secret he'd been involved in a case of sexual harassment.

Inside the firm's impressive library Evelyn walked straight to one of the computer terminals. She asked the intern who occupied it if she could look something up quickly. The intern ceded his place obediently. It avoided a login by Evelyn herself, which would have betrayed her search.

She opened the firm's document system and searched "Van Olden" as author. It revealed more than three thousand documents. *Way too many to screen one by one.* She typed "Kate Bates" in the subject field to refine the search.

0 RESULTS.

Then she tried "House of Orange." After several seconds, a list of document titles appeared on the screen, 273 in total. She studied the list briefly and noticed that some of them were marked with a lock-like symbol. She clicked on one of them, and a small warning window appeared:

CLASSIFIED. ACCESS RESTRICTED TO AUTHOR.

She was confused; she wasn't aware of this option, as the document system was for *sharing* documents. But maybe partners in the firm had additional user options she didn't know. She clicked the message away and stared at the list again. Most of the House of Orange documents were earmarked as "Correspondence"; others as "Official Documents." Some in the latter group were marked with the symbol indicating that a paper version of the document existed, which was often the case for signed contracts. Evelyn clicked on one of them, and the usual window with the archive location appeared. But to her surprise, it didn't mention the standard information. Instead, it read:

SAFE 417.

She didn't understand. She wasn't aware of any safe in the archive room; in a way the whole room itself was a safe, protecting its contents from theft and fire and the like. The only safe she knew was the tiny one at the reception, where the concierge kept a small amount of cash for deliveries.

Unless...

She quickly took the slim binder next to the telephone and opened it. She flipped through the internal telephone list until she reached Van Olden. In the column right from his name and direct line was his office number: 417.

Evelyn realized her mission wasn't over yet.

39

After leaving the Old Dutch Church, at first there had been a slightly awkward silence in the car. Or rather, in the limo, as it turned out that that was William Lent's transport method. Daniel sat back in the deep leather seat opposite Lent himself. Lent had explained that his people would take care of the rental car and that he and Daniel would drive a little to explain some more about the region's history. And about Daniel's family history.

Lent had already mentioned that the Old Dutch Church was New York State's oldest surviving church and was considered to be the center of the Dutch Hudson Valley culture. In a grandfatherly style, he had outlined the story of the Dutch settlers who had explored and inhabited the valley and even formed the spine of the nation that would become the United States.

They had continued up north, and the startling chain of Dutch references in the region had continued. First they had passed Kykuit, the Rockefeller estate meaning "lookout" in Dutch. Then they passed Van Cortland Manor, followed by several surviving Dutch colonial houses such as the Hendrick Kip House and the Van Wyck Homestead. Lent explained that the style of those houses was now generally referred to as "colonial Dutch." Their distinctive elements included gabled roofs and a raised level "stoop," from the Dutch word *stoep*. They had stopped at several of the Dutch Reformed churches of the region, often with other graveyards containing Dutch graves. Still farther north, they had crossed the town of Hyde Park, which had earlier carried the Dutch name Stoutenburgh and formed the home of the majestic Vanderbilt and Roosevelt mansions—both successful families of Dutch descent.

Daniel showed him the historic Hudson Valley map he had bought earlier. "Why do the Dutch settlements seem to stop in Albany?" he asked Lent.

"In fact, it's the other way around," Lent explained. "Albany was the starting point of the Dutch colonization. At that point in the Hudson River once stood Fort Orange, the first permanent Dutch settlement in New Netherland, which predated New Amsterdam. The settlement around Fort Orange was called Beverwyck, or 'beaver district.'"

"After the beaver skins, their main economical asset."

"Exactly. They were in high demand in back in Europe, used to make the fashionable black felt hats shown in the paintings of the Dutch masters, such as Rembrandt and Vermeer."

Daniel thought about for a second. *Had the paintings coincidentally immortalized America's first export product?*

"Albany was inhabited mostly by people of Dutch origin, so it wasn't bothered by New York's difficulties and conflicts resulting from various cultures living side by side. Over time, Albany became very prosperous, and the Dutchness of the entire Hudson Valley culture was firmly established."

"But it didn't last."

"Are you sure about that?" Lent asked rhetorically. "What's the current capital of the state of New York?"

"Albany," Daniel admitted. And not New York City, contrary to popular belief.

"Because Albany is where it all started. And there are numerous other reminiscences, often in the form of insignificant elements in daily life. Take the typically American pastry the cruller. Its name is derived from Crol, an early director general of New Netherland

and commander of Fort Orange. And talking about foodstuffs, the Dutch gave us waffles, cookies, and coleslaw!"

Daniel was surprised. "You mean, these are all Dutch words?" It sounded almost unbelievable to him.

Lent nodded.

"I guess now I understand why Albany's baseball team is called the Dutchmen."

"You're getting the picture, Daniel. And look at those flags over there!"

Daniel turned and noticed the row of shops the limo drove past. Each shop had a red-white-and-blue flag with the word Open. He immediately knew what Lent meant.

"The Dutch flag!"

"Yep. Another signal of the region's continuing Dutchness."

Daniel was stunned. Whereas the Dutch origin had mostly disappeared from the eye in New York City, in the Hudson Valley the traces had clearly remained intact. The names, the architecture, and even local customs! Now he understood why Lent had wanted him to make the trip; he would never have believed him.

The limo suddenly came to a halt, and a large gate opened automatically. They drove up a winding road, crossing what looked like a park with a large water basin on the right. Across the water stood a large mansion, and Daniel recognized the gabled roofs of colonial Dutch style.

"We have arrived," Lent said. "This is where we'll talk."

When they reached the mansion and stepped out of the limo, Daniel heard another car arriving behind them. He turned his head and immediately knew things were wrong. A black Lincoln Town Car slowly followed in their direction.

40

Oscar Smeenk decided to walk. Of course his service car, with the distinctive "AA" license plate for members of the Royal Household, had unrestricted access to The Hague's narrow pedestrian streets, but it would not have been any quicker. And the short walk would also allow him to smoke a cigarette. It had been more than ten years since he had quit, but the stress of the final stages of the operation had apparently gotten to him. *He would quit again afterward,* he assured himself.

He noticed that the preparations for the event were becoming visible now. In Dutch tradition, the population excelled at decorating everything from top to bottom in orange, with all the materials they could put their hands on. The city council had been forced to issue a special decoration directive in order to maintain a minimum of royal allure and prevent having the event resemble a soccer World Cup.

What he saw around him gave him confidence, as it confirmed that the population in its "orange mania" would swallow the additional measures without much opposition. And once recovered from their naïve drunkenness, it would be too late to protest.

He crossed Plein Square, a chilly west wind blowing in his face. He threw the cigarette butt at the base of the statue in the middle of the square. A symbolic gesture, he realized, smudging the statue of William of Orange, the "Father of the Fatherland," as he was called, the central figure in the Dutch fight for independence and the formation of the Dutch Republic. The man would surely have turned in his grave had he known that his descendants had transformed the proud republic into a kingdom.

Soon with the most powerful king it's ever had, Smeenk thought.

Putting up his collar against the wind, he walked straight to the building with the classic facade facing him. Although from the outside it appeared to be a relatively small, he knew the Defense Ministry occupied the entire block.

"Thanks for coming, Oscar," the defense minister said as he closed the door behind Smeenk.

They sat down at the large oak table in the spacious office with high ceilings.

Smeenk noticed that the minister looked exhausted, as did probably all members of their select group preparing for the de-facto coup. He saw that the documents were already waiting for him on the table. The map with the mobilized troops would be unrolled later; it interested him only marginally anyway. The real purpose of their meeting was of course the other document: the letter. He immediately recognized the American seal, with the large eagle holding arrows in one claw and the words DEPARTMENT OF JUSTICE underneath.

"As I told you over the phone," the minister started, "the letter is quite straightforward. And to be honest, I didn't expect it to be otherwise. You'll remember from what I explained some months ago that in principle, European NATO members are to inform the Allied Command Operations in Mons, Belgium, of any significant troop movements."

Smeenk nodded. "And we decided not to," he said, "in order to downplay the importance of the operation."

"Exactly. But if movements are nevertheless detected, other NATO members can submit a formal information request to a designated body of the country concerned. The Netherlands has designated the Defense Ministry for this, so the Americans sent us this letter. So far, all standard procedure. And nothing to worry about: you and I are the only people aware of the letter."

"But we'll have to respond to it."

"Of course. And that's why I wanted to have your advice. Normally I would feel obliged to inform the prime minister, but—"

"Out of the question! Imagine he mentions it to Her Majesty! You know her; she would immediately start asking questions. No, as agreed she has to be kept unaware of the operation at all cost!"

"But what if the Yanks contact her or the PM directly? How would we explain having kept things out of the reports?"

"Why would they contact them? You just said they're following standard procedure. We simply have to convince them all's in order. A military parade as part of the festivities, like the French do every *14 juillet.*"

The minister thought about the suggestion, while Smeenk studied the letter.

"It implies changing the formal nature of a mobilization that's already ongoing. An uncommon move; normally I would have to discuss that with the Chiefs of Staff first. Unless we mention the parade argument only to the Americans."

"I'll leave that up to you."

"All right, I'll find a way. For the moment I note that the PM is to be kept out of it. A look at the maps perhaps?"

"I'll leave that to your expertise too. Just keep me informed if there are any major changes."

The minister nodded obediently. Smeenk knew the man was honored enough with his role in the operation and the certainty that he would serve as head of the armed forces in the next cabinet. With considerably larger responsibilities.

41

Daniel watched in fearful resignation how the Town Car came to a halt and then gave a desperate look to Lent.

"Mr. Lent! Those men tried to—"

"Don't worry, Daniel; they're with me," Lent said, trying to appease him.

The doors of the Town Car opened, and Daniel immediately recognized one of the hitmen, who came out stumbling with his arm in a white sling.

"You surely hit him well with that millstone! They were following you to make sure you'd find your way to the Old Dutch Church. But apparently you didn't need them!"

The man with the sling gave a sheepish smile.

Daniel was totally confused now. "So where are we? And why did you take me here?"

"Welcome to my humble home!" Lent said jovially. "In the heart of Dutch America!"

Daniel looked around him again, at the mansion and the park. "You mean, you *live* here?" *The man must own a fortune,* he thought.

Lent nodded and laid his hand on Daniel's shoulder. "Let's take a stroll, and I'll explain. You surely deserved that."

Lent and Daniel walked in the direction of a fountain, while the two hitmen went back to the car.

"You know about New York City and the Hudson Valley now. But would you believe me if I said that the entire American society is based on Holland? And not on England, as is generally believed?"

Daniel hesitated. "I'm not sure what to believe anymore..."

"Name a characteristic of American society."

Daniel thought for a second. "The dominance of commerce?"

"Our mercantile nature. No doubt about it: straight from Holland! Remember, New Amsterdam was founded as a trading post. And Holland itself was a nation dominated by merchants and free enterprise. Contrary to England, where the king distributed monopolies to his cronies. Name another characteristic."

"A country founded as a republic?" Daniel tried.

"Correct. Inspired by the Dutch Republic, the world's only republic at that time. Another one, please."

"The Protestant nature?"

"Very well. Where did this come from?"

"From England, through the Puritan settlers."

"No! The state religion of England was Anglicanism. And while many of the Protestant founders of America were born in England, they were persecuted for their religious beliefs and fled that country, mostly to Holland. The Pilgrim Fathers lived in Leiden, Holland, for thirteen years before they set sail to America."

Daniel was perplexed. "What are you saying, that the Pilgrim Fathers embarked from Holland?"

"Surprising, isn't it? And in America, the Pilgrims maintained the city of Leiden's annual celebration of freedom, survival, and plenitude, which is now still an American holiday. Any idea which one?"

The sudden realization came with a shock. "Thanksgiving?"

"Exactly! Few Americans will realize it, but in fact, every year they celebrate a Dutch historical event."

Daniel had difficulty grasping the magnitude of Lent's statements and tried to find examples to counterbalance them. "What about our famous melting pot? That's an American invention for sure."

"The term, yes. But the concept already existed long before in Amsterdam, New York's spiritual father. And certainly not in feudal England! It explains why even today New York's culture is notably different from that of other American cities, such as Boston or Philadelphia, which *were* English."

Daniel thought for a moment. *So the Big Apple's unique character was in fact its Dutchness!* "What are you saying Mr. Lent, that all Americans got their history wrong?"

"In a way, yes. On almost anything in our society there's a Dutch story to tell. Do you know a Bart, Dirk, Dick, or Hank? Their names are Dutch. Santa Claus? A Dutch story, named after *Sinterklaas.* Who do you work for? A *boss,* a Dutch word."

The examples dazzled Daniel. "But I suppose the Dutch history of the country simply got snowed under by the subsequent English dominance after the take-over of New Amsterdam."

"Not really. The Duke of York and his clan were fully aware that the territory could only be profitable with the support of its inhabitants, the Dutch."

"So that's why their rights were confirmed by the Articles of Capitulation, signed by Stuyvesant!"

"Indeed. The Dutch influence continued as before. Dutchmen kept key positions, merely complemented by certain English appointments. Over time, the numerical dominance of the Dutch diminished, of course, but only slowly. Half a century after the English take-over, the Dutch still represented more than half of New York's population. And at the time of the country's independence in 1776, around one-third of its population could still speak Dutch."

"So when did the Dutch influence come to a halt?"

"You'd be surprised! Remember the Boston Tea Party and the slogan 'No Taxation without Representation'? Fully on Dutch principles! The Declaration of Independence? A copy of the Act of

Abjuration, the Dutch declaration of independence from Spain. Thomas Jefferson will certainly have known it, as it was the only existing document of that kind in the world, and widely known among political thinkers. The Articles of Confederation of 1777? Also inspired on a Dutch example, the Union of Utrecht, formalizing the cooperation of the Dutch provinces in the same battle for independence from Spain. Another Founding Father, Benjamin Franklin, was very explicit on the Dutch Republic when he said: 'In love of liberty and bravery in the defense of it, she has been our great example.'"

Daniel overthought it all for a moment. "But why would the United States *still* look at Holland even during the revolution? I mean, they countries are incomparable in terms of scale!"

"Don't forget, at that time both countries had around two million inhabitants. And Holland was still many times richer than America. It was impossible *not* to look at Holland."

"And the Constitution? Also from Holland?" Daniel asked provocatively.

"At that time Holland was the only country in the world that was a republic, a confederation of states or provinces, with a representative government."

"Now you're wrong, Mr. Lent. Our Constitution was inspired by the one of Pennsylvania and based on the enlightened and humanist ideas of William Penn. No Dutch inspiration there."

Lent smiled and turned his eyes down. "More than you may think. In fact, William Penn's own mother came from Holland."

Daniel was dumbstruck. *William Penn half-Dutch?* If it was all true what Lent was telling him, it was nothing less than revolutionary.

"Okay, so the Dutch influenced the country on a political level. But in daily life, I assume there must have been conflicts between the populations of Dutch and English origin."

"Sure, and our language still testifies of it. I'm sure you know some expressions that mock Dutch Americans."

Daniel instantly knew an example. "A Dutch treat?"

Lent nodded. "And many others—'talk like a Dutch uncle,' 'going Dutch,' and the like. There must have been equivalents mocking the English, but they disappeared with the Dutch language."

"When did that happen? I mean, today no one speaks Dutch anymore."

"It was a gradual process. Brooklyn remained largely Dutch in population and language throughout the eighteenth century. And in many other areas the local administration remained Dutch for a long time; even the draft Constitution was translated into Dutch. The last known areas of the United States where native Dutch was spoken were Bergen County in New Jersey and eastern New York State between the Mohawk and Hudson rivers. The language almost survived until our times; in the very last pockets, an American Dutch dialect known as *Jersey Dutch* was spoken until the beginning of the twentieth century. Officially, the last native speaker is assumed to have died around 1960."

Daniel was taken aback. *His own generation!*

42

Kate Bates attached her bicycle to the bridge over the Oudezijds Voorburgwal canal and walked through the large stone gate opposite the bridge. The Oudemanhuispoort, as the gate was called, was the former entrance of the "old men's house," once a home of elderly men that now housed the law faculty. She passed the stalls of the antiquarian booksellers, and in the middle of the dark corridor, she turned left, onto a stylish inner courtyard.

She came there regularly to visit the law library and consult materials she didn't have at her office. Despite the fact that she knew the place like the back of her hand, she always felt a bit awkward, well aware of the looks she received from the much-younger student population. Not that she looked *old* of course, as she knew very well that her fine face and long blond hair made her look significantly younger than her forty years. But the high heels and pearl necklace evidently created a distinct contrast with the trainers and backpacks of the students.

In the reading room on the first floor she took a place in the corner, with a view of the entrance so she could keep an eye on possible strangers looking for her. Apart from the two whispering frat boys staring at her two tables away, no one seemed to notice her, so she went to work.

The idea had come to her that morning under the shower, after having punished her brain all night long to find an explanation for the whole story. As long as neither Evelyn nor Daniel had found anything that could shed some light on the situation, it might be worth a try.

In essence, she concluded, there were three questions to be answered. The first question was about location: why would the House of Orange be interested in Daniel's research on *America*? It was to this question she hoped to find a hint of an answer in the computer in front of her.

She searched for references to the United States of America in the titles of Dutch legislation, treaties, and regulations. It yielded eighty-three results, and she started scanning the titles for anything that could be of interest. There were regulations on economic cooperation between the countries, customs treaties, tax treaties, prisoner exchange treaties, and so on. Nothing of interest.

That left the second question to be answered, which concerned time: why was the issue so important *now*? She could think of only one answer, an obvious one: it must have something to do with the sole major imminent event: the passage of the throne. Was it a security issue? Otherwise, it seemed foolish to spend time and money on checking innocent lawyers. And even more so when they were based in the United States. She sighed. *It didn't make sense.* What would the passage of the throne have to do with the United States?

In desperation, she stood up and looked around the library. She walked to a student with a red cap and borrowed his law bible. She quickly found the *Grondwet,* the Dutch constitution, and flipped through the pages to find the chapter on the passage of the throne. Most of the articles concerned situations in which there was no heir available for the throne or if he or she was for some reason indisposed. The only article that said something about the ceremony itself designated its location: it had to be in Amsterdam, the county's capital.

That surprised Kate, as most activities involving the House of Orange generally took place in The Hague, the city that served as both royal residence and government seat. She imagined that the former city hall, now Royal Palace, on Dam Square would probably be the center of the festivities.

The palace stolen from the people, Kate thought.

For the authorities, the location of Amsterdam would surely be an inconvenience. It was historically the most anarchistic of Dutch cities and notably more republican than the royalist The Hague. During Queen Beatrix's marriage in 1966, riots had broken out in Amsterdam, a repetition of which could never be excluded. In Amsterdam, the republican fire had not been fully extinguished yet.

While reading the *Grondwet,* Kate realized again what she had learned in law school, namely that the formal position of the Dutch head of state was immensely strong—almost absolutist. It seemed incredible that the power of the king had not been limited over time, as in most other monarchal democracies. Article 47 was very explicit: "The King is untouchable," it stated literally. And even if the ministers were formally responsible for the king's acts, which were in turn subjected to parliament, in practice it meant that the people didn't have effective control over the king. Moreover, as the king appointed—and dismissed—those ministers, they could hardly be expected to be impartial and independent, as may be required in a modern democracy.

But the most striking attribution of power to the king followed from Article 87. It stated that a proposition of law, once accepted by parliament, entered into force only when ratified by the king. In other words, the king had a veto on each law. A veto that could not be overruled by parliament!

In addition, to what extent the queen used this power remained secret; the contents of her weekly meetings with the prime minister were strictly confidential. But the fact that all PMs spent several hours per week of their precious time on the meeting seemed to indicate that they were more than just a formality. On the contrary: Kate knew that the meeting allowed the queen to point out at an early stage what points of a proposed bill would have to be amended before sending it to parliament, under the implied threat that otherwise she wouldn't sign the law. No PM would let it come so far, as his position fully depended on the queen. In all, even assuming the current queen didn't take advantage of her formal powers—at least, not openly—any future heir could simply seize his unlimited formal powers and impose his rule on the Dutch people. In all legality.

The conclusion filled Kate with horror. *What if the next king...*

She immediately dismissed the thought.

Somewhat frustrated she concluded that the Dutch constitution didn't provide any clue to the link between the United States and the House of Orange. It led to her third and final question: how much time would be left to discover the link? She checked her agenda and looked up in agony.

Only seven days left before the royal ceremony!

43

"Three minutes before landing," the creaking voice of the pilot announced through the headset.

Oscar Smeenk was relieved, as the deafening roar of the helicopter rotor was making him numb. He felt how drops of sweat ran from under the large headset into his neck, the spring sun heating the small cabin to unbearable temperatures.

"On the left, you see the golf course of De Pan," the pilot added.

Smeenk instinctively turned his head and saw the narrow green strips of the courses shoot underneath them, serpentining through the pine forests of central Netherlands. When the sole passenger of the helicopter flying at close range next to them greeted him, Smeenk shot back a quick military salute to the boy.

"One minute," the pilot said.

Smeenk felt how the helicopter reduced speed and started a wide downward turn toward the air base. He knew that Soesterberg Air Base had been used as a military base by the US Air Force for almost forty years during the Cold War. Following the collapse of the Soviet Union, the Americans abandoned the base in 1994, when it became a Royal Dutch Air Force helicopter base.

Once both helicopters had touched down, and the sound of the dying engines allowed conversations again, the commander of the base welcomed Smeenk and His Royal Highness. They were led to a small group of officials waiting in front of the main building. Hands were shaken.

The first part of the inspection concerned the helicopter squadron itself, and its commander proudly guided the delegation toward the first of his lined-up machines.

"These are all the same type you have just flown. As foreseen in the master plan, in the coming days twenty of them will be stationed throughout the Netherlands, ready to intervene in case of necessity. Around the clock. Their duty will of course mainly be supporting ground troops."

The commander stepped back and let his colleague of the army's ground forces take over. A general stepped forward and gestured toward the other side of the landing strip, where dozens of dark-green vehicles stood lined up.

"As you'll know, most of our troops have already taken their designated positions, such as at the Dutch Central Bank and so on. The vehicles you see here are mainly backup equipment. Apart from the ones involved in telecommunications, of course, as they will form the new network backbone when the order is given to deactivate the public communication services. Too risky to have them out there in the field already."

Smeenk doubted whether it would be necessary to go that far, but one never knew how certain media would react to the measures after the event.

"What about the base itself?" Smeenk asked the base commander.

"Fully secured, maximum level."

"And after the event?" Smeenk knew the airbase was used for humanitarian and peace missions throughout the world. In 2001, the base had gained global notoriety when it served as venue for the Lockerbie Tribunal, the trial of the Libyan perpetrators of the bombing of Pan Am Flight 103 above the Scottish town of Lockerbie.

"As instructed, all other functions have been discontinued until further orders," the base commander confirmed.

The response pleased Smeenk, as none of the financiers were happy with the Dutch "charity" activities. They certainly didn't fit into the reinforced strategy of maximizing the Orange capital. Other measures on the list were applying capital controls; nationalizing the country's largest bank, ING; diverting parts of the country's massive pension funds; leveraging the North Sea gas reserves; and attracting foreign capital through a zero-tax policy. In other words, transforming the country into a northern "Gulf State." The fact that it implied the limitation of personal freedoms was, of course, ancillary to the vast rewards. Although some resistance was to be expected, they were nevertheless convinced that the Dutch population, devotedly Orange loving as they were, would accept almost anything, as they had proven for decades.

A sudden sound blast almost made their eardrums burst, and in agony the delegation jumped to all sides. With their hands on their ears, the men looked up in confusion. They noticed how the crown prince waved to them from the cabin of the truck next to them, releasing his hand from the claxon chain. He produced a big smile.

The army men exchanged quick looks, and a soldier hurried to the truck. Smeenk was sure all men thought the same thing: they were thankful they had changed their initial plan to let the boy mount one of the fully armed fighter planes.

While the group walked over the vast tarmac in the direction of the building, Smeenk sniffed the air.

"Kerosene?" he asked the base commander.

"Yes, indeed."

"I assume you fully repleted your stocks?"

"No need for that, sir."

Smeenk immediately turned his head. "Pardon?"

"We have an unlimited supply, sir. Direct pipeline to the port of Rotterdam."

Smeenk was surprised; it meant a trajectory right across the country.

"The Yanks were thirsty," the commander added with a smile.

When the commander held open the building's door, Smeenk noticed a large wood carving with the airbase's name. He couldn't suppress a smile and recalled how they had marveled when they had heard if for the first time, at the moment the airbase was proposed as the operation's home base. The Americans had named it Camp New Amsterdam.

44

"Mr. Lent," Daniel said decidedly when they entered the mansion, "it's all extremely interesting what you're telling me, but I think it's time to give me some serious answers now. Why did I have to come here? And who are you in the first place?"

Lent halted in the middle of a hallway, at the bottom of a large wooden stairway. He looked Daniel sternly in the eyes.

"You will get your answers, Daniel. They're all related to a question, namely why the Dutch history of America in unknown. Or better, why it remains hidden. What do you know about the Dutch House of Orange?"

Daniel felt as if he had been struck by lightning. *There they were again!*

"Not too much, to be frank. It's the royal family. Why?"

Lent was silent for a while, as if searching for his words. "You should know that I used to be a member of an organization called the Dutch Republican Society. You've probably never heard of them, but they're a group of fairly influential people who wish the Netherlands to become a republic again."

"A republic? You mean, to get rid of the queen?"

"That would be the natural consequence, yes. I knew some of the society's founders from my time before my retirement, when I did business in the Netherlands. Many of its members were successful businessmen."

"Like you?" Daniel asked, gesturing to the lavish space surrounding them.

Lent didn't reply.

"But you said you *were* a member of that society."

"Indeed. They remained a discussion platform only, and the distance with the United States made it difficult. But I'm still in touch with some of my old friends there. They were the ones who informed me there's something in the relationship between the United States and the Netherlands that keeps the real history from being told. Something that's too sensitive. Or too disruptive when it comes out. And my organization wants you to find that out."

Daniel almost choked. "*Me*? But I don't know anything about it!"

Lent gestured Daniel into an immense living room, which had a balustrade on all sides. Large glass-paneled doors gave access to a terrace with view over the park.

"As I mentioned earlier, Daniel, we've selected you among our fellow Americans of Dutch descent. No one had the superb credentials you have for the mission. And that your firm sent you on leave was a godsend."

"But I'm not an historian. I'm a lawyer!"

"That's exactly what we need. We need you to analyze the historic ties between the United States and the Netherlands, which requires skills to read and interpret laws, agreements, treaties, property rights, territorial claims, etcetera."

Daniel had to admit it made sense. As one of America's top lawyers in the field of property and real estate law, he could even consider himself an expert in those activities. And with the Ground Zero case, he had unknowingly started the research already!

45

Kate returned the law bible to the student with the red cap and headed for the exit of the reading room. She descended the large staircase and crossed the courtyard again, hurrying past the groups of students enjoying their coffee break. In the main hall, she found a telephone booth and dialed a number she knew by heart.

"Evelyn, it's me, Kate. Found anything yet on Van Olden's documents?"

"Not yet. Some of his documents are classified, with restricted access. I think they're in a safe in his office."

"In a safe? Meaning you can't get them?"

"Don't worry, Kate. I'll find a way. Just give me some time."

"That's the problem, Evelyn. I found out that we've only got a few days left to find an answer."

"A few days? Why?"

"Can't tell you over the phone—you know why. And I've got to contact Daniel about it, to warn him. Did he contact you?"

"No. Nothing from his side."

"When he does, please tell him he has to contact me urgently."

"Are you all right, Kate? You sound stressed."

"Do I? Well, never mind. I guess it's just the whole situation."

"Okay, Katy. Take care. We'll get you through it!"

Kate hung up and walked in the direction of the law faculty's exit. When the student with the red cap saw her disappear in the booksellers' alley, he quickly returned inside and walked to the telephone booth.

46

In anger Oscar Smeenk threw the report against the wall of his The Hague office. It was an unexpected development: their New York agent had not been able to locate the American lawyer Van Wart. The agent only confirmed what he already knew: that the lawyer had temporarily left the firm he worked for. But since then, there was no trace of him.

When Van Wart hadn't come home at night, the agent had assumed he must have left on holiday or something. Since Van Wart didn't own a car, the agent had contacted the city's major car rental agencies. Posing as a desperate family member, he had found out that a car had been picked up in the name of Van Wart through a Hertz in Manhattan. A visit to the agency had confirmed that Van Wart had picked up the car with an open return date.

But the strange thing was that the car had been returned the same day already. And even stranger, the agency staff informed that the car had been returned by a person other than Van Wart. They didn't know what the destination of Van Wart had been and hadn't been willing to disclose the number of miles the car had traveled. The final observation in the agent's report was that Van Wart hadn't come home the night after either, so he asked for new instructions.

What was this Van Wart up to? Smeenk couldn't make sense of it. The holiday story was nonsense, of course: Van Wart was on a mission and wouldn't take a break in the middle of it. And now, other people seemed to be involved—at least, the person who had returned the car. And it seemed likely that Van Wart was not alone; otherwise, he would have kept the car.

Who were they?

One thing was sure: Van Wart had to be neutralized at all costs, despite the risks it entailed—especially the risk of entering into the spotlights of the American intelligence services. Smeenk fully realized the delicacy of such operations abroad, especially if they hadn't been cleared with the cabinet. The activity of running intelligence agents abroad and against citizens of that country fell within the definition of a universally known term: espionage.

Smeenk considered the options. The simplest one would be to bug Van Wart's cell phone. Or even better: track the phone's location. But that would require the services of an American telecom provider and, thus, cooperation from the American authorities. And contacting them was out of the question, especially now they were downplaying the significance of the troop movements.

The same difficulty applied to an alert for Van Wart at airports and borders. That option would only be possible at home in the Netherlands. Although it wouldn't solve the problem of locating him in the United States, at least it would alert them in case he tried to enter the country. One never knew what he had in mind.

Smeenk decided he would discuss the border alert with the minister of internal affairs. He would see him later that day anyway for another issue concerning the event, which was coming dangerously close now. In the meantime the instructions for the agent in New York were simple: continue surveillance on Van Wart's apartment and strike immediately whenever the lawyer reappeared.

47

The student with the red cap had seen the blond-haired lady make a call from the telephone booth. After she had hung up, he sped to the booth, inserted a phone card, and pushed the redial button.

A telephone number appeared on the tiny LCD screen.

It was a cell phone number, and he quickly scribbled it down. Then the phone was picked up on the other side.

"Evelyn speaking." the voice said.

He hung up, scribbled down the name below the number, and hurried in the direction of the exit.

Earlier, upstairs in the library, he'd had a tense moment when the blond-haired lady had approached him, but luckily she had only wanted to borrow the book had had just stolen from another table. Just after, he'd been able to recover the information she'd been looking for at the computer terminal.

He ran through the booksellers' alley, and when he reached the bridge to which the woman had earlier locked her bicycle, he caught a glimpse of her in the distance.

He unlocked his bicycle and raced after her through the narrow street, disappearing in the Amsterdam crowds.

48

Daniel followed Lent through a set of large wooden doors, and after a few meters, he paused to admire the space around him. In the dimmed light, he saw books everywhere he looked. A circular balustrade overhung a massive central table covered with countless books and documents.

"My library," Lent said. "I'm quite proud of it—the most complete collection of documents relating to America's Dutch past. I'm sure that one day, the collection will be part of a museum."

Daniel thought about the remark while running his hand along some of the leather covers.

"One thing is still not clear to me, Mr. Lent. You said the founding documents of our country and all the ideals America stands for were inspired by the Dutch. But weren't they introduced by English philosophers? John Locke and the like?"

"You're right. Locke, also named the Father of Liberalism, was one of the most influential Enlightenment thinkers and strongly influenced the American revolutionary writers. But you should know that his famous works were for a large part written when he lived in the Dutch Republic."

Daniel was stunned. "Locke actually lived in Holland?"

"And he wasn't the only one. Take John Adams, another Founding Father."

"You mean the later American President?"

"Indeed. His house in The Hague even became the very first American embassy in the world."

Daniel thought about it for a second but had difficulty grasping the implications. "What in heaven's name did a man like Adams do there?"

"Secure funding for the young American republic! The Netherlands was not only the first to salute the American flag, it also became the first state to lend money to the new country. Take a look at this."

Lent walked to one of the rows of bookshelves and pointed at a portrait painting hanging on a head of. Daniel bowed lightly to read the text below the portrait.

"The originals of the two republics are so much alike that a page from one seems a transcript of the other."

-John Adams

"Adams said this about the Netherlands?" Daniel asked in astonishment.

"Indeed. Adams was fully aware of the historical parallels between the two countries. And he left us other hints of admiration. Look."

Lent led Daniel to the central table and pointed at an image depicting a large eagle. Daniel immediately recognized it.

"The Great Seal of the United States. What about it?" Daniel asked.

"Adams was involved in the design of it. He included a subtle reference to his host country. Our world-famous eagle holds a sheaf of thirteen arrows in its left claw, one for each state. An element directly borrowed from the Dutch Republic's lion right over here."

Daniel looked at the print next to the eagle. Apparently his arrival had been prepared meticulously. Indeed both eagles held arrows in the same way.

"Around the same time, the name of the new republic was also confirmed: the United States of America—a name that unmistakably and proudly referred to the United States of the Netherlands. Or *the States*, as the European country was commonly referred to at that time."

The States! Daniel thought in amazement. He wondered how many people had ever heard this origin. "So what happened afterward? I mean, how come the Dutch influence disappeared after laying such a profound basis?"

"Who said it disappeared? Remember the Louisiana Land Purchase of 1803?"

Daniel nodded. The transaction through which the United States obtained the gigantic territory of Louisiana, composed of fifteen current states.

"Financed with Dutch money. And many schools and academies were founded by or highly influenced by the Dutch: New York University was founded by the Dutchman Myndert Van Schaick. Harvard has a Dutch Cultural Society. Several universities are even named after Dutchmen or Dutch Americans: Princeton, after the Prince of Orange; Rutgers University; Vanderbilt University; and Hofstra University."

"How come?"

"Don't forget that after the independence, the influence of the Dutch aristocracy, the descendants of the early settlers, was still very much intact. The Dutch aristocracy continued to play an important role in commerce, the army, and administration. Stephen Van Rensselaer III, for example, the heir of the huge Rensselaerswyck estate in New York State, became the tenth-richest American *of all time*. And a look at the names of past mayors of New York City will reveal that around one-fifth of them are Dutch!"

"Not to forget the other Americans of Dutch descent," Daniel remarked, proud of his knowledge. "Van Alen, the architect of the

Chrysler Building. In cinema, with Dick Van Dyke, Lee Van Cleef, the Fonda family, and Humphrey Bogart. In literature, with John Updike. In the arts, with Keith Haring. And in music, with Bruce Springsteen."

Lent produced a smile. "Born in the USA, but raised in New Netherland!"

Both men laughed out loud.

"And then the Dutch American Presidents," Lent said.

"Martin Van Buren!" Daniel knew.

"Correct. The only President whose first language wasn't English."

"What? You mean his first language was Dutch?"

Lent nodded. "And the second President of Dutch descent was Theodore Roosevelt, followed by the third one, the great Franklin Delano Roosevelt, America's longest-serving President."

FDR! Who had guided America through World War II. Daniel immediately realized the symbolism of it: America, represented by a Dutch American, came to rescue Holland in order to defend the principles of liberalism and democracy on which America was shaped after Dutch example.

"The Roosevelts," Lent continued, "were a wealthy and influential family and one of the oldest in New York State. Theodore's grandparents still spoke Dutch. By the way, the word *roosevelt* means 'rose field' in Dutch."

Roose-velt! Daniel was speechless. And instantly he felt the need to uncover everything there was to know about America's hidden Dutch past.

Standing opposite each other at the table in the middle of the library, Lent looked Daniel in the eyes.

"Daniel Van Wart, American of Dutch descent, do you accept the mission, consisting of the exploration of the common past of the Dutch and American nations, with the purpose of contributing to spread among the people the version of history most faithful to the truth?"

"Yes, I do!" Daniel replied without hesitation.

Both men raised a small glass of jenever and toasted.

Part VI

49

"I don't know what you think of it, but in my opinion the explanation's crap!" the Chief of Staff exclaimed, visibly excited.

The President finished the short letter for a second time and leaned back. "To be honest, to me it seems quite plausible."

The Chief of Staff shook his head and leaned on the Presidential desk authoritatively with three fingers of each hand. "With all due respect, sir, I don't think it's plausible at all. A military parade of this size? These vehicles don't even fit into the narrow Dutch streets! And if it only concerned a parade, why not report it in advance to NATO, as required? I tell you, this operation looks pretty strange to me."

"So what's your story?" the President retorted. "That it's some sort of cover-up? We're not talking about some banana republic!"

"That's exactly the point! If they're so honest, why not report the troop movements? And why come up with a bogus excuse when asked for an explanation?"

The President was silent for a moment. "What is it that you propose? Tell the queen they're a bunch of liars and ask them to cancel their parade?"

"The point is, there *is* no parade,"

The President looked up, puzzled. "What do you mean, no parade?"

"We did some quick intelligence work and found out that no one in the Dutch army has been briefed about any parade."

"Hold on. You spied on a NATO ally? Without consulting me first?"

"Sir, this was certainly no spying operation. We just asked some questions to our NATO staff based in the country. They're in direct contact with the local army, so they can ask questions naturally and legitimately."

The President stood up, opened the Oval Office's bulletproof veranda doors and stepped outside. He knew it was strictly forbidden by the security protocol, but he needed some air.

The Chief of Staff quietly followed him until the doorstep.

"Tell me, what's your conclusion on this?" the President asked after a while.

"For the moment, I have no conclusion. My gut feeling is that maybe some people over there have something in mind. Maybe they want to use the passage of the throne to pull off some trick. You know the mess it always creates: kings, princes, and other non-elected heads of state."

The President knew exactly what the Chief of Staff meant. Most of history's conflicts had started with a new monarch and his vision on how to run a country. Modern states had therefore abolished all hereditary functions and rightly so: otherwise eventually someone would inevitably come to power who lacked intelligence or a sense of responsibility and turn things into a mess. And if it wasn't the monarch himself, it were the people surrounding him who manipulated things. One thing was sure: the only guarantee against abuse was a republic, and any country relying on defenses as "respecting history" or "national identity" to defend monarchy was fooling itself badly.

"The only thing that puzzles me," the Chief of Staff remarked, "is that anyone with activities involving armed forces would find himself confronted with NATO. I think our country would be the first to protest and defend the Dutch people against any coup or other aggression. How the hell could the Dutch authorities ignore that?"

The President froze. *The letter from the Dutch royal house some days ago!* Suddenly he understood why it had been sent. And why now. *It was a threat!* A form of political blackmail of the highest level: a threat forcing NATO *not* to intervene!

Baffled, he stared in the direction of the Potomac River, his face turning pale.

"Mr. President, are you all right?" the Chief of Staff asked.

The President didn't respond. He knew he was caught in a devil's dilemma.

50

When the limo braked and turned right, Daniel Van Wart noticed the large sign at the entrance:

FRANKLIN D. ROOSEVELT
PRESIDENTIAL LIBRARY AND MUSEUM

After Daniel's acceptance of the mission, Lent had told him that it was here that he could find potential answers to the mystery of the hidden past: the former home of the Roosevelts in Hyde Park, NY. It was now a museum and included FDR's Presidential Library. Daniel's arrival had been arranged for, Lent had told him.

A cordial lady named Rose welcomed him and gave a short tour of the premises. Although he'd heard of the place, he'd never visited it before. To his surprise, it even contained the grave of Roosevelt and his wife, Eleanor. He was also struck by the architecture of the buildings: all in Dutch Colonial style: at the specific request of FDR himself, Rose told him.

After they had taken a quick coffee at the visitors' cafeteria, Daniel was taken to the Presidential Library itself, where Rose introduced him to the librarian. He was a tall and lean bespectacled man who in a way resembled Roosevelt himself, Daniel thought to his amusement. The man explained that Roosevelt had been the first President of the United States to make his private collection of books and papers available to the public in a Presidential library, of which he had overseen the design and construction himself.

"FDR was very conscious of his origins. It started with the fact that a certain Philippe de la Noye, a Huguenot born in Leiden, Holland, was one of the passengers of the *Mayflower.* FDR was one of his far descendants and even carried a corrupted version of his surname as *Delano.*"

"De la Noye—De-la-no. Incredible!"

"Fascinating, isn't it? And he left us some clear clues of his active interest: his sailing boat was named the *Half Moon*, after Hudson's ship when he discovered Manhattan for the Dutch. Roosevelt also became vice President of the Netherland-America Foundation, and was a trustee of the Holland Society of New York. As a Freemason he was member of one of the country's foremost lodges, the *Holland Lodge.* But most symbolic of all, it was Roosevelt who turned Thanksgiving into a national holiday."

Daniel recalled how the Pilgrims had brought the annual celebration from Leiden.

"Now, Mr. Van Wart, this is the desk I reserved for your research assignment." He explained that he would be available personally for any request and had even been instructed to close the entire premises for other visitors, should Daniel prefer so.

Lent's influence reaches far, Daniel concluded in silence.

He settled down at the desk and asked the librarian the question that had been building up in his mind for some time now: Had nothing been written before on America's Dutch origins? The librarian showed him a section in the library with most that had been written on the story. He explained that when the influence of the Dutch language dwindled and English became the dominant one, historians weren't able to study the original Dutch sources anymore. That's how the recorded history became English biased. In parallel, due to the commercial and social rivalry between the Dutch and the English, a caricature of the Netherlanders developed, discouraging any serious attention to America's Dutch origins.

"A caricature reinforced by Washington Irving," Daniel added, recalling the Sleepy Hollow cemetery.

"You're right, all starring somewhat pitiful old Dutch colonists. Irving—who could read Dutch himself, by the way—nevertheless passed the story of America's Dutch history on to new generations of Americans. His character Diedrich Knickerbocker even became a cultural icon, the word *Knickerbocker* now synonymous with 'Old Dutch' with an aristocratic flavor. Funnily, the word *Knickerbocker* also designated the typically Dutch three-quarter pants from the seventeenth century, bound just below the knee. The pants survived until our times and became today's American football pants!"

Amused, Daniel thought about the millions of American football fans who unknowingly cheered at strangely evolved Hollanders.

"And don't forget the New York Knicks!"

Daniel instantly understood the name of the iconic basketball team.

The librarian further explained that in Irving's days, the New York Historical Society had been founded, which encouraged research into the Dutch past. It led to several publications on the topic, such as Edward O'Callaghan's *History of New Netherlands* and *New York under the Dutch*, published in 1846. It was during the first centennial celebration of the American independence in 1876 that several American writers for the first time claimed that the United Provinces, rather than England, had been the "mother of America." Similar impulses were given by William Elliot Griffis's *Brave Little Holland and What She Told Us*. And the foundation of The Holland Society of New York also contributed largely to the remembrance of the city's Dutch past. The renewed interest culminated in a period of sheer "Holland Mania," roughly from 1880 to 1920. It permanently established the image of Holland composed of wooden shoes, tulips, and windmills.

"And what about today? Is there anything left of all this?" Daniel asked.

"The Mania came to an end with the hard realities of World War I. And more generally, one could say that the story fell victim to the country's extraordinary speed of development. As you know, American society has always been extremely forward looking, with the accompanying trait of forgetting to look back sometimes and contemplate its origins. The Holland Society still exists by the way, and contributed to the New Netherland Institute, which translates our Dutch colonial archives. Maybe someday that will lead to interesting new books. For the rest, we have the Dutch-American Friendship Day on April 19 of each year, and since 1990, the Dutch-American Heritage Day, celebrated on November 16."

Daniel had heard of neither of the days. "So that's all there's left?" he asked, disappointed. "What about our man Roosevelt? He seemed quite interested in the story. Why didn't he leave America with something more tangible than his library's architecture and some hidden symbols?"

"That's exactly the question we need your help with, Mr. Van Wart."

Seated alone in the middle of Roosevelt's library, Daniel glanced at the objects waiting in front of him: a brand-new laptop, several yellow legal pads and a fountain pen engraved "FDR." His thoughts returned briefly to the library at Stiglitz & Arrowsmith; it was the first time the thought didn't hurt. He was glad the situation had happened to him; he had a more important thing to do—change America's history as currently taught.

After a couple of hours, when he had finished the outline for his research, he composed an e-mail to Kate Bates. Or rather, to Evelyn of the firm's Amsterdam office, as they had agreed she would be the channel to reach Kate.

51

In the office in The Hague, the tension was almost tangible. The senior assistant sat opposite Smeenk, who held a fresh report in his hand.

Smeenk noticed how his trembling hands betrayed the fact that he had drunk too much again last night. Together with the cigarettes, it was another bad habit he'd been unable to resist lately, unable to sleep without the alcohol to stop his mind from racing, and to neutralize the stress.

It was the assistant who broke the silence. "I think we can say the report contains both good and bad news. The first part, from our Amsterdam informant, is the bad news and seems to suggest that Kate Bates, as we already suspected, has indeed a contact person through whom she probably communicates with the American lawyer. And by calling from public phone booths, as she did in the Amsterdam law faculty, the mic in her office has become useless already."

Smeenk nodded without saying a word and frowned his glasses up his nose.

"The second part contains the good news. Surprising as it may sound, Bates's contact person seems to be an associate of Van Olden's firm."

"What?" Smeenk burst out.

"It also scared us a little, as you can imagine. We screened the cell phone number the informant had obtained at the law faculty, and the Communications Ministry informed us that the number was attributed to Van Olden's firm. When we checked the number with the firm, it appeared the extension is used by a certain Evelyn."

Smeenk leaned forward and gave the assistant a severe look. "Don't tell me she works on Van Olden's team!"

"No, apparently not."

"So what's her link with Bates?"

"They were in the same class for their bar exams. Perhaps that's how they know each other; no further information on that for the moment."

Smeenk threw the report on his desk and rubbed his hands over his face. He stood up and walked aimlessly around his office, letting the news sink into his brain.

"No, it's the other way around." he suddenly said. "The contact person is the good news: now we know who it is. The bad news is that she works in Van Olden's office. Even if she doesn't work for him, god knows what information she has access to!"

"But we could ask Van Olden to keep an eye on this Evelyn. Maybe he can even get access to her correspondence with Bates."

Smeenk agreed that made sense. The girl would have to be screened thoroughly anyway. Everything in him told him her presence at Van Olden's firm was a huge and unexpected risk, one that should be taken care of immediately and at all cost. Perhaps the term *eliminating* the risk was even more appropriate.

"Put our chinny friend on her immediately," Smeenk ordered while returning to his desk. "And I mean right now! He screwed up in London; this is his last chance. And tell him that!"

"We will, sir."

"In the meantime, I'll call Van Olden."

The assistant left the office without saying a word.

Smeenk leaned on his desk and suddenly felt dizzy. He hurried to the window and opened the large sliding door. The strong west wind blew in his face, and raindrops started to form a dotted pattern on his gray suit.

He didn't know how long he had been standing there, but when he regained his thoughts, his suit was soaked. He went back inside and noticed the wind had blown some documents around his office. After he had picked them up, he took his cell phone from the desk and dialed Van Olden on his secure phone.

Dammit! Van Olden didn't answer the call. He would try again in a moment; this whole issue now had to be terminated urgently. And permanently.

52

Kate Bates walked to the pantry of her Amsterdam office and poured another cup of fair-trade coffee. She was excited that Daniel had finally sought contact. Although she regretted they hadn't been able to speak directly and tell him about the probable link between their trouble and the passage of the throne, she was comforted by the fact that he now had her cell phone number in case of urgency.

She was well aware of the security risks related to modern telecommunication, and over the years had gotten used to the methods to circumvent overcurious authorities. Prepaid SIM cards remained the best way to guarantee privacy, and she used them regularly to discuss cases with clients.

The contents of Daniel's e-mail that Evelyn had forwarded also were a consolation: the specific questions it contained proved that he too was busy trying to find answers. And she agreed with him that for some questions, she was in a better position to answer than he, as they concerned international treaties, her specialization. In essence, he asked her to check the validity of territorial claims to the New Netherland area *before* America became an independent state. And from what she had found out already, the situation seemed highly peculiar, not to say stunning.

In 1664, King Charles II of England granted parts of his North American territories to his brother James, the Duke of York. This included the Dutch colony of New Netherland. That same year, the

Duke of York sent a small army led by Nicolls to claim his property and take control of New Netherland. Stuyvesant was forced to surrender, and New York became English. This much of the history she knew.

But the validity of the land grant of King Charles II to his brother seemed highly questionable, as it was doubtful whether Charles himself had any valid legal title to the lands that constituted New Netherland. The issue concerned the *Discovery Doctrine*, the old set of principles according to which countries could establish claims to territories. The doctrine had shaped today's world by defining the exact zones of power and influence that countries could exercise: it formed the basis of many of today's culture and language frontiers.

The origins of the Discovery Doctrine dated back to the fifteenth century, when vessels became seaworthy enough to cross the oceans and discover new continents. The general principle was that a country could claim a new territory if it had not been discovered yet by another Christian country. The Catholic countries Portugal and Spain dominated the seas at that time, and they became entangled in conflicts after Columbus discovered America in 1492.

The issues were settled in the famous Treaty of Tordesillas of 1494, which drew a north-south line halfway between the Canary Islands and the Caribbean islands, which Columbus had discovered two years earlier. All territories west of the line would be free for Spain to discover; all new territories east of the line were for Portugal to claim.

Problems arose when other countries sent expeditions to the large American continent. The very general character of the Discovery Doctrine led to conflicting claims among the Spanish, English, and French explorers, especially when it became clear that all North American territories formed in fact one and the same continent. To find a solution and defend English claims, Queen Elizabeth I and her advisors therefore added an important specification to the doctrine: in order to secure a claim, new territories not only had to be discovered but also occupied.

When France and the Netherlands were confronted with English claims on their colonial territories, they defended themselves with the argument that they had purchased the land from their previous occupants, the Indians, or that they had entered into peace treaties with them. Therefore, a second specification was added to the doctrine: "occupation" would have to be interpreted as exercising *effective control* over a territory. This could be direct, through establishments, cultured lands, or forts, or indirectly through agreements with the indigenous populations.

Applied to New Netherland, discovered and occupied by the Dutch and solidly under Dutch rule either directly or through deals with natives Americans, it meant that King Charles's claims on the territory were clearly unfounded. Consequently, his grant of the territory to the Duke of York was legally void, so the latter never became the owner of New Netherland.

What about the surrender of the colony by Stuyvesant to Colonel Richard Nicolls in 1664? In his e-mail Daniel had mentioned the *Articles of Surrender* and their surprising contents, and had attached a copy of them. Kate agreed with Daniel that the most striking point was the explicit respect of full Dutch property rights. What passed to English hands was therefore the public power, or sovereignty, over New Netherland, but from a private property perspective, the entire colony remained almost fully Dutch owned.

The question Kate now had to study was whether that situation had changed during subsequent historic events. She already knew that the Treaty of Westminster of 1674 reconfirmed all Dutch property rights. She now learned that after the American War of Independence all lands of the British Crown became vested in the people of the state of New York. However, this did not trigger the forfeiture of existing property rights either. It meant that the original proprietor of New Netherland, the Dutch West India Company, remained the rightful owner all along. And since the assets of the Dutch West India Company had been acquired by the Dutch state upon the company's bankruptcy in 1792, most of New York State would still belong to the Netherlands today!

Kate couldn't suppress a laugh when she reached the conclusion. She looked at the clock and saw it was past midnight. *No wonder she came to such weird results*: she realized she'd been reading and researching for a full day without a break. Convinced she must have missed something, she did thirty sit-ups, had a cup of tea, and went to work again.

An argument that could potentially block current Dutch claims on New York was called "statute of limitations", the legal principle that if a claim was not exercised within a certain lapse of time, it lost its validity. It was a common legal principle throughout the world, to guarantee legal certainty and avoid that long-accepted situations could be challenged eternally. However, Kate knew it was far from certain whether the principle also applied to territorial claims of countries—of which the Israeli–Palestinian conflict formed a clear illustration. A key element in international law was whether a current situation had been *contested* by the other party. This had already been decided in the early 1930s in, incidentally, another dispute concerning the Netherlands and the United States: the so-called Island of Palmas case. The question therefore was whether the Netherlands had formally contested American property rights to the State of New York; information she did not have.

Kate mused about the possible consequences of it all. What if, at some point in history, the Dutch had sent a letter to the American President informing him of the Dutch prior rights, followed by a short reminder from time to time? It would mean the United States couldn't rely on a statute of limitations defense, and the Dutch claim on Manhattan would still be valid! Even if it wasn't realistic to expect an immediate hand over to the Netherlands, it could trigger a massive compensation claim, probably the biggest in the history of the world. And simply making such a claim public would create a major political conflict and wreak considerable economic havoc. Which American President would like to become associated with that?

53

An unexpected knock on the door broke Van Olden's concentration and agitated him. It was the reason he hated Wednesdays, when his assistant was absent and no one else fenced off unscheduled visits from bothering colleagues.

"Yes!" he barked in the direction of the door.

The door slowly opened, and to his surprise a young female associate entered. He wasn't sure she'd already been introduced to him, but he thought he vaguely remembered her smile. *A beautiful smile.*

"I'm busy, as you can see. Whom are you looking for?" His question came out less biting than intended.

The girl closed the door behind her, which struck Van Olden as peculiar. He watched her as she stepped to his desk, holding a shoulder bag in one hand and a large envelope in the other one.

"I'm so sorry to disturb you, Mr. Van Olden, but I need a partner's signature on a counterstatement that has to be filed before tomorrow. And in view of the hour, you're the only partner left."

When the girl had taken the document from the envelope and bent forward to hand it over to him, he had a clear view inside her blouse. He almost sighed out loud, so close they were.

"I'll have to read it first before signing anything; I hope it's not too long."

"Don't worry; it's just a two-page formal application. It'll be a quickie."

Van Olden's heart almost missed a beat. Had she winked at him while making that remark?

"Let's go through it together," the girl said as she walked around the desk and placed herself next to him.

This was quite a lady! Van Olden thought. With a self-confident and determined act he'd rarely seen from a junior!

His cell phone vibrated on his desk. He picked it up and saw on the display it was Smeenk. *He would have to wait.*

While poring over the document, he felt her hip briefly touch his arm. He looked up at her: the slim neck, the pearl earrings, the blond hair.

She noticed his stares and replied with a quick smile.

Van Olden couldn't read a letter of the paper in front of them. He knew very well he had to be careful in view of his past. But this had never happened to him before: *she* was taking the initiative!

While pretending to read, the tantalizing mix of her scent filled his nostrils. Instinctively his right hand left the desk and touched the fine legs next to him. She didn't protest, so his hand moved up slowly and hesitated shortly when he reached her skirt. Then it continued its explorative journey.

His head was turning. He had to reshuffle slightly to ease the tension that was building up in his crotch. It was almost unbelievable; the girl even seemed to spread her legs slightly, giving his hand more space to maneuver. Then she suddenly moved her legs together, trapping his hand between her thighs.

"Do you want to know what's up there, Van Olden?"

"I surely do," he murmured, his throat dry from excitement.

"I thought so. But I'll keep you longing a little more. Look, I brought you something. I want you to think about me."

She took another sheet from the envelope and laid it in front of him.

He immediately saw what is was: a picture taken from under her skirt.

"You have to promise me one thing, Van Olden. This has to remain our little secret."

He couldn't agree more. "Of course it will."

"No, you have to prove you're serious."

"Prove it?" he asked impatiently. "How?"

She looked up and pointed in front of them. "Let's put the picture in that safe. Just to be sure."

He nodded in agreement and felt how she loosened her thighs' grip, releasing his hand. He took the picture, stood up, and walked to the safe. To his surprise, she walked with him. *Was she going to watch as he typed in the combination?* He hesitated: the files of his most important client!

She smiled at him, and he decided he would change the code later on.

Just when he had closed the safe again, his desk phone rang. He walked back to his desk and took the call.

"Can't you bring it up to my office? I'm busy now." He listened for a few more seconds, muttered a few angry words, and hung up. "I have to go down to sign for a courier delivery," he told the girl. He accompanied her out of his office, said good-bye, and took the elevator down.

When he returned, he was surprised to find the girl standing next to his desk again.

"You forgot to sign this!" she said, holding the document in the air.

He sat down, took his fountain pen, and placed his signature at the bottom of the document.

"Good boy," she said, imitating a kiss with her lips. With the document and the envelope she headed for the door and gave him a last wink.

Van Olden hung back in his chair. *What a girl!* On the badge clipped to her skirt he had seen her name: Evelyn. Even without the picture she would be difficult to forget.

—

It was only after some minutes that he remembered that Oscar Smeenk had tried to reach him.

"Oscar, Hein Van Olden here. What can I do for you?"

"Hein! Thank God you called me back. We have an awkward situation. It concerns your firm."

"My firm?" Van Olden asked in surprise.

"Yes. We found out that someone at your firm is a friend of Kate Bates! And acts as her intermediary to communicate with Daniel Van Wart!"

Van Olden was silent for a moment, his brain still distracted. "And who would that person be?"

"An associate named Evelyn. Do you know her?"

Van Olden was paralyzed.

"Hein, does she have access to anything? I mean, information concerning the operation? Imagine her feeding things to Bates!"

"Unlikely, Hein. She's not in my team. She must have access to the firm's document system, but our files are not in it. They're in my safe, here in front of me."

Van Olden looked at the safe, and to his shock he noticed that the lever was not in the "closed" position anymore.

54

Apparently his client was in some sort of trouble. After London recently, this was the second time that he'd been called on a hurried mission consisting of shadowing a target. Fortunately he'd been in Amsterdam that morning, where he had been posting in front of the World Trade Center for almost twelve hours now. The wooden bench opposite the entrance of the law firm Stiglitz & Arrowsmith was hurting his back. He still had his helmet on, but he had loosened the strap around his protruding chin.

He looked at the image of the girl for the hundredth time. The screen of his cell phone was small, but her features were clear enough to recognize her among the surprisingly large number of people that still exited the building, despite the late hour.

Suddenly the cell phone vibrated in his hand, and without saying a word, he listened to the voice. The new instructions were surprising, but much more to his taste: apparently the target had just stolen a file inside the building, and he needed to recover it—at any cost.

He doubled his concentration on the entrance, and after only a few minutes, he noticed the blond-haired girl passing through the revolving doors. She was carrying a bag across her shoulder, which he assumed held the file. When she unlocked a bicycle that was attached to the railing left of the entrance, he didn't hesitate and quickly ran back to the Kawasaki. While igniting the engine and fastening the strap of his helmet, he kept observing her as she started cycling in the direction of the WTC train station. He let the bike roll down the ramp and followed her at a distance, lights off. He didn't know the area very well but recalled there were several short tunnels ahead, probably passing underneath the train tracks and the Ring, the expressway around Amsterdam. It was there that he would have to strike, he decided.

—

Evelyn pedaled quickly, still full of emotion about what had just happened. She tasted the salt of her tears. *That creep Van Olden.* He hadn't changed a bit since that interview after the bar exam. She'd been surprised at how quickly he had touched her leg; he had surpassed his reputation. The rest had passed in a rush of near unconsciousness.

But the strategy had worked. And thanks to the unexpected courier delivery she had even obtained the documents right away, without the need for a second visit to his office. The safe had contained a drawer with suspended files. In fact, she had no idea what she was looking for; confidential documents concerning the House of Orange, Kate had mentioned. But which ones? Among the titles printed on the covers she had read: ORANGE FAMILY, INVESTMENTS, PRIME MINISTER, and many others. When she had heard the elevator tone at the far end of the corridor, she had quickly pulled out a slim file marked OFFICIAL DOCUMENTS, closed the safe, and sped back to the desk. She had just had enough time to slip the file into the envelope with Kate's home address before Van Olden entered the office again. He hadn't noticed anything, she thought.

She had wanted to run out of the building but forced herself not to act suspiciously. At a quick pace, her knees weak from fear, she had descended into the entrance hall, greeted the man from the mail pickup service, and now cycled off into the night.

—

The first tunnel was too light, he decided, still following the girl at a distance. If someone were to accidentally witness the action, the bike's license plate could be read, and in view of the last-minute instructions, he hadn't had time to swap them with a set of stolen ones.

The second tunnel looked better. The flickering tube light made it very difficult for the eye to read, something he knew from the stint he had worked as security guard at a discotheque. From the distance, he tried to time the moment she would enter the tunnel. Then he accelerated sharply.

He noticed how the girl briefly looked behind her, probably because of the roaring sound of the motorbike. When he entered the tunnel, he extended his right arm, and when he was beside her, he reached for the shoulder strap of the bag. She turned away in a reflex, but he managed to get hold of the strap.

Just when he wanted to accelerate again, a violent pull on the strap surprised him, and he felt how it escaped from his gloved hand. The sudden change of balance made him sway heavily to keep the bike under control, swinging from left to right and back over the pavement.

After he regained control and stood still with one foot on the ground, he looked back. The girl was sitting on the pavement in the middle of the tunnel, like an abandoned doll on a playground. Next to her lay the bicycle, one wheel still turning. He didn't know what had happened: maybe the strap had gotten stuck behind the bicycle's handlebar.

He watched her standing up slowly, walking to the bag lying a couple of yards farther, and picking it up. To his surprise, she didn't pick up the bicycle but instead started to run toward the entrance of the tunnel.

With a loud roar and a spinning back wheel he turned the bike and accelerated in her direction. When he had almost reached her at the end of the tunnel and prepared himself for the impact, she suddenly moved left sharply and started to climb up the grass ramp on the side of the road.

The ramp was way too steep for the motorbike, he judged, so he brought it to a standstill and stepped off. A slight panic caught him now: uphill was unknown terrain, and without the bike, he lost a clear advantage over her.

He jumped on the ramp in pursuit of the girl but felt how his sneakers immediately lost grip on the wet grass. He slipped and fell hard on his face; the girl's high heels had given her an edge.

Lying at the bottom of the ramp, he saw the girl almost reached the top. He was absolutely sure his client had used the code phrase "*at any cost,*" so there was only one way left. He zipped open his jacket and took out the gun with silencer. He positioned himself, and when he saw the blond hair catch the wind on the top of the ramp, he aimed and pulled the trigger.

55

The early morning jazz musicians in the New York subway woke Daniel up. He had dozed off, he realized—no wonder after working on the memo at the Roosevelt library throughout the night. He was at Penn Station, and was just in time to jump out of the carriage before the doors closed.

William Penn, half Dutchman! he recalled while starting his ten-minute walk home.

Although the unexpected stay at the Hudson Valley had been revealing and not unpleasant, he was glad to go home to get a couple of hours of sleep and sort out some affairs. For the following day, Lent had reserved another mission: presenting his findings to Lent's Dutch historical society.

The memo itself was in a well-advanced state now. It started with a general introduction to the Dutch history of America, reproducing parts of the memo the intern had prepared earlier. Followed by a chapter on the circumstances of the transfer of the colony in 1664, with in particular the remarkable *Articles of Surrender* guaranteeing all existing property rights.

The third chapter would have to be completed by Kate, about the intertwined English and Dutch history, illustrating the fact that the Dutch culture of America could remain intact after New York's "transfer" to England.

The fourth part of the memo concerned the actual "chain of title" issue, analyzing existing case law on property claims from the colonial period. That had yielded another extremely interesting story: several individuals, mainly descendants of Dutch settlers in New Amsterdam, had indeed claimed ownership of American property invoking imperfections in the chain of title in the past. And one property in particular: Manhattan's Trinity Church! The ground the church had been built on had previously been a farm owned by Dutch settler Roeloff Jansen and his wife, Anneke Jans. The validity of the subsequent chain of title to the Trinity Church had been contested by several heirs of Anneke Jans in a series of lawsuits spanning two centuries. Until present, the actions had been without success, but it confirmed what Daniel saw as the memo's main conclusion: that serious questions could indeed be asked about current property rights to New York soil.

For completeness' sake, Daniel included a fifth chapter on potential property rights of the indigenous population. After all, the Indian tribes were the first habitants of the American continent. The issue had been the subject of serious legal debates and litigation in court, notably in the 1823 the Supreme Court case *Johnson v. M'Intosh.* The Supreme Court characterized the rights of the tribes merely as a "right of occupancy," effectively validating European claims. Therefore, indigenous rights did not trump Dutch claims either.

The sixth and last chapter was also reserved for Kate's input. It concerned the competing territorial claims of the Netherlands, Britain, and the United States in the light of international law. He hoped she had managed to finish this part, as for some reason, Lent had been adamant about finishing the memo as quickly as possible.

While entering the hall of his apartment building he thought maybe he should call Kate right away, and from a public phone booth, in line with her instructions. He turned around, making the man entering behind him bump into him. He apologized and went out again in search for a phone booth.

56

Kate had been devastated when she had received the news. She had cried out loud and fallen onto the floor when Evelyn's mother had told her over the phone about the death of her daughter. She had immediately taken the train to Evelyn's parents in the town of Aerdenhout, not far from the city of Haarlem. As Evelyn's longtime friend, she had joined the small group of intimates that had gathered to digest the news and to support Evelyn's parents. They had told her about the circumstances, which, for the moment, remained under investigation. Evelyn's body also remained under autopsy.

The police had told them the body had been found accidentally that morning by rail workers replacing cables close to the WTC in the south of Amsterdam. The body had been found just beside the train tracks and was mutilated on one side, possibly resulting from a train impact. For the moment, the police were investigating the causes of the incident and couldn't exclude a suicide.

A suicide! Kate almost flew to the wall when the word had been mentioned. Of all imaginable causes, this was impossible. Evelyn's character, attitude, perseverance—they simply didn't allow that. Besides, Kate was not aware of any problems Evelyn had at the moment, and she would have been the first to know if anything had been the matter. The only concern Evelyn currently had, she knew, was for Kate herself: she considered it *her* fault she was being followed again after putting her in touch with Daniel Van Wart.

It was, of course, that same case that worried Kate, and it had made her feel nauseous from the moment she had heard the news. The question was whether Evelyn's death was linked to the case, as her intuition told her. That would mean her death was not an accident and implied she had been… murdered! Had Van Olden found out she was fishing for something? Had she discovered something?

On the one hand, it seemed unthinkable that Evelyn's firm would physically harm her in any way; if something had gone wrong, they could have sanctioned her otherwise. But on the other hand, Van Olden was of course only a legal executioner of his clients, who were far less scrupulous, something she had experienced herself firsthand in the past.

Sitting on a bench at the monumental Haarlem Central Station waiting for the train back to Amsterdam, she was lost in a thousand thoughts. *Haarlem was the name giver of New York's Harlem,* she recalled. Had Evelyn somehow become a victim of the mysterious ties between Holland and the United States? Or had the news of her death simply affected her brain, and she was seeing ghosts?

She had decided not to tell Evelyn's parents about the story and the delicate—if not illegal—mission her daughter had been on. It made her feel extremely guilty, hiding a possible clue to their daughter's death. But first she needed answers. And she wouldn't rest before she had all of them.

She opened her handbag and took out a tissue to wipe her mascara again. The skin around her eyes felt painful after the countless identical gestures of that morning. When she put the package back in her bag, she heard her cell phone ringing. The one with the prepaid SIM card.

57

Kate briefly recomposed herself before picking up the cell phone.

"Kate, it's Daniel speaking. How are you?"

"Daniel! Not too well actually. Have you heard about Evelyn?"

"No, what about her?" Daniel asked.

She told him the news. And about the absence of the exact circumstances of Evelyn's death, which made her fear the worst.

"This is dramatic, Kate! So you think it's them? But why would they do that? Take such a risk?"

"It's a long story. Can you talk? Where are you?"

"I can talk. I'm in a hotel lobby. Couldn't find a public pay phone. I'm just returning home from an interesting guy I spent a couple of days with. He told me incredible things about the Dutch heritage of the United States. You won't believe it! In essence, the whole country is based on the Netherlands. The culture, its symbols, the Declaration of Independence—everything!"

Daniel briefly told her the story of the GPS and the meeting at the Sleepy Hollow Cemetery. How he had been selected by the wealthy Lent and his Dutch historic society to contribute the legal part to their research, all in quest of answers as to why the Dutch past had been erased from America's history.

"But the memo still needs your input, Kate. I found out there's an issue with the ownership of Manhattan. But I still can't see how that can be of interest to the House of Orange."

"I may have found an answer to that, Daniel."

"I beg your pardon?"

"I researched the situation from an international law perspective and came to the conclusion that the Dutch state might be able to claim ownership."

"The Dutch state? Why?"

Kate told him the story of the Discovery Doctrine and the invalidity of English claims right from the start.

"But asserting the claim now would cause a major diplomatic incident. I don't see why the Dutch government would do that."

"Under normal circumstances, they wouldn't. But there will be a new king shortly."

Daniel laughed. "And why would the new king do that? Gain popularity by showing that Holland founded the United States? Besides, I assume he would require government approval, and presumably the king doesn't have the power to impose his will."

"That's another thing I found out Daniel. In fact he *does* have that power." She told him of the sheer unlimited constitutional powers of the Dutch king, in contrast to most other surviving monarchies.

"So what you're saying is that the new Dutch king could simply invoke his constitutional rights and do as he pleases?"

"In essence, yes."

Daniel was silent for a moment. "But I assume there are limits to what other countries would accept. I think the United States would be the first to protest in case of a violation of democratic principles."

"Unless the king has knowledge he can use as a defensive threat against the United States."

"Knowledge? But what—" Daniel stopped in the middle of his phrase.

The claim on Manhattan!

"My goodness, Kate, I see what you mean. A scheme to enlarge royal powers, covered by the United States. Noninterference in exchange for abandoning territorial claims!"

"And supposing that's the strategy, it'll be crucial for the king to keep the threat intact and the knowledge in the bottle. That's possibly why we're being chased, Daniel: the chain-of-title issue automatically leads to the discovery of the claim. We came too close to what they're up to!"

"But how? I mean, if my Ground Zero research appeared on their radar, they must have put in place drastic security measures."

"Our royals have the means for it, I tell you."

"And without knowing it, I dragged Evelyn with me. And you."

"I probably only made the situation worse. There's something I didn't tell you, Daniel. I've been in a fight with the House of Orange before. Some years ago, for a client. I caused them hard times, so probably they panicked when they found out you and I were corresponding on the chain-of-title issue. I'm sorry for that, Daniel."

"Kate, do you think Evelyn was on to something?"

"Probably. Does the name Van Olden tell you something?"

"I think I know a partner in our Dutch office with that name. Why?"

Kate told him that he was the lawyer of the House of Orange and that he must be the link between Daniel's chain-of-title issue and the subsequent action of the House of Orange.

Daniel was dumbstruck. *The queen's lawyer!* It would explain why he had been taken from the case: Van Olden must have worked Sutherland, the firm's chairman…

"Evelyn tried to find out more about Van Olden's role," Kate explained. "Somehow they must have found out."

The information dazzled Daniel. The seriousness of the case was beyond his imagination. "So what do we do now?"

"I don't know, Daniel. That memo you wrote—where is it?"

Daniel reached in the pocket of his jacket and held the small USB stick. It suddenly felt as if he held the detonator to a nuclear bomb. "I have it with me here. All it needs is your input. Just one question, Kate. When will this new king take his powers?"

"In four days from now."

"In *four days*?"

"I'm afraid so. The whole country's been in an Orange fever for weeks now. The Dutch go crazy on events like these."

"And no one's asking questions about this new king?"

"That's the point, Daniel. The Dutch people don't realize anymore that it's the republic that made them great. They don't realize the gravity of the situation and think a kingdom is just fun. The only thing we can do to stop them from executing their plan is to make it public before the king's accession to the throne. But for that we not only need your memo, but also some proof. If only Evelyn had found something!"

"Maybe that gentleman I mentioned earlier can help us. He mentioned he was a member of some sort of Dutch republican society in the past. I'll see him later on."

"Just make it quick; time's running out! And something else: you should be very careful, Daniel. If they did kill Evelyn, we're also in danger. We're probably the only other people who know about the story. You're probably being shadowed too."

In a reflex Daniel looked around the lobby conspicuously, but didn't notice anyone.

"Whatever you do, don't go home; they'll probably be waiting for you."

Kate's warning suddenly made him realize something. *The man at the entrance of his apartment building!* Had he narrowly escaped trouble?

58

Oscar Smeenk held the empty bag in his hand and rubbed the steel Hermès logo with his thumb. He was furious. The agent had been able to recover the bag from the girl, but to their astonishment it had not contained the file. On top of that, the death of the girl had served them with another major complication.

This time, the agent was not to blame. On the contrary: he had been at the location when needed, despite the last-minute instructions. Smeenk even had to admit that it was pure professionalism that the agent had dragged the body to the train tracks to make it look like a suicide. But the trick would only work for a short moment: the labs would surely report the bullet hole. And then? The investigation would undoubtedly start with Stiglitz & Arrowsmith, her employer and the last point of contact before her death. Van Olden would have to clean up that mess himself, he thought.

The culprit sat opposite him, tucked away in the deep couch like a scared little bird. He was unshaven and looked exhausted. When his mistake had become apparent last night during their call, Van Olden had immediately confessed what had happened. The girl had played him masterfully, both men agreed. But after the immediate instructions to the agent observing the girl, both had been confident the mistake would be corrected quickly and the file retrieved.

That hope was now gone: the bag had been empty, apart from some irrelevant paperwork and personal belongings.

"Dammit!" Smeenk shouted, throwing the bag into a corner of the office. He knew the roles between them were back now to where they had been in the very beginning: he was in the driver seat again. Van Olden was all his. But it was of little comfort in view of the huge problem they now had: the documents! The operation stood or fell with retrieving them.

At first, they didn't understood how the file could have disappeared from the bag. The law firm's security team confirmed the girl hadn't returned to her floor after she had left Van Olden's office, so they assumed her bag must have contained the file when the agent started his pursuit.

It was during his debrief that the agent mentioned the passing of the firm's courier service. When Van Olden recalled the girl had a large envelope with her in his office, they realized she must have sent the file by mail on her way out.

The girl had been clever. Very clever.

They had subsequently verified the outgoing registered mail of that day, but unfortunately it hadn't revealed anything. So they concluded the envelope had probably been sent by regular mail, meaning impossible to trace and retrieve.

When someone knocked at the door, Van Olden quickly sat upright.

"Yes!" Smeenk shouted.

The assistant stepped in, holding a paper in the air.

"From our man in New York! Thought you may want to read it."

"Just tell me," Smeenk commanded.

"It's very short. The American agent reports he finally spotted Van Wart. After his disappearance during the last few days he suddenly turned up at his apartment building, by foot."

"Excellent. Did he capture him?"

"Afraid not. Van Wart entered the hallway but didn't go up to his floor; when the agent followed him, he immediately left the building again, just seconds later. The agent didn't have time to move. Van Wart hasn't returned since."

"That's all? That damn Van Wart!" Smeenk shouted. "He must be aware. It cannot be explained otherwise! But what in God's name can he do from the States? And at this stage?"

After a long silence in the room Van Olden slowly rose from the couch. "If Van Wart is too far away from the action, it seems there's only one person to whom the envelope could have been sent."

Smeenk looked up in surprise, but instantly realized whom Olden referred to. When the assistant responded to Smeenk's inquisitive look with a nod, Smeenk's face relaxed somewhat.

"Our men are already on her," Smeenk said. "I'm afraid it's your only hope, Van Olden."

59

Daniel had quickly realized that Kate's warning about not going home to his apartment had not been exaggerated, and it had not taken long to spot the blinded van parked right across the entrance. Going home for the night had not been an option anymore, so had spent the night at a small hotel in north Manhattan. The room was shabby, and the shower irregular, but he had had little choice. Lent had sent the limo to pick him up in the morning, and Daniel was now savoring the coffee at their meeting point, the Beekman Arms Inn, in the town of Rhinebeck, NY, on the banks of the Hudson River. Sitting opposite Daniel at a table at the inn's classic columned porch, Lent explained it was America's oldest operating inn, founded in 1766 by Dutch colonists. Later on, it was from the inn's front porch that President Roosevelt started every one of his four election campaigns.

Roosevelt. It struck Daniel that Lent must have some sort of fascination for the man, as the name kept coming back every now and then.

The inn's current owners seemed to know Lent, and didn't make the slightest remark about the orange bow ties Daniel and Lent were now wearing. Lent had just given the thing to Daniel and insisted he wear it, assuring him it was the dress code for the society's meeting.

They left the inn, and after a short drive Daniel noticed the roads were getting narrower and bumpy, the soft suspension of the limo making them shake gently.

Where was Lent taking him?

Lent lowered one of the limo's windows, and Daniel observed the rural surroundings. Small valleys, villages, farms—he knew they were in the heart of Dutch America. As if time had stood still since his ancestors had started inhabiting the region.

With every mile the curves in the road were becoming more frequent, and the driver had to make an effort to keep the heavy vehicle under control. When at a certain point the car almost came to a halt to make a sharp left turn, Daniel managed to see the street name.

"Binnewater," he read out loud.

"It means 'inland water' in Dutch," Lent remarked. "In a moment, you'll see why our forefathers chose that name."

Without saying a word, Daniel observed the lush environment, and after a few minutes indeed something like a lake or creek appeared.

Some miles farther still, the car made some sharp turns again, at the village of Rosendale.

"This name also," Daniel remarked.

Lent grinned. "We're in Dutch America, Daniel."

When the road turned into a steep and swirling mountain road, both of them had difficulty remaining seated.

"Where are we going, Lent?" Daniel asked with some anger in his voice. "This doesn't look like a conference destination to me. We're climbing the Catskill Mountains, if you ask me. But the skiing season's over."

"We're there." Lent said, pointing in front of them.

Daniel peered through the dark windows of the limo and couldn't believe his eyes. In front of them appeared a castle-like silhouette, towering over the mountainous landscape. With the foggy air moving up from the valley, it looked like a Disney setting.

"What the—" Daniel started. The place was huge, and with its composition of different buildings and styles, it almost looked like a miniature city.

The limo passed the crowded parking lots, and when they approached the building Lent pointed upward.

"Do you see that top gable over there, at the center? Does it remind you of anything?"

"A gable of a Dutch canal house? What is this, Lent, some sort of Dutch city?"

"You could see it that way. Consider it the capital of Dutch America."

They stepped out of the limo, and Daniel instantly noticed that the other arriving people spoke a different language.

It can't be: Dutch!

"Welcome to Mohonk," Lent said to him when they entered the stately wood-paneled hallway.

There was a notable buzz around them, and Lent nodded gently to some of the other people. Daniel noticed that all of the men were wearing orange bow ties. He looked at Lent, who seemed to enjoy his amazement.

"This is the Hudson Valley's old Dutch community, Daniel," he said while gently pushing him through the crowd. "The place was constructed at the end of the nineteenth century to preserve the Dutch culture and language. Every year, thousands of descendants of Dutch settlers come here to keep the Dutch American culture alive. Some of them have learned Dutch directly from their parents, grandparents, and so on."

Daniel was flabbergasted. It meant the language had in fact survived in the United States throughout the times! An unbroken chain going back to the Dutch founders of New York!

They were led into a huge room where hundreds of people had gathered. The room's large windows gave a panoramic view over the surrounding valleys. When Daniel noticed the podium and microphone at the far end, he realized the crowd hadn't come here to enjoy the view. They were waiting for *him*.

60

Kate was still inconsolable over the loss of Evelyn. It felt as if part of herself had died with Evelyn. Her mind and body were in disorder: it was impossible to eat or sleep. Going to the office was out of the question, so she had stayed home. It had taken the whole morning to calm down again after Evelyn's mom had called her, this time to inform her that the autopsy had revealed a bullet wound.

According to Evelyn's mom, it suggested that her daughter's death had been the result of an armed robbery, which seemed to be confirmed by the fact that her handbag was missing. The police had said that a pattern of robberies had indeed been observed in the WTC area in the past months. Although they could not fully explain why she had been found near the train tracks, they assumed she had been killed in a pursuit. The formal investigation was not closed yet, and they hoped to find witnesses.

Kate knew it was all nonsense, of course. The bullet wound proved that her intuition had been right and that Evelyn had been killed by her adversaries. *Murdered!* Apart from the immense anger and fury it had caused, another sentiment was equally strong: that of outright fear. What would they do next? Would she also be on their list? *Are they watching me now?* she wondered. She defiantly opened the large windows with the view on the Egelantiersgracht and looked at both sides of the canal. There was no one to see, apart from the mailman in his yellow suit right below her, pushing his cart toward her door. Several seconds later, her doorbell rang.

Just when she wanted to press the buzzer, she hesitated. Why would the man ring instead of using the postbox? *It could be a trap!*

She walked back to the window, and when the man noticed Kate above her, he held up a package.

"It doesn't fit through!" the man shouted in her direction.

Relieved, Kate descended, and when she studied the thick envelope, she immediately recognized the handwriting. *Evelyn's!*

At the table, she opened the envelope with curiosity. It contained a file marked OFFICIAL DOCUMENTS.

What was this? Evelyn hadn't mentioned that she would send something.

The file contained several dozen documents, each wrapped in a transparent protective cover. She took the first one and noticed its letterhead was the official seal of the Kingdom of the Netherlands. Underneath it read, "To the President of the United States of America." Something started to dawn on her. She scanned through the letter and saw that it had something to do with military troop movements, in connection with the passing of the throne. She was baffled. *Where did the file come from?*

At random she took another document. It was also a letter to the American President, but this time many years earlier. The rusted staple had stained the paper in the top corner. When she tried to take the document from the plastic cover, she noticed there were several pages of thin paper with grayish patches all over them and the full stops had pierced the paper. *The time of typewriters and carbon copies,* she realized. She read the subject line and instantly understood why Evelyn had sent her the file: it was for this letter she had been killed.

TOP SECRET—NEW COMMUNICATION IN THE MATTER RELATING TO CERTAIN AMERICAN TERRITORIES.

Her heart jumped when she read the rest of the short letter. In fact, it was a simple reminder of letters sent earlier, listed in the attachment, which referred to Dutch American territories. She looked up, her eyes wide open.

The statute of limitations issue! The letters precluded the United States from stating that the claim had lapsed. It was the proof that the theory she had discussed with Daniel was true. The territorial claim over New York exercised by the Netherlands was a reality! A reality abused by the House of Orange to blackmail the American President in order not to interfere in the Dutch situation. And to continuously accept the constitutional position and privileges of the House of Orange, which were in blatant opposition to all the founding principles of both countries. And now, America would even have to close its eyes when the new king seized his full powers, and God knows what else he had in mind.

What an incredible scheme! Kate thought. She suddenly understood why the secret had to be protected at all cost. The surveilling of Daniel's research, herself being followed again, the killing of Evelyn—nothing was spared in order to protect the secret claim!

She realized it also made perfect sense that it was Van Olden who kept the underpinning documents. Not only because he was the House of Orange's legal advisor and had probably drafted the recent correspondence with the Americans, but also because his client's documents were covered by *legal privilege*, adding an extra layer of security: in case of trouble, none of the royal papers could be requisitioned, not even by a public prosecutor or judge. It all seemed masterfully well prepared.

A sudden sound in the kitchen frightened her. She shot up but saw it was the cat jumping onto the kitchen dresser. The rush of fear nevertheless reminded her of the danger she was in: Evelyn's killers would undoubtedly turn to recover the file from her most probable accomplice—Kate herself!

She raced up the steep wooden stairs, pulled a large bag from the closet, and filled it randomly with some clothes. In a single gesture, she wiped her beauty products from the mirror shelf into the bag and raced downstairs again. She let out the cat, hoping the neighbors would take care of it. Then she took the file and put it in the bag, together with her purse and passport which she snatched from the small shelf underneath her coats.

When she unlocked the front door, she hesitated and quickly locked it again. Instead, she took the door to the cellar and walked through it in the dark, her hands touching the walls for guidance. She unlocked and opened the wooden hatch, which gave access to the small alley behind the house. When she had climbed out, she noticed her neighbor's Batavus bike. *She would explain later.* With the bag on the bike's front carrier, she hurried through the alley until she reached the Nieuwe Leliestraat, and pedaled away in quick strokes.

Just as Kate's silhouette disappeared behind the bridge over the Prinsengracht canal, the men who had appeared from the van parked opposite her flat opened the front door with a loud crack.

61

The applause was overwhelming, and Daniel slowly descended from the podium. Lent, in the first row, gave him a quick nod. Apparently his conclusion on potential Dutch claims on Manhattan had not disappointed Lent. A crowd surrounded Daniel, and he didn't know which face to look at. He was congratulated by several people, while waiters in tuxedos started serving drinks. It was all very surreal.

When he had answered many questions from interested guests, someone pulled at his sleeve. An old man with a long, white beard, leaning on a stick. He murmured something, but due to the buzz of the remaining crowd Daniel couldn't hear what, so he lowered his head.

"I think you found it," the old man said.

"Excuse me sir? Found what?"

"The answer to the Roosevelt question."

Daniel wasn't sure he understood. He could only think of the remark from the man in the Roosevelt library as to why FDR hadn't left more obvious traces to America's Dutch origins.

The old man pulled Daniel by his sleeve so that he had no choice but to follow him. They settled in the adjacent room, with a large fireplace and comfortable chairs. The large windows gave an extraordinary view of a lake stretching out in front of them.

"Tell me," the old man said, "what do you know about our man Roosevelt?"

Daniel told him what he knew.

The man nodded in approval. "FDR has been studied extensively, but there's one aspect to him that has always remained a mystery: his relationship with the Netherlands."

"It looks like he pretty much admired the country," Daniel said.

"He admired the Dutch past but not its present. He was repulsed by the way the Netherlands treated its colonies. It was against his ideals, which he later summarized in his famous Four Freedoms speech. More principally, Roosevelt was a staunch defender of democracy and had strong objections against kingdoms and other nonelected heads of state. And he had reserved feelings about the Dutch queen Wilhelmina personally, sometime calling her 'pretentious.' But here comes the strange thing: Roosevelt nevertheless developed very close ties with the House of Orange!"

Daniel thought for a second. "I suppose he had close ties with many heads of state," he said, trying to put the fact in perspective.

"But these ties went exceptionally far. He offered the Dutch royal family shelter at his own home when Germany invaded Holland in World War II. They declined, but Queen Wilhelmina nevertheless visited the Roosevelts in August 1942. And the ties with her daughter, Juliana, the future queen, were closer still. Princess Juliana often spent her summer holidays in upstate New York, where Roosevelt came to see her. Juliana's husband, Prince Bernhard, also paid regular visits to the Roosevelts during the war, and in 1943, Roosevelt even became the godfather of their daughter Princess Margriet. All in a period when full attention was needed for the war, and even when Roosevelt's health was declining. It was almost as if he *had* to keep close ties. As if he was actively pursuing something."

"Pursuing something?" Daniel asked, intrigued.

"As if he needed a favor from them. Some thought it was the abandonment of the Dutch colonies, especially Indonesia. But after the war, Roosevelt's pressure on Juliana continued, even *after* the independence of Indonesia. So it had to be something else."

"But wait a second—Roosevelt died before the end of the war!"

"Sharp remark, young man. In fact, it was his wife who continued the mission."

"Eleanor Roosevelt?" Daniel asked in surprise.

"Exactly. Did you know her maiden name was also Roosevelt? Their families were related; in fact her family line was more Dutch than his. It was Eleanor Roosevelt who maintained the close relationship with Juliana, who became the Dutch queen in 1948. Eleanor Roosevelt visited the Netherlands herself in 1948, 1950, 1951, and 1956. Interestingly, during a visit of Juliana to the United States in 1952, she made a symbolic visit to St. Mark's Church in-the-Bowery and the tomb of Stuyvesant, the emblematic figure from America's Dutch past. Eleanor Roosevelt knew Juliana had a strongly developed sense of justice: was she trying to convince the queen of something? What power did the queen hold that could be so important for America?"

Daniel's eyes suddenly widened. "The claim!"

"I think today we found the answer, young man. After so many years of doubts, questions, and hypotheses, that must be it."

Daniel stared over the lake, thinking out loud. "So the Roosevelts were aware of the claim! And they were trying to convince Juliana to give it up, to safeguard America from turmoil in case the claim would be made public."

"Not only that. If the claim would be out of the way, America would also have its hands free to continue one of the most important projects of human civilization: making the world free for democracy and progress. Without kingdoms. Without dictatorships. Roosevelt realized more than anyone else that the old Dutch Republic, the inventors of self-government, had handed over the baton of freedom and prosperity to America, which was supposed to hand it over again to the rest of the world. But the story had become considerably less convincing when the country that had started the movement, Holland, became a kingdom itself. And their secret claim on

American territory impeded the United States from acting against too openly against kings and other non-elected heads of state."

Daniel hesitated. "But the United States *did* fight for democracy and freedom in the world. Take the two world wars. And its resistance against communism during the Cold War."

"You're right, but look at the map of the world today. Since the Dutch Republic, we know that only the magic potion of democracy, civil liberties, and capitalism can guarantee prosperity. But still half of the countries today are some sort of dictatorship! How can you make a credible coalition and send troops to free people from dictators and promote democracy when coalition partners are kingdoms themselves?"

Daniel agreed it made sense. Despite his obvious age, the old man hadn't lost his sharpness.

"Gentlemen!" Lent said, who had apparently been listening to the conversation for some time. "The important conclusion is that we finally have an idea what our great brother Roosevelt was after."

Daniel veered up. "Roosevelt tried, but he didn't succeed! And Eleanor Roosevelt neither!"

The two other men looked at each other in surprise.

"It's a long story, but something's going on in the Netherlands at the moment, and the House of Orange is fully asserting the claim. Gentlemen, we have to rescue Roosevelt!"

62

Kate was still out of breath from the bike ride from her house. She had hurried, despite the fact that she had no plan and nowhere to go.

She stared at the church's wooden pulpit in front of her. Instinctively, she had chosen the small church at Amsterdam's Begijnhof as refuge. It made her feel closer to Dad, whom she really needed now. He had taken her here countless times and told her how the Pilgrim Fathers had once settled there after they had fled England in search for a place to live in peace. The Pilgrims had later moved on to Leiden, before eventually setting sail to America. Kate wondered whether Daniel Van Wart was aware of the Pilgrim's Dutch connection.

She needed to think now. What would the Royal House's next move be? She couldn't count on protection from the Dutch state, with its structural weakness toward to everything royal. And so close to the coronation, the public authorities would surely be fully on the royal side.

She sighed in desperation. How had Holland, with its republican tradition, been able to let it come so far? She knew the country had become a kingdom only relatively recently. It was a peculiar development, as most countries had followed the reverse path, from kingdom to republic. In fact, the republic as a modern state organization was more or less invented in Holland. There had been rudimentary republics earlier of course, such as the Roman Republic some one and a half millennia earlier, and the Republic of Venice. They all shared the same characteristic: a period of great expansion and prosperity.

It was always the same story, she knew. *Without* democracy, supported by civil rights and capitalism, a society was doomed to fail. And even if some kingdoms had adopted a democratic political structure, the problem was a principal one: how could kingdoms ever promote democratic principles in regions of the world still lacking them? It was an ideological issue, about removing obstacles for the progress of human civilization.

Kate knew that the end of the Dutch Republic had ironically started with Holland's recognition of America's independence from England, which had caused the Fourth Anglo-Dutch War. Holland could hardly bear the financial consequences of the war, and together with the social unrest caused by popular movements elsewhere in Europe, it caused serious conflicts in the Dutch Republic. Its central powers, once the shining example for the world, were accused of mismanagement, and the office of stadtholder was exercised in an autocratic style. The Orange-Nassau family, habitually invited to supply the stadtholder, even managed to have the office declared hereditary. It symbolized the definitive decline of Holland's power, the inevitable fate of countries not selecting leaders on the basis of quality or merit.

The subsequent Dutch Patriot movement wanted to reverse the situation and restore the glory and power of the Golden Age under a more democratic government, in line with the Dutch republican tradition. The movement was also heavily inspired by the ongoing American Revolution, reversing history: it was now Holland that took inspiration from America in the defense of its freedom and ideals.

The Dutch Patriot revolt was violently suppressed, however. It was not the first time the Orange-Nassau family showed despotic and ruthless tendencies: in 1617, Maurice of Orange ordered the arrest of the highly respected statesman Van Oldenbarnevelt, who was beheaded publicly. In 1646, stadtholder William II of Orange unsuccessfully tried a coup to obtain absolute power. In 1672, his son William III of Orange rewarded the murderers of his political rivals, the De Witt brothers, who had reigned over the Dutch Republic at the zenith of its power and glory, during a stadtholderless period referred to in Dutch history as the "true freedom." Other occasions on which the Orange family defended their power, often in blatant conflict with the values the Netherlands stood for, would present themselves throughout history.

Until present, Kate thought.

The Dutch hope of returning to a republic received a definitive blow after the fall of Napoleon in 1813. William Frederik of Orange-Nassau, the son of the last stadtholder William V, was granted the title Sovereign of the Netherlands. Two years later, he autoproclaimed himself King William I of the Netherlands, attributed with almost absolute power. Starting with King William I, the Netherlands would remain a kingdom until today.

The Dutch monarchy meant above all the definitive end of the globally admired Dutch Republic, which had lasted for more than two centuries. During this period, the country had propelled itself from a collection of unrelated damp territories on the outskirts of Europe, destined to remain poor forever due to the lack of natural resources, to the most powerful, prosperous, and advanced country in the world. Becoming a kingdom shattered the dreams of those who believed in liberty, equality, and democracy—and of social, economic, and moral progress, at that. The only spiritual consolation would be that another country, by adopting and transforming the principles and ideas of the Dutch Republic, was in the middle of an equally stellar ascent: the United States of America.

The Dutch monarchy almost came to an end naturally several times. The first time was at the end of the reign of King William III, when the Orange family lacked sufficient male offspring as a result of early deaths and childlessness. The only person left to inherit the crown was his four-year-old daughter Wilhelmina; the Netherlands' head of state thus became a four-year-old girl.

The second time the reign of the House of Orange-Nassau almost ended—and probably the monarchy, at that—also concerned Wilhelmina. As she did not have any brothers and sisters, it was imperative for her to have children, otherwise the crown would pass to her relatives of the German house of Saxe-Weimar-Eisenach, with complete annexation by the German Empire as a possible result. However, Wilhelmina had four consecutive miscarriages, probably caused by her husband Hendrik's syphilis, a result of his extensive adultery. Wilhelmina also almost fell victim to typhus in 1902 and narrowly escaped death in a car accident in 1908. It was only in 1909 that Wilhelmina secured succession and gave birth to a child: Princess Juliana. It was later questioned whether Juliana was the actual child of the royal couple. Due to Hendrik's syphilis, he may have been unable to produce any vital offspring at all. Support for this thesis was that Wilhelmina suffered two further miscarriages in the following years. Whether the House of Orange thus turned to "outsiders" to save their position could easily be established through DNA analysis, something refused by the Dutch royal family until today.

Kate stared at the bag lying next to her on the wooden church bench. She knew it contained documents that could finally put an end to the royal injustice. Remove an obstacle for progress. Continue the spiritual heritage of the Pilgrims.

63

"Kate, it's Daniel here."

"Oh, thank God, you called, Daniel!"

"Why, is there a problem? You sound desperate."

"You could call it that. I'm on the run."

"On the run? What do you mean?"

"They're hunting me, Daniel. You know who. I just got a call from my neighbors that they broke into my apartment. They were looking for a stolen file, and I'm sure they hoped to catch me too! I think I'm lucky I got away just in time."

"A stolen file? What are you talking about?"

"Evelyn stole a file from your firm. From Van Olden. She managed to send it to me before she got killed. You won't believe it, Daniel: it contains documents that prove the plan of the House of Orange with the claim on America! Correspondence with the American President and all. I'm sure the documents were the reason they killed Evelyn; they must have found out she stole the file."

"And now they're chasing you? But how do they know you have the file?"

"I don't know. Maybe they assumed Evelyn sent it to me."

"My God. Where are you now?"

"Running around Amsterdam. I don't know where to go; I'm sure they're still following me. I'm scared, Daniel."

"Hang on, Kate; I'm coming your way. We have to block their plans before it's too late. I also have new information. Incredible information."

"What about?"

"You remember that man I told you about, Mr. Lent? He took me to a meeting of his Dutch historical society. Guess what? There's still a whole Dutch community out there! Going back to the early settlement of New Netherland. They speak the language and all!"

Kate reflected on Daniel's statements. It would mean an uninterrupted presence since the beginning of the country!

"And there's something else," Daniel continued excitedly. "It seems that Roosevelt was already on a mission to eradicate the claim!"

"Roosevelt? You mean the American President?"

"Yep. He was of Dutch descent and close to the House of Orange."

Kate was silent for a moment as she tried to fathom the implications. "Daniel, as discussed we have to combine it all in the memo," she finally said. "We'll join the royal correspondence as proof and create an irrefutable document, then make it public. It's the only way to neutralize the claim and stop them! There's only one problem."

"What?"

"We have less than three days left before the coronation. That's seventy-two hours!"

"I know. I borrowed a car from Lent and I'm on my way to the airport right now. I have to hang up, otherwise I'll miss my flight. It's in three hours from now and I'm still in the Hudson Valley."

"Where's the flight to?"

"To Amsterdam, of course."

"No! Don't go there!"

"What? Why not?"

"I can't stay in Amsterdam. The file can't stay here. They'll do anything to get it back. It has to be brought to a safe place, somewhere the House of Orange cannot exercise their power."

"My flight has a stopover in London."

Kate considered the suggestion. It would be easy for her to get there, with several flights from Amsterdam every hour. She realized the destination was far from safe either, of course; the House of Orange could surely obtain immediate cooperation from the British crown—and unlimited cooperation at that, not only because the families were related but because the British crown could also expect head winds should the issue explode.

"Okay, we'll meet at Heathrow," Kate said. "But stay in transit! Whatever you do, don't go through immigration!"

"Okay, understood. But how will I find you? I don't even know what you look like!"

"Don't worry. I'll find you."

64

Seated in the back of his service car, Oscar Smeenk served himself his habitual jenever. While savoring the cold liquid, he looked through the bulletproof window and saw how workers were putting steel barriers in place on both sides of the road. In less than three days from now, the barriers would serve to fence off the crowds from the royal procession.

He had often marveled at the simplicity of the idea. The potential Dutch American claim had been there to spot for centuries, right under the world's nose. Someday it had to be used! Ideally the legal claim would be supported by a continuous Dutch presence in the United States, such as through the survival of Dutch culture and language in certain areas. But of course everybody knew that all Dutchness had vanished after the English take-over of New York; so the chain of reminder letters from the Dutch monarchs to the American Presidents would have to do the job.

The royal financiers were the ones who had come up with the idea to leverage the claim for the current operation. Smeenk had tried to find out which bright satanic spirit among them, but as usual, they had kept their lips sealed. Smeenk sighed. *The financiers. Always calling the shots.* But this time, the stakes were exceptionally high, even for them. He knew they were just as nervous as he was.

The financiers derived their power from managing one of the largest private fortunes in the world. Its exact size was one of the best-kept secrets in the world of finance; even he was kept in the dark about it. The Oranges had of course earned some money during their days as stadtholders during the Dutch Republic, but the start of the real fortune coincided with the moment the Oranges became royals. As in any kingdom, they could grab money as they pleased. And the Oranges had been masters at it, right from the start. King William I received 1.5 million guilders annually, an immense fortune at that time. Moreover, under his authoritarian regime he exercised shrewd capitalistic entrepreneurship for his own account. The "merchant king", as he was known, mixed personal and general interests in a way people would qualify today as corrupt. While the population of the Netherlands suffered and lost its great wealth, the king amassed a fortune, which formed the basis of the current royal family's huge capital. A more recent notorious gatherer was Prince Bernard, the husband of Queen Juliana, who, after World War II, sold war planes confiscated by the Dutch state while keeping the proceeds himself. And later on in his life he took a million-dollar bribe to push the Dutch army to buy Lockheed fighter planes.

Although the strong republican culture in the Netherlands had always caused criticism on the royal behavior—the three kings in particular were never popular—it was the civil revolts of the 1960s during the reign of Queen Juliana that finally forced more control on the royal finances. But the financiers had played the game masterfully and presented the royal finances as being in a deplorable state, not sufficient to cover its costs. It led to the Financial Statute Royal Household Act of 1972, which, in essence, allowed the queen to charge the costs of the royal household, such as the palace staff, fully to the state. And by also formally transferring the royal palaces to the Dutch state, while keeping a perpetual right of use, the Oranges freed themselves from the considerable maintenance costs. A royal salary was also maintained, currently at a level of almost ten times that of the President of the United States. In addition, a new article in the Dutch constitution was introduced by which the sovereign was exempted from taxes. In all, the Oranges managed to consolidate their wealth, making them richer than the British royal family. And the Orange capital would, of course, increase vastly after the imminent passage of the throne, the main purpose of the whole operation. Smeenk recalled the financiers' joke during one of the early preparatory meetings: "In the United States money is king; in the Netherlands king is money!"

At various moments during the preparations Smeenk had felt something like pity for the crown prince, the new king in a few days from now. For him, the whole operation was probably a "flight forward," as he realized that he wasn't up to his future role and functions. Unlike his younger brothers, who were smart and had a natural authority, he lacked the necessary charisma to be the head of state. But such was the tragedy of royal heritage: he was designated by birth. He had been given some minor responsibilities to start with, notably in the area of "water management," which had quickly been mocked at as "aqua-planning." Things wouldn't be so bad if the country's royal functions had been purely ceremonial, but the Dutch constitution attributed a central role to them in the legislative process. It had become clear that the boy lacked the courage to face the consequences of his two only alternatives to change his fate: either abdicating, or putting in motion the painful process to change the role of the king. For Smeenk, so much was sure: it must be a comforting thought for the boy—even a relief—to be taken by the hand by the men involved in the operation. Together with the claim, it was a pillar of the operation's success.

Smeenk's cell phone rang. *The call he had been waiting for.*

"For some reason, she wasn't there," the caller informed him.

"What?! But you said your men were watching her just before the raid!"

"That's right, sir. She was at the apartment; her teacup was still warm. She must have left right before the strike. Probably through the cellar, which has access to an alley behind the block."

"And the file?"

"Nothing either. We searched the entire apartment. She must have taken it with her. We did find the envelope that probably contained it, the one delivered by the mailman just before."

"Dammit! A tip-off?" Smeenk asked.

"I cannot think how. Maybe there was a message in the envelope."

Smeenk was silent for a while and then burst out in anger. "You bunch of amateurs! This was our best chance! Now she's on the run and hiding from us!"

"There was another thing missing, sir."

"What?"

"Her passport."

Smeenk instantly knew what that meant. "Inform the border authorities at once! As long as she's in the country, we can still take action; once she's out, things may be lost definitively. Get the justice minister, and ask for Bates' immediate arrest!"

"Are you sure he'll cooperate? What do we tell him? After all, for the moment she hasn't committed any crime. He would probably need charges."

"Theft of state property. Do it now!"

65

Daniel had left the Dutch community behind at the Mohonk mountain resort and was racing toward the airport. The last days had been extremely interesting, with Mohonk as surprising culmination, but only when Kate told him she was on the run he realized how much time he had lost. He was glad he had accepted the lighter and more agile alternative to the limo.

He crossed the Hudson River at Poughkeepsie and took the Taconic State Parkway in a southern direction. It was not the shortest route, but it avoided the congestion-prone George Washington Bridge. Any minute lost in traffic could cause him to miss the flight, meaning the loss of a crucial day before the passing of the throne.

The Taconic State Parkway continued as the *Bronx* River Parkway, past *Van Nest* and on to the Interstate 95 in the direction of *Schuyler*ville. Then it went over the toll bridge to *Flushing*. Daniel was still impressed by the number of Dutch names still in use.

To his annoyance, traffic had become dense now. When he entered the *Van Wyck* Expressway in the direction of JFK Airport, he looked at his watch.

One hour before takeoff!

He pressed the accelerator; there was not a minute to lose now.

—

NYPD agent Lawson hesitated for a moment. The meal in the Styrofoam container was still warm and only half-eaten. But the speed of the car that just passed him didn't leave him much choice so he placed the container onto the seat next to him and started the pursuit.

It took some time before he spotted the car again, still driving frantically. He managed to overtake it, and its driver finally pulled over right after the Nassau Expressway flyover.

"You're in trouble, young man," he said after the driver had lowered the window. "I can cite you for speeding and cutting in front of other drivers. And both multiple times. ID and papers, please!"

"I'm sorry, Officer," Daniel said while handing them over. "I'm in some sort of emergency. I have a flight to Europe leaving in forty minutes. It's crucial I don't miss it."

"And who are you that it's so important? The President of the United States? That's not what it says here," the officer said while returning the ID card. "It says your name is Van Wart."

"Correct, Officer. But in a way, it does concern the President.

The officer looked up from the driver's license. "Taken any drugs or alcohol?"

"No, Officer, I'm very serious. The President is being blackmailed, and I have some papers to take to Holland to put an end to it! I'm an attorney; here's my badge of the New York Bar."

"Slowly!" the officer shouted instinctively when Daniel fumbled in his affairs before giving him a plastic card. "And who would that bad guy be who's blackmailing the President?"

"It's a long story, but it involves some people in the Netherlands."

"The Netherlands? One minute ago, it was still Holland. I think you're talking bullshit. A serious offense, Mr. Attorney." He handed back the card.

"They're one and the same country, Officer. The founders of New York, remember? New Amsterdam, Peter Stuyvesant."

"Holland the founders of New York? I've had enough of this. There ain't no windmills in New York. Please step out of the car; hands where I can see them!"

Daniel obeyed but suddenly noticed something. "Please, Officer, I can prove it!"

"You can prove it to the district attorney. Now put your hands on the roof, please!"

"I'll show you a windmill, and you let me go, okay? And I promise I'll drive slowly."

The officer shook his head with a smile. "If you show me a windmill, you must indeed be the President." He took his ticket book from his pocket and walked back to his car to write one.

"Look at your cap!" the officer heard the attorney shout. Intrigued, he took off his cap and looked at the steel NYPD logo on the front.

"*What the—*" he mumbled, amazed by what he saw.

When he looked up again, he watched the attorney's car pull onto the highway and disappear in the direction of the airport. Then he looked at his cap's logo once more: a colonial figure that was indeed holding a windmill. He scratched his head in confusion while crumpling the ticket.

66

Kate never understood why a country that excelled in logistics couldn't get the trains to run properly. Her train arrived ten minutes late at its destination, Amsterdam Schiphol Airport. For once, the delay didn't matter though, as she hadn't booked a flight yet.

"One return ticket to London Heathrow, please. Open return date, immediate departure," she said to the woman at the KLM ticketing desk.

"Let me see. Our first flight is due in fifty minutes, boarding in twenty. You should be able to make it with only hand luggage. Your passport, please."

Kate nodded and gave her passport to the woman. As always when she traveled to England she used her British passport. It was a question of habit and also facilitated UK immigration formalities, as the country wasn't party to the Schengen agreement.

She was nervous when she arrived at customs and noticed that her hand trembled when she handed over her passport. She knew she was taking a risk: it was possible that her adversaries had put her on some sort of surveillance list. And with the file in her bag, there would be no way out; it would mean the end of the whole story.

But nothing happened, and after she passed through security, she took a seat in the waiting area at the departure gate, relieved. Through the large windows she looked at the airplane that would take her aboard at any moment. On the side of its nose she read the slogan carried by all planes of the KLM fleet: THE FLYING DUTCHMAN.

How appropriate, she thought. The Flying Dutchman, the story of a ghost ship that never reaches shore, as a punishment for its sailors. It was a centuries-old Dutch mariners' tale, but also the symbol of the lost cause for the Dutch ideals—the ideals that had metaphorically set sail to conquer the rest of the world but that were for some reason precluded from harboring. It was a story of silent political protest, of which the first written traces date back to exactly the time the Dutch Republic ceased to exist.

Perhaps it was deserved, Kate mused. Perhaps the sailors, representing the Dutch population, earned their punishment: they had let their precious republic turn into a kingdom and had spoiled its founding ideals.

Perhaps the time had come to set things straight.

The loud boarding announcement woke her up from her thoughts, and she joined the other passengers in the queue before the gate. She nervously shuffled forward while observing how the KLM ground staff checked the boarding passes and passports of the passengers before her.

As she waited, two uniformed officers walked to the boarding desk and joined the KLM staff. They discussed something, and some paperwork changed hands. One of the officers studied a document. Suddenly Kate feared the worst.

"Keep your boarding passes and passports ready for inspection, please!" a KLM hostess announced through the microphone.

When it was Kate's turn, she handed her boarding pass to the hostess, who inserted it into the machine. When it came out again, she ripped off the small passenger part and gave it a quick look.

"Ah! Are you Miss Bates?"

Kate felt as if she had received a punch to her stomach. *This was it, they got her!*

"Can I see your passport, please?"

A million thoughts crossed her mind. Should she simply walk away? She could still turn around, run to the exit, and leave the airport. She looked at the woman, who stared back at her firmly. Then she obediently gave her passport.

The woman took the passport and looked back and forth twice between Kate and the document. "Just a moment please, Miss Bates." She walked with the passport to the officers.

Kate watched one of them study the passport carefully, flipping through the pages. Then he started to discuss something with his colleague.

Kate was absent minded, lost in a mixture of fear and resignation over the hopelessness of her situation and the terrible things that were now awaiting her. She almost didn't notice the hostess appearing in front of her again, handing back her passport.

"Have a good flight, Miss Bates!"

Part VII

67

Back at his The Hague office again, Oscar Smeenk scribbled his initials on the last page of the binder in front of him and closed it. He felt his energy was wearing thin after another night of little sleep and many worries. During the morning meeting with the financiers and the rest of the team, he had had difficulty hiding his anxiety. It had been one of the last meetings before the event, and he had been questioned thoroughly on the outstanding risks.

The most pressing issue was, of course, Van Olden's screw-up and the theft of the documents. The group had praised Smeenk for his reactivity after the incident and had confirmed that Van Olden would from now on walk on his lead. But his failure so far to retrieve the documents had brought him scorn. Smeenk had pleaded for all the assistance they had in their power, referring to their vast network of contacts within the country and abroad. It had been confirmed to him with limitations.

Most of the issues contained in the stolen file were now covered. Van Olden had reconstructed the contents of the file, and, together with his team, prepared an action plan on how to react in case they were made public. They had involved the Rijksvoorlichtingsdienst, the state's official communication service that also handled press issues regarding the royal family, which had prepared statements that could be issued immediately in case of need.

There remained, however, the issue that dwarfed all others: the letters to the American Presidents about the territorial claim.

They had the potential to expose the whole operation, and the current secrecy of the claim was the cork on which it floated. Nothing should be spared to retrieve or destroy the letters—with or without the person carrying them. But for that, the person would first have to be caught.

Smeenk took the note on which he had scribbled the direct line of Lieutenant General Bastiaans, commander of the Koninklijke Marechaussee, the Dutch military police in charge of border protection. Smeenk dialed the number and waited.

"Bastiaans speaking."

"Smeenk, of the royal cabinet."

"Ah, yes, good afternoon sir. I think my assistant left you a message to confirm all is fine; the person has been added to our surveillance database. We received the immediate go-ahead from the Ministry of Justice."

"Thank you. I'm glad about their expedience in this matter."

"Nothing to thank us about, sir. Now, I understand it concerns a theft, but in view of the urgency I have to admit I didn't have the time yet to look into the matter. Are you in the position to tell me what it's about?"

"The lady stole a file belonging to Her Majesty."

"To Her Majesty?" the commander asked in surprise. "Sounds serious indeed. But there's something I don't really understand: I heard the lady's a lawyer. Isn't that strange? I mean, a lawyer stealing files?"

"She's working on a case against Her Majesty," Smeenk responded dryly.

"Oh, I see. Well, let's hope we catch her quickly then. As I said, my men are fully instructed. Borders, airports, seaports. What was her name again?"

"Bates. Kate Bates."

"Ah yes, that was it. That reminds me: I just got a call from my general in charge of border patrol, Schiphol Airport District. They thought they had a catch, but it turned out to be false alarm."

"False alarm? What was it about?" Smeenk asked impatiently.

"Another lady with the name Bates. Booked on a flight to London. But she didn't match the profile, as she wasn't Dutch. And her first name wasn't Kate but Catherine. Mr. Smeenk? Are you still there?"

68

While waiting at the busy Heathrow terminal, Kate studied the picture for the hundredth time. It was small, but detailed enough to perceive the characteristics of the face. The website of Stiglitz & Arrowsmith had presented the firm as a clone factory: all lawyers had an identical pose, with soft smiles, dark suits, and a graded background. Daniel Van Wart had dark hair—almost black, she thought—and a well-formed, oval face, with small, piercing, clear eyes. She couldn't suppress a certain excitement when the first passengers off the British Airways flight from JFK to London Heathrow appeared. She had wondered what their meeting would be like. Until that point, they had only spoken over the phone, and the dramatic turn the story had taken surely added weight to their encounter.

It wasn't difficult to spot him among the passengers. Although taller than expected and wearing khakis instead of a suit, the blue eyes caught her attention immediately.

"Daniel?" she shouted in the direction of the crowd.

He looked up, searching for the caller, and then he noticed the waving hand.

"Are you Kate?"

"Yeah! Good to see you Daniel. I hope you had a good flight."

"It was all right. A bit short notice, but we didn't have the choice. Have you been waiting here for long?"

"A couple of hours. I think I got away in the nick of time, it feels as if I narrowly escaped."

"I'm very sorry for you, Kate. And for Evelyn. It's all my fault; I got you both involved."

"Don't be sorry, Daniel. My involvement in royal issues wasn't exactly neutral. I think it was a coincidence our paths crossed this way."

In a slightly awkward silence they followed the stream of passengers, both a duffel bag across their shoulders.

"What time's your connecting flight to Amsterdam?" Kate asked when they passed a monitor terminal.

Daniel looked at his watch and calculated the local time. "In two hours from now."

"Then we'd better get to work. I already found a good spot."

They settled in a coffee area at a slightly isolated table next to a huge glass window. The view showed several airplanes being serviced at their gates, like ant queens being cared for by their colonies of workers.

They briefly discussed their respective adventures. Both were taken aback by the scale of their discoveries and the implications. The misrepresentation of American history, the territorial claim, the blackmailing by the House of Orange—in a way, it all contributed to the sabotage of one of the most ambitious projects in history: bringing democracy to the world.

They started assembling the different parts of the memo on Daniel's laptop. Then they reviewed some arguments and formulations together and drafted a conclusion. It went quickly and smoothly; it was clear to each of them that the other was a highly skilled professional.

"You could become an intern at my firm," Kate joked.

Next came the documents. Daniel noticed how Kate's hand trembled when she took the file from her bag. He quickly read the letters to the American Presidents and agreed they were the critical pieces of the puzzle.

Daniel then took the file from the Roosevelt library.

"What are these documents?" Kate asked with curiosity.

"Call it circumstantial evidence. They illustrate Roosevelt's determination in promoting democracy. And Eleanor Roosevelt's continuation where her husband left off. Did you know she was the first chairperson of the UN Commission behind the Universal Declaration of Human Rights?"

Kate nodded. "The declaration that was signed but never fully enforced."

"What do you mean?"

"The text of the declaration is crystal clear: *"All men are born equal."* A more public and direct denunciation of kings wouldn't be possible, don't you think?"

Daniel instantly understood Kate's remark: no privileges by birth. "So now you know why it wasn't enforced," Daniel said. "America couldn't insist on its full execution globally as it was handicapped by the threat of the Dutch claim dangling above it like the Sword of Damocles!"

Kate nodded. "Royal families around the world have been obstructing America's push for republicanism for centuries. But I didn't know the Dutch role went this far."

They looked at each other in silence, both realizing the importance of their mission again.

"Daniel," Kate finally said, "we're up against one of the richest and most powerful families in the world. They have everything to lose and will do anything to protect their situation. The memo and the supporting documents have to be brought to safety. To a neutral country. One that isn't a kingdom that can assist their fellow royals."

Daniel thought for a moment. "Switzerland?"

Kate nodded. One of Europe's staunchly neutral republics.

Daniel looked at his watch. "So I abandon my flight to Amsterdam, and we go to Switzerland?"

Kate pulled a difficult face. "I'm afraid it's not that easy."

"What do you mean?"

"We have to pick up the original documents first."

"*The originals*? You mean these are only copies?" In disbelief Daniel waved the slim plastic file containing the letters in front of her.

"I didn't dare to take the originals across the border. I wouldn't be surprised if there's a search warrant outstanding for me."

"So what do we do now? Go back to the Netherlands and pick them up?"

"I can't, Daniel. I'm sure they'll arrest me the moment I set foot at the airport."

"I hope you're not suggesting what I think you are," Daniel said, his eyes wide open.

"You have to do it, Daniel. We have no choice. We need the originals as proof."

"But they can arrest me too!"

"They could. But you're a foreigner, so they that would probably only do that when you pass customs. And you don't need to."

Daniel was perplexed. "What exactly do you have in mind, Kate?"

"I'll explain. Now let's go, or you'll miss your flight to Amsterdam."

Daniel saved the completed memo on a USB stick that he put in his pocket, and confided the laptop to Kate. During the walk to the transfer terminal Daniel listened in silence while Kate gave him instructions. And a tiny object.

69

The service car stopped in front of the ivy-covered building at The Hague's Raamweg and let out its sole passenger. Oscar Smeenk looked at the sky and judged that his umbrella wouldn't withstand the strong northwestern wind. He could smell the sea, at only a few minutes' drive west from there, and the seagulls flying land inward announced a storm coming in. He walked to the entrance at a quick pace. Three minutes later, he sat opposite the deputy director of Europol.

"So the first person, the woman, has been added to our register immediately after you called," the deputy director said with a satisfied air. "The situation with the second person, the gentleman, is a little bit more complicated. As there was no formal arrest warrant for him yet, we had to request one from the Ministry of Justice. That may still take some time, because the charges you described, high treason, are not that common."

"As I explained, there's no time to lose," Smeenk insisted. "They're making their moves as we speak! We have to immobilize them before the event!"

The deputy director looked up over his reading glasses and now understood what the surly man opposite him insinuated. *So it concerned an activist of some sort,* he thought. Or possibly even a terrorist, trying to stage an action during the passage of the throne. It explained the urgency and also why man had come to their offices in person.

"Let me call the agent who's handling the case," the deputy director said. "Maybe he's got some progress to report." He dialed a number and waited.

"Yes, it's me. Any news?"

While he listened to the person on the other side of the line, he stared at Smeenk intently. "Ah, I see," he said loudly, winking at him. "So that will be in a few hours then. Yes, it's urgent."

Smeenk had already gotten the message: delay. *Damn!* He stood up, threw a quick salute to the deputy director who hadn't finished the phone conversation yet, and left the office. Outside the building, he was surprised by a gust of wind and staggered briefly. He waved to the service car waiting on the opposite side of the road.

The headlights lit up instantly, and with a quick and agile turn the car crossed the road toward Smeenk.

"Dammit, Albert!" he shouted when a tire hit a puddle and splashed up water. He stepped back and observed his pants, which were covered in mud spots.

Seated in the car he looked at his watch. *Some valuable hours without border control!* In foreign countries, that was: in the Netherlands both targets were already on the search list and would be grabbed instantly when they tried to enter the territory.

But his biggest frustration was not with Europol but with Interpol. *The bureaucrats!* His team had contacted them before anyone else. Since the American lawyer had disappeared again, it was crucial to have an arrest warrant globally, not only in Europe. But the French snails at their Lyon headquarters had blankly refused any action regarding the American! Their explanation was that a so called "Interpol Red Notice," the closest thing to an international arrest warrant, could not be issued regarding activities of a political nature. And in absence of any violent acts, "high treason" was regarded as such!

He had considered changing the charges to theft of state property, just as for the Bates woman, but he had dismissed the idea as it would probably raise suspicion.

His cell phone rang.

"Sir, we just received another alert from the Marechaussee. Schiphol Airport District. It appears the American lawyer, Van Wart, may be coming this way."

"*What?*" Smeenk lurched up excitedly. "Where? What time?"

"Schiphol Airport. On a flight from London. In half an hour from now."

Smeenk frantically looked at his watch. There was a slim chance he could make it there in time by car. *What an extraordinary chance!* How wonderful it would be to nail him! He would certainly lead them to the documents, one way or the other. He looked out the window and saw that the traffic was already heavy, and with the rain things would only get worse. He decided to leave it to the pros.

"Make sure they don't miss him! And send someone over, just in case!" he ordered and hung up.

He leaned back on the headrest and stared at the car's ceiling. It was an unexpected turn in their favor. But what on earth was he coming to the Netherlands for? Bates had just left the county, so they couldn't meet. Maybe he wasn't aware she had left? In any case, he didn't have the stolen file in his possession, so he would have to be "worked" to reveal his secrets.

Unless…

Smeenk's eyes widened. *Of course!*

He calculated again and concluded it was possible: *they had met in London!* Bates's arrival and Van Wart's departure had overlapped; so she could have given him the file!

He quickly called back the caller's number.

"He's got the file! So don't scare him off. No signals, no violence. Just arrest him when he enters the country!"

70

Daniel was surprised by the very short duration of the flight: apparently it took only forty-five minutes from London to Amsterdam. The cabin staff hardly had the time to serve everyone a drink and distribute the ridiculously small pouch of minipretzels.

Together with the other passengers, he walked down the gate in the direction of the terminals, and he couldn't suppress a certain tension.

Would the authorities be waiting for him?

He hadn't been in the Netherlands for years, and all the research he had done into the Dutch American history had provoked a burning desire to visit the country. *His family's fatherland.* It was a strange feeling. At the same time, somehow he didn't feel overly welcome at the moment.

As instructed by Kate, instead of following the Exit signs he proceeded to Transfers at the main terminal. There he joined the large streams of other passengers and headed for gates B and C. She had warned him about the considerable walk; Amsterdam Schiphol was one of Europe's main air hubs. Coming from the United Kingdom he had to pass passport control. Kate had assured him that the control shouldn't pose a problem as long as it was to go from one gate to the other; things would be different if he exited the terminals and officially entered Dutch soil.

He passed the check indeed without incident and entered the huge waiting area of Lounge 1. There he walked straight to the impressive Grand Café Het Paleis and took the stool at the end of the bar. He was tempted by the inviting Heineken beer taps a few feet away from him but ordered a coffee instead; he had to fight his jet lag and, above all, stay fully concentrated.

While sipping from his coffee, he observed the passengers, the ground staff, the cabin crews, the cleaners, and all other people around until he was sure none of them were observing him. Then he moved.

In the middle of Lounge 1 he took the stairs one floor up to the food court. There he followed the Toilet signs, which led him to a bright corridor facing the planes waiting at the gates. He followed the Men's sign and checked the number of the room at the end: 2874-24.

So far, all according to plan.

He entered one of the toilet cabins and closed the door. Fumbling in his pocket, he found the object Kate had given him in London before his departure: a tiny spool with yarn. After he had found the end of the thread, he made a knot around his index finger and held the spool in the same hand. He unlocked the cabin door again and opened it an inch, allowing him to peep in the mirror opposite the door. There was no one to see.

He quickly walked to the glass facade, and when he stood a few inches away from it he looked to his right.

It was there! A small space, just wide enough to squeeze through, between the facade and the first toilet stall.

He entered the space sideways and moved on to its end, invisible now for other possible lavatory visitors. Through the glass he was still visible of course from outside, but he hoped the busy schedules of ground staff would protect him from suspicious looks.

Seated, he pushed against the lower corner of the huge glass pane with his right foot.

Nothing happened.

A wave of heat swarmed over him. *Had Kate been wrong?*

He tried again, with more force.

Nothing again.

In a slight panic he studied the suspension system and noticed the rubber around a large screw had been tampered with. He removed the rubber strip and pushed again.

This time it moved slightly.

He pushed with both feet, and the gap widened until the glass pane left a space about two inches wide. He let the spool drop through it, the end of the thread still attached to his finger. The spool unwound as it tumbled.

Then he waited.

71

It must have been the sixth time that Ali drove the vehicle along the trajectory. He started to worry, as his team would certainly not appreciate his prolonged absence during a busy day with a tight schedule. But he had no choice: he needed to complete his mission.

The empty luggage trolley behind his vehicle rattled and rumbled violently. He was tired but still had some hours to go. Hours more of heavy suitcases, loud engines, and kerosene fumes. It was tough work, but he was grateful he had it.

His brothers back home had reasons to envy him. Tacim had lost his leg in the battle when he stepped on a mine. Zerdûs had spent three years in a Turkish prison. And the little Pawan had never been to school and had been absorbed by the fight for the Kurdish people's freedom and independence since he was seven years old. He hadn't seen them in years.

He had been lucky, though. Very lucky. Almost every day he recalled how he had reached Rotterdam, more dead than alive, after many days without light or food. It had been freezing cold in the container he shared with some other men, hidden in a secret compartment. When they had been discovered upon arrival by the Dutch port authorities and handed over to the immigration services, the decision had been quick and disastrous: they were expelled back to Istanbul, Turkey, their point of embarkation. As he was a known member of the PKK, the Kurdish organization of independence fighters, a harsh destiny of torture in Turkish prisons would surely await him.

But then she had appeared and had saved his life. At first, he hadn't understood a word of the blond lady. But with an interpreter, Miss Bates had guided him through the labyrinth of interrogations and procedures. And ultimately, she had managed to have him recognized as political refugee. He later heard her action had been a legal masterpiece, since the Dutch state didn't recognize the violent and long-lasting Kurdish conflict as serious enough. Some years later, even their leader Abdullah Öcalan was refused asylum: while trying to reach the International Court of Justice in The Hague! As a result of the refusal, on direct orders from Prime Minister Wim Kok and the Dutch queen, the Kurdish case was never tried, and Öcalan, after a desperate flight path, was finally captured by the Turks and put in prison. Ali still didn't understand how the Dutch could accept a queen like that.

When Miss Bates had contacted him earlier this morning with the peculiar request, he had been very pleased. It was the only thing he could reward her with. He owed it to her.

He drove the trajectory in vain twice more before heading back again to his team.

Then he saw it. A small glistening object hanging on a thread, dangling in the wind.

It was the sign!

He immediately braked and maneuvered the vehicle right underneath the object. He removed his gloves and carefully inspected the object. It was a tiny wheel or something. From his jacket he took the slim steel tube containing the papers, wound the thread around it several times, and attached it with a knot. When he was done, he gently pulled the thread twice and got back behind the wheel of the vehicle.

He accelerated and looked up at the glass facade above him; someone put up his thumb to him.

When ten minutes later a Boeing 777 was connected to its gate, none of its passengers noticed that among the ground staff unloading their luggage was one person with a very broad smile.

72

The general of the Marechaussee glanced at his watch again and exchanged looks with the agent standing next to him. Both had the same thought: *This is taking too long.*

The flight from Heathrow had landed almost an hour ago now, but so far their target had not shown up. Of course, it always took some time for passengers to leave the aircraft, walk through the gate to the main lounges, maybe visit the lavatories, and proceed to customs. But this was taking too long.

The general regretted following the request from the royal cabinet to strictly limit action to the immigration zone; normally he would have posted one of his men right at the gate.

"Maybe we should extend the alert to the entire airport," the general suggested to the cabinet man. "Then we'll have him quickly."

"No, let's wait just a little bit more. He has to pass through here," the cabinet man said, convinced of his logic. His superior, Smeenk, had been very insistent: 'don't scare him off.'

"Maybe he received a tip-off and changed his plan, taking a flight back," the general suggested.

"Not likely. He's carrying something that has to enter the country urgently, at any cost. And the other target, Bates, is still out of the country, so apparently it's up to him to do the job. He's got no choice."

The general stroked his neck while thinking over the situation. Some twenty yards away, just behind the fence, he noticed the questioning faces of his men, waiting impatiently.

"Besides," the cabinet man continued, "even if he wanted to take another flight, he would have to pass through here anyway."

The general looked up, surprised by the ignorance of the man. "Not necessarily! If he doesn't have any luggage to reclaim, he can proceed directly to the transfer hall."

The cabinet man shot a concerned look at the general.

"I propose that we check the option," the general said. "I can send one of my men."

The cabinet man looked at his watch again and then nodded at the general.

With two fingers, the general beckoned one of his agents and gave him instructions. The agent scurried away and disappeared behind the barrier.

Seven minutes later, the agent reappeared, running toward them while holding some papers in the air.

"General, general!" he shouted excitedly. "He's on a flight to Geneva!"

The two other men looked at each other, perplexed.

"A flight to Geneva?" the general asked.

"Yes, sir, right now. Boarding was finished, so they must be at takeoff now."

"See if you can still stop them! At once!" the general commanded, snatching the printout from the agent's hands. He knew it would probably be too late.

"How's that possible?" Smeenk's man asked, visibly angered.

"As I just explained, he must have proceeded to the transfer hall directly. Maybe he already had a ticket. Let's see. This is the printout of immigration's file."

The general studied the document, his gloved hand sliding over the pages.

"There you are. Van Wart, Daniel. Yes indeed, from Amsterdam Schiphol to Geneva Airport. On a ticket reserved in advance online. But hey, this may surprise you!"

"What?" Smeenk's man asked impatiently.

"The credit card used for the purchase was in the name of Miss Bates!"

73

Still at the Heathrow terminal, Kate took a last moment of rest before the next episode of her plan would commence.

The crucial episode.

In silence, she stared in front of her at the coming and going of airplanes. On the runway, a 747 of Aerolineas Argentinas landed; she recognized the airline's distinctive blue color from a couple of years ago.

Her first trip to Argentina in mid-2001 had made an unforgettable impression on her. She recalled how in Buenos Aires she had visited the Mothers of the Plaza de Mayo, protesting the unsolved disappearance of their children, a stunning thirty thousand in total, during the Videla dictatorship in the 1970s and 80s. Despite her sympathy for the mothers, she had been shocked by their violent reaction when she mentioned she came from the Netherlands. In agony, she found out that a week earlier, the Netherlands had happily announced the wedding of its future king with the daughter of Videla's right hand, Jorge Zorreguieta. For the mothers, it was inexplicable and intolerable that a country advocating justice internationally could disregard their cause so lightheartedly.

Once back in the Netherlands, she had followed the brief political discussion that followed. The girl couldn't be blamed of course for her father's acts. But as all acts of a royal family are political ones, the crown prince should have taken the only right decision:

simply renounce the throne and let one of his brothers take the job. Instead, he denied the gravity of the situation by contending that the disappearance of the thirty thousand people was "just an opinion"! It convinced Kate, as well as many others, that the prince was definitively unfit for his future job.

Kate closed her eyes. *Would the Dutch still be open for becoming a republic again?* Or had it been too far in the past now, and had the spirit to fight for its ideals faded over time?

Not necessarily, she mused. After all, the Dutch were still a freedom- and justice-loving people. It seemed to be in their genes, transmitted through the Frisians. And it had been only a few generations ago that the Dutch still played a major role in improving the world. The concrete proof was still there: even today, the world's main peace institutions were located in the Netherlands, such as the International Criminal Court, the International Criminal Tribunal for the former Yugoslavia, the Organisation for the Prohibition of Chemical Weapons, and above all, the International Court of Justice. Roosevelt had seen right that the cause wasn't lost yet.

It reminded Kate of her internship at the International Court of Justice at the beginning of her career, in the wonderful Peace Palace in The Hague. She recalled that the construction of the castle-like building had been financed entirely by Andrew Carnegie, the American industrialist and philanthropist. Only now she realized the symbolism of it: the two countries in the world that had contributed most to freedom and democracy, united in a logical next step—freeing the world from the disasters of war.

But there was one dissonant element in this image, and Kate knew that Carnegie was certainly aware of it: he had written about the topic in his book *The Triumphant Democracy*. It was the fact that the Netherlands was represented by a *queen*. And royalty was an inferior and outdated institution, largely surpassed by republicanism; royalty was in blatant conflict with democratic principles and the values of equality and merit. Carnegie knew that monarchy formed a serious brake on the development of the world, and during the opening ceremony of the Peace Palace he must have realized the job wasn't finished yet.

Kate sighed. More pieces of the puzzle were coming together. *Apparently Roosevelt had continued where others had left off.* Had Carnegie known about the current developments, he would certainly have turned in his grave, wherever that was.

Kate veered up: in fact she *did know* where Carnegie's grave was! Somewhere in Daniel's memo she had read that he and several other American icons had symbolically chosen the Sleepy Hollow Cemetery, next to the Old Dutch Church. *Was it another hidden clue?*

74

Smeenk was raging when he heard that Van Wart had left the country again. It was the second time the authorities had failed! Worst of all, it meant the file was also out of the country again and therefore difficult to recover. With the event imminent now, the situation had become an outright emergency.

He took the small bottle from his briefcase. He took several large gulps from the strong liquid and let the alcohol do its work. He needed to calm his nerves and think clearly now.

From now on he would handle things himself.

He kicked one of the carton boxes scattered everywhere. The boxes indicated that the endgame had begun: during the event the team's headquarters would be relocated close to the action. He closed the door of his office and picked up the telephone.

His first call was to the justice minister. After having reprimanded him about the double failure of the Marechaussee at Schiphol Airport, he urged him to contact his Swiss counterpart to make sure Van Wart would be captured upon his arrival at Geneva Airport. The minister raised possible obstacles, pointing out that the Europol search warrant may not be applicable to Switzerland, a non-EU country. And the Interpol Red Notice warrant concerned only Bates, not the American. But the minister's objections evaporated when Smeenk mentioned that he considered reporting the ministry's failures, which had put the royal family in danger.

Smeenk's second call was to the Dutch embassy in Bern, the Swiss capital. He was lucky he got the ambassador on the line personally, and briefly explained the situation. Although the man had strong reservations about sending agents without first consulting with the Swiss authorities, he promised he would instruct the Dutch consul general in Geneva to find a solution.

Smeenk hesitated briefly before he placed his next call. What he was about to do was against all rules and security measures: contacting informants and agents directly. It was against the rules for or obvious reasons: they were often doubtful figures with shady connections, so providing them with information on staff, whatever their rank, could provoke dangerous situations. But Smeenk knew he had no choice anymore, so shortly before the passage of the throne. If he didn't get things under control, it would mean the end for himself.

The call was to a firm, not a person. He knew the firm had been used in the past and could supply experienced hitmen anywhere, anytime. The fact that they operated from Geneva could prove an advantage in view of Van Wart's destination. It was all very short notice.

His fourth and last call was to the usual person. He had recently made some mistakes, notably in London, but over the years, he had always impressed with his professionalism and astuteness. He would have to strike decisively now. The only challenge would be to get him to Geneva immediately. Maybe the royal jets would be available; in the coming days they wouldn't be needed anyway.

75

"Your seat belt, sir. We're landing."

The stewardess gently tapped on Daniel's shoulder, and when he opened his eyes, he realized he had dozed off. Drowsy, he moved the seat forward according to her instructions and closed his eyes again. He was exhausted, but something told him that sleeping would be for later.

At least he was free from trouble now, he thought. Kate's plan had worked. At Amsterdam airport he had obtained the original documents through the trick with the tube, and he had been able to proceed to his connecting flight without trouble. All that remained now was to put them in safety in Geneva for proof, while Kate would break the story in the Netherlands before the royal ceremony.

He looked sideways through the window and saw that the airplane was descending rapidly. Several lakes passed underneath the wing, and the snowcapped Alps sloped up in the distance. The plane suddenly made a sharp turn to the left and continued its descent. A few minutes later the plane hit the tarmac on Swiss soil.

With the other passengers, Daniel walked through the gate, following the Exit signs—or *Sortie,* as it was called in this French-speaking part of the country. During the walk he switched on his cell phone. Or better, Kate's cell phone: she had given him her prepaid one, which was still safer despite having been used several times already. They had agreed he would call her as soon as he was in Geneva and had passed immigration.

He had been to Switzerland once before on a skiing trip, and the abundant ads for chocolate, watches, and banks confirmed that nothing had changed since. He joined the queue for passport control and waited patiently, trying to recall some French words from school to greet people or buy a train ticket.

Then suddenly he saw them.

There were three of them, standing together somewhat behind the immigration cabins.

It was unmistakable.

They were talking to a uniformed Swiss officer, and each of them was holding a piece of paper. The three men themselves were not in uniform but in plain clothes. But that was exactly what had betrayed them: underneath their buttoned shirts all three of them wore white T-shirts, the edge visible at the collar. In the entire world, only Americans and Dutchmen had this sartorial habit! There was no doubt about it: *the Dutchmen were waiting for him.*

Daniel felt as if the ground disappeared under his feet and a rush of panic came over him. Kate hadn't anticipated this. *He was trapped!*

He tried to stay on his feet and stay as calm as possible in order not to attract attention. He looked in their direction from time to time to make sure they hadn't spotted him already. The pressure was unbearable, and he nervously scanned the information panels around him. He didn't understand the French texts, and for several minutes he just stood there, unsure what to do. Then the small Swiss and French flags on the information panels suddenly sparked a possible solution in his brain.

He looked at his waiting committee once more and then slowly left the queue, out of their sight. He walked back in the direction he'd come from, but instead of going to the gates again he quickly turned left into a long corridor. He look back, and noticed to his relief that for the moment, no one was running after him. He continued and passed a large, arrow-shaped sign:

FRANCE

76

Although he had the Swiss nationality and had spent most of his life in that country, Martello Rompivetro was proud of his Italian origins. Therefore he had chosen the Segafredo coffee corner as observation point.

He was sipping his third espresso since he had arrived, sweetened with the habitual two sugars. Before him lay the *Gazzetta Dello Sport,* but he had little attention for its contents. Not only because he had lost interest in sports in recent years—which the growing belly under his Armani pullover testified—but also because he couldn't relax his view of the gates, spitting out new groups of passengers every time a flight landed.

Some ten minutes ago he had spotted him. The target's plane had arrived from Amsterdam on schedule, and as expected the man had proceeded to the Swiss immigration checkpoint. There he had taken a place in the long queue.

A typical American, Martello concluded. Dressed as a businessman on holidays: a light-blue button-down shirt, khakis, and white sneakers. His hair was well cut, he had to admit, but it seemed very dark so he wondered whether the man dyed it, just as he did himself.

Martello noticed something was going on when all of a sudden the American started to look around frantically. First he thought that maybe the man had lost or forgotten something. That seemed confirmed a few minutes later, when the man left the queue and walked back the way he had come. But when the man subsequently chose the opposite direction from the gates he knew he had to be on full alert. He left the coffee bar in pursuit.

He was surprised the American had apparently chosen to leave the airport on the French side; from the short and urgent briefing he had received from his agents a few hours ago, he understood the target was heading for Switzerland, not France. But he knew from experience that anything could change. The man could have been scared off or simply have chosen the French side because it was generally less busy. He would have to follow him anyway.

The American passed the French customs without notable difficulty. In fact, the unexpected choice for the French side posed a slight practical problem for Martello himself, as his Alfa Romeo was on the Swiss side. On the French side he had a Ducati motorbike stationed permanently, but he wasn't dressed for it. He didn't even have a helmet, an object quite necessary for a dirty job like this—not so much for his safety but simply to avoid recognition.

From a distance he observed how the American entered one of the car rental agencies and was accompanied to the parking lot some ten minutes later. After the customary damage check, the American drove off.

Martello knew it would be crucial to predetermine the right spot for the job, so he simply followed him at a distance to get a clue about where the American was heading. If it was the city of Geneva, things could become difficult, as it meant a lot of bystanders and witnesses. But the fact that the man had rented a car hinted at a farther destination.

And to his relief it was. The American chose the D884 in a western direction, away from the city. After the village of Collonges he took the D1206 along the beautiful valley of the river Rhône and continued west for several miles in the direction of Bellegarde-sur-Valserine.

When they had almost crossed the village, the American slowed down considerably, as if looking for the right direction. Then he suddenly stopped altogether on the side of a roundabout, just opposite a small gas station. In order not to appear suspicious, Martello had no choice but to drive past the American and choose a direction on the roundabout. He decided to go north; it would be unlikely the American would do the same.

He was wrong. Two minutes later, the car passed him and accelerated sharply on the same road.

Damn! The American had looked at him.

The man's choice was inexplicable: he was going in the opposite direction of Switzerland.

Martello kept following him on the D101F, and a few minutes later the car's right indicator started blinking. It was the answer: he was taking the A40 highway!

Martello briefly panicked, as he knew the entry point of the highway had a toll station. Passing without a helmet could trigger alarms, and more importantly, he would be registered on camera! There was only one solution: *he had to strike before.*

With his right hand, he took the Beretta from the clip underneath the gas tank. When they had rounded the bend in the road, he noticed the viaduct somewhat farther on and decided that would be the point.

He accelerated the Ducati until he was right behind the American, and just before the viaduct, he overtook him on the opposite lane. When he was directly next to the car, he stretched out his right arm and aimed the gun in concentration. He briefly saw that the American noticed him, an expression of panic on his face.

Then there was a loud bang.

77

When Oscar Smeenk pulled aside the heavy curtain, a cloud of dust swirled up in the ray of light. *Very old dust,* he thought. Just as old as everything else in the room. Both the room and the endless hallway leading to it smelled of floor wax. It was no surprise: the floor, the ceiling, the furniture—everything was made of marvelously beautiful wood, the best available in the vast Dutch Empire during the palace's construction at the zenith of the Dutch Republic.

Through the window Smeenk looked down over Amsterdam's Dam Square beneath him and observed the busy buzz of bicycles, trams, and pedestrians. On two sides of the square huge podiums had been erected for the VIP guests to be seated during the ceremony. The other folks would have to content themselves with places behind the steel barriers in the far corners of the square, or watch one of the giant screens on which the live broadcast could be followed. Smeenk saw how the television teams were already busy installing the necessary cable work coming from the satellite vans that dotted the vicinity of the square.

Their temporary offices in the Royal Palace on Dam Square were truly *royal.* He had never been inside the famous building before, and he had to admit it was all splendor. Especially the large marble hall on the ground floor had impressed him; its lightness stood in stark contrast with the somewhat dark exterior. The stained exterior was, of course, mostly due to the town council's stupid decision to allow cars to circulate the streets directly around it, even after the costly cleansing operation some years ago.

In The Hague, they would have known better, he mused.

Although initially he had had his reserves when it was proposed to have the teams close to the new king during the event, he agreed it was a sensible idea after all. It would avoid losing valuable time in case critical decisions would have to be made. And above all, it meant they could keep an eye on the royal boy, making sure he would stick to the plan and not let him deviate from it by his mother, who was still ignorant of the whole scheme.

There was a knock on the heavy oak-paneled door. Smeenk turned away from the window, and his assistant entered, holding up some papers.

"Three new developments, sir! First a message from Madame Brise-Vitre, the lady from the consulate in Geneva. She informed us that Van Wart hasn't passed through the Swiss customs at Geneva Airport."

"What?" Smeenk roared in anger. "But how..."

"She thinks he left through the airport's French side. But has no means to check that."

Smeenk didn't understand. "The French side?" He tried to map Geneva's location in his brain. "Why would he go to France?"

"Maybe to avoid the Swiss side?" the assistant suggested. "Maybe somehow he knew they were waiting for him."

"Impossible! Unless that woman messed up somehow."

It wouldn't surprise him; he didn't have a high opinion of embassies in general. Their usefulness was highly overestimated, especially in Europe where all decisions were made in Brussels anyway. He started pacing around the room impatiently.

"France! Why would he go to France? I cannot think of any explanation! And certainly not so close to the event. We're talking *hours* now!"

"Maybe the other interesting piece of information may help, sir. The prepaid phone of Bates has finally been traced. And it looks as if the phone is traveling the same route as Van Wart."

"What?"

"The signal has been picked up a few kilometers from Geneva Airport."

"Incredible!" Smeenk exclaimed. "So they're traveling together! But how come we weren't informed of that?"

"Not necessarily, sir. Maybe Van Wart is simply traveling with her phone. Because there's some other information we just received."

"Tell me!"

"Bates is booked on a flight to Amsterdam."

Smeenk almost choked. It took a few seconds before he could speak.

"To Amsterdam? When? Today?"

"In a few hours. Coming from London."

Smeenk thought for a moment, rubbing his chin with his hand. "It may be a ruse. To put us on a false trail."

"Could be. But the ticket was booked with her credit card, also from London."

"It would be suicide! She knows she's being hunted. She may have been lucky when leaving the country, but when she reenters she'll be arrested immediately!"

"I already instructed the Marechaussee at Schiphol Airport again. Right after I received a confirmation call from Lieutenant General Bastiaans himself. The man knows a second failure is not an option."

"Good! But let our minister call London immediately to make sure they let her leave British territory, despite the international search warrant. We need to get her ourselves!"

"Very well, sir. Hadn't thought of that. And what about Van Wart? I would say he's our biggest problem; he has the file!"

Smeenk looked at him with a penetrating look. "There's something I haven't told you yet. I already sent someone after him. Two people, to be exact, including our chinny friend."

His assistant looked at him quizzically. "But, how did you...I assume you didn't contact them personally? It would be against the rules!"

"To hell with the rules! Things have become too critical now. From now on there're no rules anymore!"

The assistant didn't respond.

"Just make sure that our friend constantly gets the most recent info on where Bates's phone is going. It'll be crucial for him!"

The assistant nodded, and just when he wanted to leave the room there was a loud explosion.

Both men looked at each other in a slight panic and hurried to the window.

On the other side of the Dam Square they saw a cloud of white smoke hanging in the air, with several groups of horses behind it.

"It's nothing," Smeenk said. "They're just training the horses for possible riots."

78

Daniel opened his eyes and saw the thousands of pieces of broken glass lying in his lap. He barely dared to move, afraid that the pieces inside his collar would cut his skin. He didn't recall exactly what had happened, but there had been a loud bang, and the window of the car was smashed to pieces. He had ducked away in a reflex, at first he had thought it was the end of his life.

Shot by the biker with the gun.

But when he'd heard the noise behind him and saw the motorbike bouncing over the road violently, he immediately realized what had happened. The biker, too concentrated on the gun, hadn't seen the tractor coming from the dirt road. He must have hit him right at the moment he pulled the trigger.

The biker without helmet. Where had he come from?

Daniel recalled how relieved he had been earlier after passing customs at the French side of Geneva Airport, escaping the welcome committee on the Swiss side. But he knew things were still terribly wrong when he'd seen the biker a second time, waiting for him after the rotunda where he had looked at the road map. He had desperately tried to lose him, but he was no match against the fast and flexible motorbike. Then he had suddenly looked at the man, and the gun barrel pointed at him.

He was still completely numb from the action and couldn't remember how long he had driven since. He realized he desperately needed a break to calm down. And maybe eat something; his last meal had been at the airplane, just after takeoff from JFK. He exited the highway at Cluses, and along the main street of the small French town he found a bar restaurant.

A waiter wearing a red apron gestured him to the corner table, and it was only after he had devoured the first half of the plat du jour consisting of a steak served with *tartiflette*, followed by a double espresso, that he came back to life.

He recalled how he had stopped the car on the side of the road directly after the accident. But when the farmer stepped off the tractor seemingly unharmed, he had decided not to take the risk and look at the biker; after all, he had tried to assassinate him! So much had become clear from the action: he and Kate had largely underestimated their opponents—instead of being followed, they were hunted.

He noticed the numerous scratches on his hands and recalled how the woman at the toll station at the exit of the highway had looked at him strangely, probably surprised by the smashed window and the glass all over; he looked like a criminal on the run, and he realized she may have notified the police. And maybe the killer's masters also knew about the rental car. There was only one solution: abandon the car as soon as possible.

While drinking a second *double express*, he observed the comings and goings at the tiny gas station across the street. A pattern materialized. He decided it was his only chance. But it required a larger gas station with more people. He paid for his meal, memorized the waiter's directions, and drove off.

The Total gas station was not far and close to the highway. With close to a dozen pumps it was large enough for his purposes. He parked the rental car two blocks farther, then walked back to the gas station where he lingered around for a while, observing the cars around him. He noticed to his satisfaction that the station was operated by personnel and not self-service, which would have spoiled the plan.

When the owner of the Renault at pump number five walked to the building to pay, Daniel sneaked to it and grabbed the keys, which the employee had routinely put on the roof while filling up. He opened the door, started the engine, and drove off.

His heart was bouncing. Never in his life had he done such a thing before. And he never imagined that one day he would. He was now a carjacker, putting his career, his freedom, his life at risk.

He wondered how much time it would take before they came after him; in his mind he could already hear the cars with wailing sirens and angry French cops. It was a huge gamble, and he hoped the confusion at the pump would last long enough to allow him to escape.

And proceed with his plan.

Leaving Cluses behind him, he switched on his own cell phone. He knew it created a risk, as they could possibly track him through the signal. But he had no choice; he needed a phone number from his contact list. He wasn't sure whether he had kept it since the last time, and he was relieved when he found it.

He typed the number into Kate's secure cell phone and pressed Call.

79

Kate put the lipstick in her bag and threw a last look in the tiny airplane mirror. It was visible she had been under strain for quite some time now, but she decided her looks were good enough for the challenges that were awaiting her.

She readjusted the thin file taped to her body and breathed deeply. Then she opened the door of the onboard toilet and took her seat again. Five minutes later, the jetliner began the landing approach to Amsterdam Schiphol Airport.

After the aircraft was connected to the pier and Kate exited the plane, she immediately noticed the three officers waiting there. Two she recognized by their uniforms as Marechaussee, the other one was ordinary police. There was no doubt about it: they were waiting for her. The moment she set foot on the air bridge, one of the Marechaussees stepped forward.

"Are you Miss Bates?" he asked.

She swallowed. The muscled reception made her fear the worst.

"Not today," she answered defiantly.

The officers exchanged surprised looks. "No time for jokes, madam. You're under arrest."

"Under arrest? And on what charges, if I may ask?"

"That will be explained later. First, you have to come with us. And you'll have to wear these." The officer held a set of handcuffs on two fingers. "Please put your hands forward."

Knowing resistance would be useless, Kate silently stretched out her hands and felt two clicks. She followed the officers through the gate under the curious looks of the other passengers. She had heard from clients it was a humiliating experience, and now she witnessed it herself.

At immigration level she was guided through a labyrinth of corridors until they reached a room that was clearly an interrogation room: light, sober, and with the habitual see-through mirror.

"Miss Bates, you're under arrest, and you know why."

"Not at all; you just refused to tell me."

"Theft of state property. You're in possession of documents stolen from the Dutch state. Can I see your bag, please?"

"Never look in a lady's purse. Didn't your mother tell you?"

The officer ignored the remark and started emptying the bag on a table underneath the mirror. He quickly concluded it didn't contain what they were looking for.

"So where are the documents?" the officer asked when he turned around.

"Assuming I have them, I can't share them. They belong to a client of mine, so they're protected by legal privilege."

"So you do have them in your possession right now?"

"I didn't say that."

The officer looked at his colleague, then back at Kate. "Miss Bates, please hand them over voluntarily right now or we'll have to search you."

"You can't. You know the rules; you need a female colleague for that."

"I don't need anyone for that," the officer replied, visibly irritated.

"That qualifies as harassment. Can I see your ID, please? And also of the people on the other side." She pointed to the mirror. "They're witnesses."

The second officer stood up now. "Miss Bates, as you seem to know your rights so well, you'll also know exactly how long we can keep you detained. I suggest that you cooperate; it'll save you some uncomfortable hours. Now, I'll repeat the request one more time: please give us the documents."

"And what's my reward then for handing them over?"

"Maybe the public prosecutor will be more lenient."

"Now we're getting somewhere. So you confirm he'll press charges?"

"I'm sure he will, Miss Bates."

"Thanks very much, my boy, very smart. That confirmation means I now have the right to consult a lawyer first."

There was a brief silence in the room.

"I'm not sure it's in your interest to play smartass now, lady. For the last time: give us the documents."

"Ask your female colleague."

The officer nodded to his colleague, and two minutes later a big lady entered the room holding a pair of plastic gloves. "Follow me," she barked at Kate.

Kate followed her to the adjacent room and let the lady remove the documents from her waist. The tape left a burning sensation on her skin. An instant later, she sat opposite the officers again. One of them flipped hastily through the recovered documents and then stood up.

"They're copies!" he said, smashing the documents on the table. "So where are the originals?"

"On their way to a safe place," Kate replied.

The officers shot a surprised look to each other. "And where would that be?"

"I can't tell you yet. I need to see my lawyer first."

"Very well, Miss Bates. We'll get you a lawyer. While you spend the time in one of our cozy cells. And it may take some time before your lawyer gets here, I can tell you."

"I don't think so," she said with a smile.

The officer took his pen from his pocket. “Now who would your lawyer be?”

“His name is Van Olden. Hein Van Olden.”

On the other side of the mirror, Smeenk almost had a heart attack.

80

"Message received. Over and out." The Chin closed the satellite cell phone and leaned forward to the driver. "To Cluses! As fast as possible!"

The driver nodded, and one second later both men were pressed against their seats by the power of the accelerating V12 Mercedes.

It was a luxury he had rarely seen, even after so many years of work for the world's rich and powerful. What was curious, however, was that the identity of his client had been revealed to him so directly.

The Dutch royal family!

Of course he considered it an honor to work for them. He had marveled at the top-priority treatment, with a police escort directly to the airport. And the royal jet, for him alone. And the V12 with driver picking him up right at Geneva Airport's tarmac. It was his finest hour.

At the same time, he was curious about why his current target required such drastic measures. He imagined the operation wasn't without risk for the family itself; his mission would be political dynamite if the press got wind of it. But that wasn't his problem, of course, and his job was not to ask questions.

He looked at his Swiss Army watch. They had lost valuable minutes while waiting for the precise instructions on where to go; he knew his client's team first had to pinpoint the location where the target had made his call.

The V12 at full throttle, he switched on the reading light and unfolded the map the driver had given him.

Cluses, in France! Why leave the highway there? he thought, stroking his chin while studying the map attentively.

He recalled the briefing he had received earlier about his target's probable goal: Switzerland. When he saw the dotted line on the map, he suddenly had an idea what his target might be up to.

81

After having passed through the ski resort of Les Gets, Daniel drove the stolen Renault into Morzine, a pleasant valley town with high mountains sloping up on both sides. As it was in the middle of a skiing area, he passed large numbers of hotels and holiday chalets. They were mostly empty and the streets were deserted: it was early spring and the skiing season had just ended.

He had been there before during a ski trip some years ago; it had been his first holiday together with Melissa, and some memories started to surface. Although they had stayed on the Swiss side of the area in a tiny but marvelous mountain village named Champoussin, its ski slopes gave direct access to the French side, all without border checks. He was betting the free passage would still serve today.

A practical problem was of course that she ski season was over and the lifts were closed. But he had an alternative. During the same holiday that they had also made a slightly more adventurous trip, starting on the French side. It had been with a guide and he didn't remember the exact route, but he hoped his memory would be enough for the mission.

It had to be.

On the eastern side of Morzine he stopped the car briefly to look for directions. Then he turned right and sped away in the direction of l'Erigné. The road was narrow and winding and sloped up gently. From the trees and vegetation he could see that spring was arriving.

In the lower parts of the valley the snow had already melted away; only higher up was the white cover still visible. He hoped the snow would still be thick enough there, as doing the trail on foot would take far too long—the documents wouldn't be delivered before the event, and the mission would be a failure. It was a race against the clock.

He noticed how with every mile up the valley the human presence became less visible. There were a farmhouse every now and then and some telephone or electricity poles along the road. The road had become rough, and the stones and potholes tortured the car's suspension and bodywork incessantly. The sun climbed over the mountain ridge and illuminated one side of the enclosed valley; birds circled in the air enthusiastically. The view was spectacular, but also somewhat threatening due to the impressive rock formations enclosing the valley on three sides. It was the end of the world.

When he had reached the end of the paved road he parked the car. He left the keys inside, in an effort to limit the damage for its owner. He walked to the only building, a small inn, and knocked on the door. After minute he knocked again.

There was not a sound. Not inside the inn nor in the entire valley around him. He panicked slightly; his plan fully depended on what he needed from here.

Only after he had loudly called *"bonjour"* a few times someone opened the door. He was relieved when he recognized the weathered, oak-wood face.

The man had prepared the backpack and accessories just as he had requested over the phone. It had been a clumsy conversation in a mixture of bad English and even worse French, but apparently the man had understood what he needed and had preserved the earlier list in the name of Van Wart.

After Daniel had filled up the water bottle, put on the semi-flexible Asolo ski boots and paid for the equipment, he was ready—except for one thing: he had to call Kate to announce that he was still on his way to Switzerland. His escape from Geneva Airport and the catastrophic detour through France had slowed down the plan dramatically, and he could only hope it hadn't caused problems on her side.

He switched on her prepaid cell phone again, waited for it to find a network, and then dialed the number of her other cell phone. As it was probably being monitored, he kept the message short and cryptic. He waited for the call to be picked up, but after it had rung a few times he was transferred to voice mail.

Damn! He had hoped to hear her voice and know she was all right; her mission was at least as perilous as his. He left her a short message to announce the delay and then switched off the phone again.

He looked up and saw that the sun was already high in the sky. He knew he had to hurry in order to reach the summit of the range before sunset, a critical moment in unknown terrain. He fastened the hip belt of the backpack and started walking to the point where the snowfield started, on the shadow side of the valley.

Once in the snow, he clicked on the skis equipped with skins, and adjusted the length of the telescopic ski poles. He looked up at the mountains one more time, and from then on only focused at the advancing tips of his skis, gliding through the snow in regular traits. Left. Right. Left. Right. He felt how the spring snow was wet and heavy. The skis sank deeply into it, leaving a clear and uninterrupted trail behind him.

82

Because Schiphol Airport fell within the jurisdiction of the city of Haarlem, it was no surprise for Kate where they took her. Suspects arrested at the airport were often transferred for further prosecution to the large police complex on the banks of the Spaarne River, in the heart of Haarlem's city center.

Kate was led into one of the interrogation rooms on the ground floor, and the warden removed her handcuffs and left the room. It wasn't her first time here, and she may even have been in the same room before. But as a visiting attorney of course, not as a crime suspect.

Sitting alone in the room her thoughts went to Daniel. It was strange he hadn't called her the moment he had arrived in Switzerland, as agreed.

Had something gone wrong? Unless he had called within the last hour, after her cell phone had been taken from her.

The door of the room suddenly opened, and she recognized her visitor immediately. Hein Van Olden had become older, but the face was still the same as during that courtesy interview when he had been president of the bar, many years back.

"Well, what a pleasant surprise, Miss Bates!" Van Olden said, not hiding his sarcasm.

Kate stared at him without saying a word.

"So I understand you're in trouble and need a lawyer. Huh! I have to say, Miss Bates, from what I've been told, your case doesn't look good. Theft of state property is a serious offense. And even more so for an attorney! I'm sure you'll know what it means for your career." Van Olden remained standing, his arms crossed.

"I didn't steal anything, Mr. Van Olden. I was entrusted certain documents by a client."

"A *client*, you say? I'd say Evelyn was a friend!"

"May I remind you that under Dutch law, a lawyer's word cannot be questioned when it comes to his relationship with clients? Evelyn was a client, full stop. There's no rule excluding friends from clients—you taught that to me yourself."

"*Me?*" Van Olden asked in surprised. He quickly understood she must have been referring to his time as bar president. "That could be, Miss Bates. But then there's another thing you may remember. The fact that a lawyer cannot accept conflicting cases. And the file you have in your possession belongs to another client of mine, so I cannot accept your case. Quite painful you didn't remember that."

"So then why did you come here? Let's stop your formalities Van Olden, they're not going to save you. I have a file, and in view of its contents, your client understandably wants it back. So you'll have to deal with me to get it. Now let's come to business."

"That's blackmail, Miss Bates. Your position isn't getting any stronger with that. You're digging your own grave here."

"You're completely right—this is blackmail. Something your client is quite familiar with, so it seems we're working on equal terms."

Van Olden took the chair opposite her and looked her in the eyes sharply. "What is it that you want, Miss Bates?"

"Do you have a pen and paper? I have a shopping list. Number one, I'll be released from here immediately, and charges against me are dropped."

Van Olden's throat produced a quick laugh. "Miss Bates, you must have lost your mind. It's up to the public prosecutor to make such decision. You're talking to the wrong person!"

"No I'm not. If you can organize my arrest on bogus charges, you can also organize my release. Just talk to your friends again."

Van Olden was silent for a moment. "What else is on that list of yours?" He leaned sideways to a notepad from his briefcase.

"Second, a letter will be sent to the President of the United States of America, in which the Kingdom of the Netherlands renounces any and all claims, past or present, to American territory."

She paused a moment, while Van Olden scribbled frantically.

"Third, the new king will announce publicly that he will refrain from any form of political influence. Accordingly, he will publicly demand an amendment of the Dutch constitution, abolishing all royal rights and privileges."

Van Olden shook his head. "A change of the constitution no less! You're out of your mind, lady."

"Fourth," Kate continued, undisturbed, "that the Dutch royal family, from their personal fortune, will create a fund with the value of one billion US dollars to be administered by the Dutch state with a purpose I'll disclose later on.

"And fifth and last, that no Dutch king or queen will ever set foot anymore in the town hall on Dam Square, the symbol of the lost Dutch Republic."

Van Olden looked up. "You're not serious, are you? I'm wasting my time here with this nonsense. You know very well that none of it is feasible." He put the writing pad in his briefcase and stood up.

"You can think of it what you like, Van Olden; these are the conditions. To be met before the event, of course. Just try to imagine what will happen to your clients should the documents become public. The blackmailing of America. The scheme for the new king and his accomplices to abuse power. It may well cause the end of the

Dutch monarchy. In that perspective the conditions are quite reasonable, don't you think?"

"They're outrageous," Van Olden retorted.

"You better be careful, otherwise I'll add some more. What about the king wearing wooden shoes to all public events?"

"Miss Bates, I'm happy you haven't lost your sense of humor; it may come in handy when you're spending the rest of your life in jail. Because there's something you seem to forget: What proof do you have? The worthless copies you were carrying? Don't make me laugh. You'll have to come up with something better. And you can't, because the person you're relying on for the originals has been taken care of. Good-bye, Miss Bates."

Van Olden walked to the door and was let out by the ward.

A shockwave went through Kate's body. *Had something gone wrong with Daniel?*

83

The image of the small but powerful Swarovski binoculars came into focus, and for several minutes the Chin scanned the mountain range facing him.

Still nothing, apart from a herd of ibexes, high up against the rocks on the south face of the valley.

He put away the binoculars, drank some water from the aluminum bottle and continued his ascent. It was only a matter of time before his target would become visible. Luckily the man had been so stupid to leave clear traces right from the edge of the snow field, so it was child's play to follow him.

Earlier, when he had received the message that his target had made a call from the tiny dot on the map called l'Erigné, just after Morzine, the driver of the V12 had sped there and continued along the narrow and bumpy road until it became an unpaved trail. He had despaired, as the massive Mercedes couldn't continue there. But then he had heard the tinkling engine sounds of the other car parked there: the hot hood confirmed his target had also stopped there. He had walked to the inn across the road but found no one but the innkeeper. The man had been difficult to understand, but his own level of French obtained during his years in the Brussels crime scene was sufficient to understand that the target had just left. *On skis!*

The man had initially not been very cooperative, and it was only after he'd shown him the gun that the man understood the urgency and handed over the necessary equipment. Unfortunately he didn't have boots in his size 46, so blisters were building up already, the hard plastic scrubbing his skin at every step.

But what bothered him most were the small UFO-shaped clouds above the mountain summits combined with the sudden brisk wind: it meant the weather was worsening. The fact that the ibexes were already visible from low altitudes confirmed his diagnosis.

He continued his ascent, increasing his speed slightly. In the beginning the terrain was easy, with softly sloping fields and pine woods, passing an uninhabited farmhouse every now and then. But above a certain altitude, the terrain became rougher, and the ski trail became less straight in order to circumvent the large boulders and rock formations. Before him, he saw his own shadow, plodding through the snow: a lean man with ski poles and a bulky rucksack. And sticking out in the air a pointy object he had also taken from the inn: a long-barreled hunting rifle.

84

The climb in the heavy snow exhausted Daniel. Panting profoundly, he leaned on his ski poles for a moment and regretted his unhealthy lifestyle as office worker. His weekly jog in Central Park was clearly not enough, and his body was unfit for such effort. In addition, the mountain air had become thinner now he had reached a considerable altitude after several hours of climbing.

On the map he had seen that the crossing point at the top, named Col de Cou, was at 1,921 meters, which he estimated as more than six thousand feet. The tour guide of the previous trip had explained that the pass was heavily used by migrating birds and even had a small bird observation cabin on the top. As the pass formed the exact border between France and Switzerland, in the past it had also served as smuggling route. Daniel was betting the route still functioned today.

The sun gone now, the combination of altitude and wind had made the temperature drop considerably. It made walking easier, but from time to time he had to turn his face away to shelter from the whirlwinds that blew up icy crystals. Even more bothersome was the reduced visibility. At moments he card hardly see the tips of his skis.

He slogged on, knowing that it couldn't be too far to the top of the pass anymore. Even without visibility he would know when he reached it, because the earth would simply start sloping downward again. On the top he would only have to find the mountain shack he remembered, which he could use as shelter. It was probably closed and he would have to break in, but inside he would eat the small cheese and sausage the innkeeper had packed, and roll out his sleeping bag to get a few hours of sleep. It was a stimulating thought, as the cold, the hunger, and the fatigue were testing his strength incessantly.

It had started snowing, and his clothes were already covered by a layer of white powder. It worried him; he was not at all prepared for such weather conditions. In vain he had searched the backpack for goggles; the icy wind entering his eyes from the sides of his sunglasses caused stings of pain, the first symptoms of freezing of the retina.

Just walk on, Daniel. There was no alternative.

The terrain became very steep now, which seemed to indicate he almost reached the top. But without visibility he wasn't sure where he was going; if he walked too far to the side, he could miss the pass and continue climbing the mountains on either side of it, with steep rock formations and abysses. Maybe he had embarked on the hazardous mission too lightheartedly.

No, he shouldn't worry, he told himself. He would just have to walk on, and the cabin could appear from the mist and snow anytime now.

But it did not happen. When he had walked on for another hour, he noticed the start of twilight. The wind had turned into a gale, sometimes almost making him lose balance. He stood still for another moment, leaning forward on his ski poles. He was exhausted. All he wanted was to lie down in the snow. Just for a short while. Just to get his breath back.

The thought scared him. He knew it was a mountaineer's kiss of death: lie down, fall asleep, and freeze to death. He had to continue until he found shelter. He forced his legs to continue the slow and desperate climb. His mind had become numb, his legs were senseless, and his toes and fingertips were frozen.

He was going nowhere.

Daniel had lost all sense of time and direction when his skis suddenly hit something frontally. He tumbled over in the snow, dizzy for a moment.

What had happened? A boulder?

With one of the poles he groped in front of him. He felt a hard object. He took off his sunglasses and tried to see something while pressing his eyes to keep out the hurting crystals. He saw the dark contours of something. It looked like a huge rock, covered with a large overhanging layer of ice and snow. Had he reached the rocks? *It meant he had missed the house!*

He lay back in desperation. Looking at the snowflakes racing by in the wind, he felt a smooth sort of peace drifting over him. Despite the frozen cheeks and ice patches around his mouth and nose, he pulled a smile.

It was wonderful! He wanted to doze off slowly again.

No! A last convulsion of consciousness made him veer up. With all the power he had left, he ejected his skis and crawled toward the rock. He stashed the backpack against the rock, and with one of the skis started hacking in the icy mass underneath the rock until a cave-like hole formed, protected from the wind by the overhanging ice cap. The effort was almost unbearable. With his feet, he pushed the removed snow and ice toward the exterior of the hole, forming a protective rampart. He fenced the hole off as best as he could with the skis, the poles, and the climbing skins.

Inside the cave he spread out the aluminum emergency blanket and emptied the backpack. He wrapped himself in the sleeping bag and put the backpack around his feet for extra warmth. From the pile of gear, he retrieved the two cell phones and dropped them through his collar under his T-shirt. Their cold surface made him shiver, but there was no other solution to keep their batteries alive.

With a Swiss Army knife he cut some slices of the sausage. It was almost frozen, just like his senseless fingers. While he sat there chewing the salty meat, he felt how the cold slowly crept up and paralyzed everything. He looked outside through an opening and saw that it was completely dark now. The wind howled, and snowflakes shot by horizontally. For a moment he thought he saw a light moving some few hundred yards lower; the cold was probably making him mad.

In his insanity he thought about ways to warm up. He was tempted to pee in his pants, but the brief moment of warmth would quickly transform into a mortal cold. He felt and touched the objects next to him and held up the lighter.

He could make fire! Burn his skis? His backpack? He needed paper.

He touched next to him again until his fingers found the slim steel tube.

The documents! Paper!

He took off one glove and unscrewed the tube's cap, letting the roll of documents fall out into his lap. He took a sheet and lit the lighter: the magic yellow light instantly transformed the pitch-dark cave into a cozy space.

Fire. Warm fire!

The document he held looked old, and he stared at the American eagle logo on its top holding the arrows, transmitted from the Dutch lion as a symbolic Olympic flame, to be transmitted again and again until all countries lived in freedom.

In a last spark of consciousness, he put the lighter away from the document.

He was holding that flame!

85

In the palace on Dam Square, Oscar Smeenk stood up from the high oak-wood chair and looked at Van Olden in astonishment.

"Release her? For the moment she's all we got!"

Van Olden fumbled with his golden pen and tried to remain unmoved by the physical aggressiveness that was facing him.

"By releasing her she won't escape, Oscar. Don't forget, she came back from England intentionally to let us arrest her. She also needs *us* for her mission to succeed!"

Smeenk reflected on the statement and frowned his glasses back up his nose. *It was typical Van Olden,* he thought. He didn't like the man, but he had to admit he was brilliant at recognizing interests and transforming them into something manageable, manipulating them to align them with his own interests. A form of intellectual judo, which had made him the top lawyer he was.

"She'll get back to us with the original documents," Van Olden continued. "She'll understand very well that's the least we need in exchange for her demands. And for the moment she can't, not only because she's in captivity but also because your man is taking care of Van Wart and the documents as we speak."

"But that's the point. When we release her, she'll do everything she can to help him!"

"But what can she do? You just told me Van Wart is somewhere high up in the mountains, with a killer on his back."

Smeenk nodded. "What about Bates' other terms? We all know they're unacceptable."

"Are they really?" Van Olden asked rhetorically. "Did you discuss them with the Orange family?"

"Good God, no!"

"And the financiers?"

"I informed them an hour ago. But you know them. They didn't move an inch and insisted on proceeding with the entire operation. They said it was up to us to solve the problem. Immediately. Anyhow."

The men looked at each other in desperation.

Van Olden now also stood up, putting him on an equal level with Smeenk. "I'm not so sure the demands are so unrealistic. Think about it. If the Oranges are faced with the choice between sacrificing a small portion of their rights and capital, or risking a major media frenzy that has the potential to end the Dutch monarchy, they'd better choose the first option. Remember, Bates didn't ask for renunciation of the throne. Nor for the Orange capital to be handed over entirely. She could have, though."

Smeenk agreed Van Olden had a point. "The money won't be the problem. But a change of the constitution, dammit! How can we ever manage that?"

"That's only for later! It would take time, and she knows it. It can't be done in a day. At the moment, it would only be a promise. It would buy us time!"

Both men looked up in surprise when a bright light moved over the room's wood-paneled ceiling. They realized it came from the spotlights being installed below on Dam Square. The preparations continued day and night now.

"One day, Van Olden. That's all that's left!"

"All is in the hands of the killer now. Do you know who he is, if I may ask?"

"The same who took care of your colleague. Well, former colleague."

"Seems to be a pro then. So I confirm to Bates that we agree, and we'll wait for the agent's final confirmation."

Smeenk didn't answer, but Van Olden knew enough. He noticed how Smeenk's hands trembled when he unscrewed the cap of his bottle again. The coming hours would be decisive, and transform the rest of their lives in either heaven or hell. Without saying a word Van Olden left the room and started his descent through the palace, until the echo of his footsteps on the marble floors died away.

86

The soft light of daybreak lit the white mountain landscape, and the eastern flanks of the summits bathed in a pink glow. The beams that penetrated the cave woke Daniel up, and he slowly opened his eyes.

He noticed the small space around him, and it took some time to remember who and where he was. But then he realized he was alive. Cold to the bone, but alive. He raised the upper half of his cramped body and peered through the tiny hole the snow had left. The gale had stopped, and the sky was blue.

He cleared some of the snow and looked at the landscape in front of him. Lightly sloping pristine white plains, with the majestic rock formations of the Dents du Midi towering behind them, small clouds of white powder blowing from the summits. It was beautiful, and under normal circumstances a mountaineer's dream.

Where would he be? How far from the cabin on Col de Cou? He took a sip from the water and noticed the bottle was almost frozen. He bit off a remainder of the cheese and only when the first crumbs entered his empty stomach he felt how hungry he was. While devouring the cheese, he moved his fingers and toes to try to warm them up, but it was in vain. He put some of the stuff back into the backpack and decided to leave the voluminous sleeping bag behind.

A massive layer of snow had fallen, and he had some difficulty freeing himself from the ice cave. Standing outside, he let the sunrays warm his face. Then he walked some steps in the deep snow to look beyond the rock.

The cabin! A few hundred yards below him on his right. He had simply walked past it, invisible in the gale. A high serpentine of snow had been blown around it by the wind, and one of the shutters was open. Probably by the storm, he guessed.

He removed the skis from the cave and placed them in parallel before him. No need for the skins anymore. From now on, it would all be downhill. The snow made crispy sounds when he clicked his shoes in the bindings. Then he fastened the backpack and put his hands through the loops of the ski poles.

Suddenly he heard a loud bang, immediately followed by its echoes through the surrounding valleys. He felt something had hit him, and when he looked sideways, he saw a tiny stream of water pouring out of the steel bottle through a round bullet hole.

A shot!

Instinctively, he let himself fall on the ground. *A hunter? Swiss border patrol?*

Over the edge of snow he looked in the direction the shot had come from. He saw how the cabin door opened, and a man in a black-and-yellow parka walked out in a quick pace. *The open shutter! Someone had been there!* Had they chased him all the way up here?

He quickly got up and tried to accelerate. But the deep snow was heavy, so the skis didn't collaborate. With all his strength he plowed forward, his arms making spastic movements to gather extra speed.

A second shot resonated in the valley.

Daniel watched how in the distance the shooter also tried to accelerate on skis. Luckily the cave had been in slightly steeper terrain than the cabin, allowing him to gain speed more quickly. He put himself in the low *schuss* position to reduce air resistance—and limit exposure to the gunman.

He quickly scanned the landscape in front of him. He didn't exactly recall the route they had taken last time, but they had kept somewhat to the left, he thought. With a wide turn he steered around a hump in the mountain, giving him temporary cover from behind.

The snow was even deeper here, not blown away by the winds higher up. Waves of powder snow gulfed up unto his middle, sometimes even touching his face. His speed was so high now that he made as few turns as possible. A fall would mean the end for him, as a lost ski would be impossible to retrieve.

He continued to the left side of the crescent-shaped valley and looked back: the gunman was still following in the distance.

Bang! Another shot.

In the open landscape, there was nowhere to hide, and Daniel realized he was a lame duck for the gunman. He steered sharply to the steeper right, increasing his speed even more. He decided to cut through a small group of trees for temporary shelter, although he had no idea what was behind them. Branches laden with snow slapped him violently as he slalomed between the pine trees. Then suddenly, the earth disappeared beneath him. The trees had hidden a crevasse.

A wave of panic shot through his body, and several seconds later he landed in the snow again, his lungs pressed by the impact. What followed was a balancing act to stay upright, one ski in the air. *He had been lucky.*

Just before another cliff he steered sharply to the left and noticed he was on the right track: somewhat farther he saw the colored poles demarking the remains of the Ripaille ski slope. He looked back and saw the gunman passing the bush on the side, avoiding the crevasse. The man was closing in.

The ski slope was still in the shadow and as hard as rock. His straight tour skis weren't adapted to the surface and he had difficulty mastering them. The hard surface also made his speed increase instantly, and the bumps in the slope made his legs numb.

At high speed he passed Chez Marius, the cozy terrace with panoramic views he recalled so well from before. From there, the slope became a path, and in schuss he tried to gain maximum speed. At the hairpin turns in the route, he hung so low that his hand touched the snow.

After the bridge over the small stream, the path continued through the pinewoods. In a sharp bend he was just able to avoid a Ratrac transport caterpillar coming from below, and when he cut off another hairpin, he lost a ski pole in the balancing act that followed. They were at far lower altitude now, and at certain points the snow had completely disappeared; from time to time a jump was necessary to avoid the grass and mud.

Once they approached the flat clearing at the end of the slope, his speed decreased, and he knew it would be a decisive moment.

Another shot echoed through the valley, with flocks of black rooks flying up from the trees in panic.

He noticed the barrier in front of him marking the end of the slope and the beginning of the road.

Now there was nowhere to go!

Then he saw the contours of the yellow Postbus approaching behind the trees, and didn't hesitate a second. He passed underneath the barrier and slid onto the road. The skis made a terrible noise on the asphalt as he slid toward the Postbus in front of him. Once in reach, he clung on to the ski rack mounted at the back of the vehicle and pulled himself up. The bus accelerated, and when he slammed off his first ski on the road beneath him it bounced violently several times on the asphalt before disappearing in the bushes.

There was a shot again, and a fraction of a second later his other ski transformed into a bundle of splinters of wood, steel, and plastic. In the distance Daniel caught a last glimpse of the gunman in the black-and-yellow parka, throwing the rifle on the ground in anger.

87

The Chin picked up the rifle again and hung it over his shoulder, still blaming himself for the missed shots. There was not a minute to lose. He could still follow the bus if he was quick enough. He scanned the situation around him for a solution, and he found one immediately. He kicked off his skis and walked to the ground station of the chairlift where two men were busy with maintenance work.

"Le moto est à vous?" he asked, pointing to the Honda TransAlp motorbike standing next to the lift's ground station.

One of the men looked up and nodded.

"Les clés! Vite!" the Chin commanded, taking the rifle in his hands again.

Perplexed, the two men looked at each other, and one of them started to search his pockets frantically.

The Chin took the key and walked to the motorbike. When its powerful engine started, he slung the rifle over his shoulder and accelerated across the muddy field onto the road.

After a few bends in the narrow road, he entered a town called Champéry. He followed the main road and suddenly saw the Postbus. It was standing in front of a strange, cathedral-like building with an open facade. He braked sharply and studied the building more carefully.

A cable car station!

He parked the motorbike in front of the entrance ramp, and when he saw numerous people around the place, he realized he couldn't take the rifle. He took it from his shoulder and pushed its barrel in a flower bed. A waste, he thought, as he had been surprised by its pleasant use; it lacked only a gunsight for precision. Now he would have to rely on his handgun again.

He ran up the ramp and instantly saw a small red train putting itself in motion. *The cable car station was also a train station!* He quickly looked inside the station, but it was empty, so he concluded his target must be on the train.

"Ce train, quelle destination?" he asked the first person he saw.

"Aigle."

He knew the word meant "eagle" in French, but he had never heard of the place. He studied the regional transport map on the wall and found it, just below the eastern tip of Lake Geneva. He ran down the ramp, kick-started the TransAlp, and drove off again.

From Champéry he followed the winding road down to Val d'Illiez. It offered magnificent views but he had to concentrate exclusively on the road with its continuous play of turns and bends. From time to time he caught glimpses of the red train, which followed a separate track, not parallel to the road. He continued through the village of Troistorrents until he reached Monthey, at the foot of the mountains and on the edge of the flat Rhône Valley. The train tracks led him to the station, but when he entered the place the sight of several similar red trains surprised him. *It could be any of them!*

He hesitated, not sure his target's train had already arrived. Should he ask? Or simply continue the route to Aigle and wait for him there?

His cell phone rang.

"He's going to Chillon!" the voice said.

He immediately recognized the heavy Dutch accent but didn't understand what he was saying. "Going where?"

"Chateau de Chillon. It's a castle on Lake Geneva shore, close to Aigle. We just intercepted a telephone conversation between the target and the woman. She told him to go there."

"Okay, understood. I'll be there."

"It's taking too much time. Do it now!"

He wanted to reply but heard the man had already hung up.

He made an inquiry at the ticket desk, and two minutes later he sped away on the motorbike. *This time his target had no way out.*

88

There it was: Lake Geneva. The vastness of the view was breathtaking, and Daniel was surprised how close the train came to the waterfront. The lake's surface was so flat that it was almost a mirror, and the morning fog hanging just above it gave it a fairy-tale atmosphere. He looked back in the direction had come and saw the contours of the snow-capped Dents du Midi mountain range. He couldn't imagine he'd been up there only moments ago.

He had no idea where he was going. Kate's instructions had been very cryptic: a chateau just after Aigle. In the cozy old train from Champéry, he had inquired from an old couple about the chateau. They had given him directions, and pointing to his backpack they had asked if he was a mountaineer. He had nodded and quickly put his leg before the drinking bottle with the bullet hole. Then he changed his ski boots for his sneakers.

The next stop couldn't be far anymore.

The destination could hardly be missed: the massive stone walls and round towers of a typical castle from the Middle Ages rose from Lake Geneva, just as the old couple had described. The train slowed down, and the station of Chillon was announced through the speaker.

Daniel got off and walked through the tunnel underneath the train tracks to the footpath along the lake. He admired the contours of the castle, with the lake and the mountains in the back. It was one of the most stunning views he'd ever seen.

He looked back to see if anyone suspicious was following him, but apart from some obvious tourists nobody seemed to have left the train. He took the steel tube containing the documents from the backpack and put it in his jacket. He dropped the now useless backpack behind the bushes.

Once he approached the entrance of the castle, he hesitated. *Was he supposed to go in?* Or would someone to pick him up here? He had no idea; Kate hadn't given him any further instructions.

Should he try to call her? He wondered if his mission still made sense anyway. In twenty-four hours the royal ceremony would already be over, and the documents were still stuck in a remote castle in another country!

It was probably all lost.

He walked to the bridge connecting the castle to the shore but didn't see anyone waiting for him. He looked around in confusion; all he could see was a coach parked on the opposite side and some tourists crossing the pedestrian bridge over the train tracks.

Then he suddenly heard loud screams.

Tourists jumped aside in panic as a motorcycle came racing across the bridge. The bike skillfully steered down the ramp in the direction of the castle, and only when it came straight at him Daniel recognized the black-and-yellow parka.

He didn't hesitate a moment and sprinted to the castle. At the stone gate he jumped over the turnstile, staff shouting after him. He reached an open inside courtyard and looked back; the man came running toward him over the bridge.

He ran through a small porch that led to another courtyard, with a stone staircase. In big strides he mounted the spiral steps until he suddenly found himself in a large, majestic hall.

Unsure what to do next he briefly observed the hall, with its small widows and huge fireplace. In the middle stood a group of visitors, listening to a guide. He walked nonchalantly in their direction, as if admiring the abundantly decorated walls and ceilings, and joined the group; maybe the killer wouldn't notice him now.

Just when he realized his colored ski jacket could reveal him, the killer entered the hall. Daniel froze in fear.

The man scanned the room for a moment, then looked at the group.

Daniel quickly lowered himself, picked the cell phone from his pocket, and dialed Kate's number. He slowly rose again, but the first thing he saw was the killer's eyes. And his strangely protruding chin.

"Daniel, is that you?" Kate's voice creaked from the phone's speaker.

He couldn't answer, paralyzed by the killer's stare. From the other side of the group the man now came slowly walking toward him, holding his right hand inside his parka.

"Daniel, where are you? In the chateau?"

"Yes, I am," he whispered. "I'm dead, Kate. He's got me."

"Can you see the lake from there?"

He hesitated, not understanding her pointless question. He turned his head to the open window hole just behind him.

"Yeah. Why?"

The killer rounded the group and slowly came his way.

"Daniel, jump!" Kate shouted.

He was confused. *Jump through the window?* He looked at the lake deep down. *He was way too high!* He would undoubtedly crush all his bones in the shallow water at the castle's base.

The group of visitors started to move in the direction of the door. He was now alone against the killer.

"Daniel, are you there? Jump!"

The Chin took his hand from his pocket and pointed the gun toward Daniel.

Daniel's hands felt the granite contours of the hole behind him and he acted instinctively. He fell backward, ejecting himself from the window. In the dazzling free fall that followed, he heard the sound of a shot. Then everything went black.

89

The sudden appearance of the animal before the window scared Smeenk. He watched how the bird held several short branches in its claw and inserted them cleverly in the half-finished nest in the corner of the windowsill.

A pigeon, the most harmless of animals, he thought. He realized it was probably his general state of fear that caused the overreaction. Then his eyes focused again on Dam Square below him, his thoughts back on track.

How was it possible? Or was it pure bluff of the Bates woman? According to Van Olden she stated that the American had been able to get the documents into safety, and therefore insisted on her demands. *It would mean the hitman had failed.* But Bates had not provided them with any proof.

There was only one way to verify things: call the hitman himself again. But that was something he couldn't do in the presence of everyone there at the palace—he didn't know how he would react if the hitman's failure would be confirmed. It would mean the case against them was complete now; it would mean the game was over. The masterful plan and several years of planning all gone up in smoke.

While putting some items in his briefcase he contemplated his own fate. There was no doubt about it that all traces of the operation would lead to him. The preemptive measures. The illegal wiretaps. And even the killing of Van Olden's colleague. If the plan succeeded, none of it would matter, as the team's almost-limitless power would protect them against any indictment. But now, all could be different. Not for the House of Orange, of course, or for the financiers. Although they would probably have to accept most of the conditions and give up a considerable part of their power and wealth, he was sure their lives would continue more or less unaltered. But for him, and possibly for that fool Van Olden, things were not the same. His knowledge was now a liability for the House of Orange. He would be the hunted man himself. Gone was the prospect of the quiet life at the cottage in France.

As a doomed man he descended the marble palace stairs, past the hundreds of people busy with the preparations for the next morning. Stylists, television cameras, florists, security men—the Royal Palace had transformed into a beehive. He had to flash his badge several times to get through the hermetic security fences, then walked past the thick walls to the palace's backside on the Nieuwezijds Voorburgwal.

He forced his overweight body to run for the yellow tram that was waiting at the stop, knowing that it could very well be the last one before the entire area of the city was closed off. There was a notable buzz in the city, and the tram in the direction of Central Station was packed. He noticed he sweated profusely when he left the tram and walked into the station.

The local train in the direction of Utrecht was supposed to be gone already, but the large information panel indicated a delay of about ten minutes. He moved up the escalator to platform 2b, and only when he'd already taken a seat in the first-class compartment he realized he'd forgotten to buy a ticket. The last time he had used public transport was years ago, now used to moving around the royal way, separate from the herds.

When the train finally set itself in motion, his trembling hand took his cell phone, and he finally made the call.

"Tell me what happened," he simply commanded.

"Difficult to say at the moment," the Chin answered.

"What do you mean? I understood you missed, and the target got away!"

"Not necessarily. I shot at him, but not sure I hit him."

"How can you not be sure?" Smeenk asked angrily.

"He fell through a window twenty meters high into the water. Must have been shallow there, so he's probably broken his neck on the bottom."

"Probably? I have to be absolutely sure!"

"I immediately went down to verify, but there was no trace of him."

"So he survived and swam to the shore."

"Impossible. No one came out of the water."

"So what are you saying? That he simply disappeared?"

"I say he probably drowned. The impact and then the ice-cold water. No person can survive more than ten minutes in it."

"A boat?"

"Negative. The lake was deserted."

Smeenk was silent for a moment. *It didn't make sense.* Unless the Bates woman *was* bluffing and didn't have the documents at all! A sudden wave of optimism hit him. *Maybe things were not lost yet!* Maybe he had despaired too early. But he was already on the train now, moving away from the action. He looked through the window and saw the A2 highway in the distance with miniature cars slowly moving forward. It didn't matter, he concluded. There was no doubt that if the American had really survived—and with him, the documents—they would send the proof any moment. It would be better to be far away. Without anyone knowing where.

He decided to push for a last mission anyway. A horrible one, he admitted, but it was best for his daughter Jennifer's own future. Whatever the final outcome of the operation, it would mean at least one victory.

"Listen," he said calmly, "I have a new mission for you."

He gave him the name of his Jennifer's boyfriend.

90

The strong, gloved hand pinched Daniel's arm once more and shook it heavily.

Daniel opened his eyes hazily.

"Are you all right?" the black figure in front of him asked.

He looked around him and studied the narrow, tubular space around him. In the dimmed orange lights, he perceived another man, sitting in a cockpit-like space and handling a joystick. Lights flashed on a dashboard.

Where was he? A spaceship of some sort?

He felt a pinch in the arm again.

"Are you all right, sir?" he heard the man asking again. Daniel stared at him and noticed he was wearing a black diving suit.

Daniel nodded, still groggy.

"Great. Welcome aboard!" the frogman replied.

Daniel started to recall what had happened some moments earlier. The sudden tight grip around his ankle that had made him come back to his senses. Being dragged through the ice-cold water for what felt like ages, unable to breathe. Then something had been pushed into his mouth violently. He had wanted to resist, but when the flow of oxygen started he instinctively gave up and let his deprived lungs fill up again. Hands had pushed him inside a steel container, and after a shutter closed behind him, a machine was set in motion in high gear. After some seconds, his head came out of the water, and despite everything still being pitch black, he felt how the level of the ice water slowly dropped around his body. The warm air had felt like heaven.

When all the water had drained away, another hatch opened, and it was the man in black that grabbed him by his shoulders and pulled him through the hole. Only then did he realize he was breathing. *He was alive!*

"Do you have them?" the man asked in a heavy French accent.

Daniel didn't understand. "Have what?" he asked, still half-dazed.

"The documents!"

It took some more seconds before the question sank in. *The documents!* He immediately opened his soaking ski jacket, water seeping onto the steel floor. He touched and felt the object sticking out of his inside pocket. The steel tube.

The man took it and gave a thumbs-up and then turned back to the pilot.

"Got it! Full steam back."

The pilot pushed the joystick forward, and the sudden acceleration of the vehicle made both other men struggle for balance. The cabin light was dimmed even more and the green light of the radar screen was all that remained, giving a Martian-like glow to their faces. The frogman turned to the wall and pushed some buttons on a panel. Then he started a series of clicking sounds.

Daniel recognized them as Morse code. "Where the hell am I?" he asked the frogman.

"Lake Geneva! Can't you see?" the man said with a broad smile, pointing at a porthole.

Daniel saw nothing but blackness.

So they were underwater, in a tiny submarine!

"How deep?" he asked.

"Not much, about fifteen meters. But the lake's deepest point is around three hundred."

Daniel tried to calculate how many feet that was, but his mind wasn't ready.

"Where are we going? And who are you?"

"Don't worry, Mr. Van Wart. Just be patient. And take those wet clothes off; you might catch a cold. There's a towel hanging behind you."

Daniel realized that all he could do was obey.

91

The tiny submarine surfaced in a boathouse, and Daniel and the two other men climbed out of the vehicle through the narrow top hatch. Someone handed Daniel a thick bathrobe.

It felt like sheer luxury; he was still shivering from the cold water of Lake Geneva.

From the boathouse he was escorted over a neatly cut lawn, to a white mansion some two hundred yards from the water. He thought he'd seen the place before, in a movie or something. Or comic album. *Was it Tintin?*

They entered the villa through what looked like the kitchen, and Daniel was seated at the large table standing in the middle. A hot coffee was handed to him, and the smell of it alone already resuscitated him. He sat there in silence, warming his hands on the mug and contemplating where in God's name he had ended up. A door opened, and a look at the person's face made his jaw drop.

"Kate!"

"Hi Daniel. Good to see you again," she said with a broad smile. "I'm so glad you made it!"

"What the...But what are you doing here?" he stammered in disbelief. "I thought you were in the Netherlands and—"

"Don't worry, Daniel. Everything's all right now; we're completely safe here. Did they already tell you where we are?"

Daniel shook his head.

"On the northern shore of Lake Geneva. The Swiss side, so you made it. The villa belongs to a friend. Oh Daniel, I'm so glad you survived! You don't know how much I worried about you!"

"Thanks," Daniel muttered, still not understanding the situation. "I think I had some close calls coming down here."

Kate gave him a kiss on the cheek, making him feel slightly embarrassed.

"You owe me several explanations, Kate. What about this submarine? What about you here? Was it all planned?"

"You owe *me* an explanation, Daniel!" She took a seat at the table. "Why didn't you enter the country through Geneva Airport, as agreed? Our people were waiting for you there!"

"And so were others!" He explained how he had recognized the Dutch waiting committee.

"But what kept you so long afterward?"

"I knew an alternative route through the mountains. But I was surprised by a snowstorm. And chased by an assassin."

"The storm was on the news. Several mountaineers are still reported missing. But what assassin are you taking about?"

"In fact, there were two. One that chased me on a motorbike, from the airport. I lost him by chance in a road accident." He told her about the collision of the motorbike and a tractor.

"And the second one?"

"He suddenly appeared in the mountains this morning. Chased me on skis. I thought I'd lost him, but then he turned up again at the chateau. The last thing I saw of him was that he pointed a gun at me, then I jumped through the window. He fired a shot but apparently missed."

Both were silent for a while, contemplating how close it had all been.

Kate finally broke the silence.

"I didn't congratulate you yet," she said, taking Daniel's hand. "You saved the tube with the documents. And therefore the whole mission."

"I thought it would be too late. The coronation is tomorrow morning, isn't it?"

"Yep. But a scan of the documents is being sent to Holland as we speak, together with some proof we have the originals. It'll make some people very angry. Their game is over now, thanks to you."

"I'm not the only person to thank, Kate. I assume it was *you* who sent that yellow submarine and saved my life."

"That wasn't me, Daniel. All I knew was to guide you to the Chateau de Chillon. Apparently, it's built on some sort of large rock with a steep underwater cliff at its base, giving direct access to the submarine."

"So that's why I didn't break my neck. The depth of the water saved my life."

"And for the rest, you'll have to thank my friend next door." Kate nodded sideways.

"You mean the owner of this place?"

"I sincerely don't know if he's the owner, Daniel. I don't know him very well. In fact he's expecting us, so maybe he can explain everything to you. Shall we go in?"

Daniel looked down at his bathrobe and then back to Kate.

"Don't worry," she said. "We'll get you some clothes afterward."

They stood up and walked through the large hallway leading up to two massive wood-paneled doors. Daniel felt less exhausted now and was excited to know who the mysterious person was who had saved his life. And why!

Kate opened one of the doors, and when he looked inside he saw a man sitting at a desk at the far end of the room.

"Welcome to Switzerland, Daniel!" the man shouted in his direction.

He recognized the voice. *What the—it can't be!*

He was looking at William Lent.

92

The GSM telephone waves didn't take long to reach the yellow regional train that was advancing through the flat green landscape of the Dutch polders. Oscar Smeenk passively observed the narrow canals shoot by the window when his cell phone rang. He frowned his glasses up his nose and saw it was Van Olden.

It was all or nothing, Smeenk thought.

He listened to the message without saying a word and then pressed the red button to end the call. After staring out the window absent-mindedly for ten more minutes, he started composing a text message, which he saved as draft.

At the train's stop at the town of Breukelen, Smeenk got off and left the station in a westerly direction. He passed the large windmill and walked through the tunnel underneath the A2 highway. Immediately after, he took the small land road named Galgerwaard, parallel to a straight canal in the middle of the flat meadows. He knew the route like the back of his hand. He and his wife Hedwig had often sought the quietness of the town and the surrounding countryside as a retreat in the weekends.

He took his cell phone from his pocket and sent her the text message.

He looked back over his shoulder and saw the pointing summit of a small church towering over the village in the distance.

Breukelen.

Only now did he realize the irony of the location, as the name giver of Brooklyn in New York. The city where the whole adventure had started. He couldn't help thinking of the people some centuries ago who had made the brave leap from the earths he was standing on to the new and unknown territories on the other side of the Atlantic. People who may even have walked the same route he was now walking now. People in search of hope, forming the basis of a new, better society that would eventually grow into the world's most powerful country. A country that was now held hostage by a small group of descendants from its founders.

He was a traitor to his country, Smeenk realized.

He just stood there, staring at the horizon of the empty landscape. Large clouds quietly floated by, projecting their shadows diagonally in the bright Dutch light. On the other side of the water a group of black-and-white Frisian cows was grazing quietly, undisturbed by the sole man's presence.

Smeenk slowly raised his right arm.

A sudden shot ended the peaceful silence.

93

In the villa on the Lake Geneva shore, Daniel slowly walked over the thick carpet in the direction of the man on the other side of the room. He was flabbergasted and utterly confused.

"Hello, Mr. Lent," he said dryly. He didn't know what to feel. On the one hand he was very pleased to see him again, but at the same time he and Kate had clearly hidden information from him about the mission.

A mission that could have caused his death.

"I can see what you're thinking, Daniel, and we're going to set the record straight right away. But first of all, I have to compliment you on your courage. You did a fantastic job!"

"So you and Kate knw each other?" Daniel asked, straight to the point.

Lent briefly looked at Kate, then stood up and gestured Daniel to the lounge-like sitting area overlooking the lake. "Have a seat."

Daniel obeyed.

"The answer to your question is yes, we did know each other before. But our cooperation in this case was a coincidence. Do you remember I told you about that Dutch Republican Society?"

Daniel nodded.

"Both Kate and I were members, and we met many years ago. But since I left the society and retired, we lost touch until very recently, when Kate sought contact again for advice in a case concerning the

Dutch royal family. It was at exactly the same moment the Dutch Historical Society you met back in the Hudson Valley selected you for researching the property claims. At first, we didn't make the link between the two cases; it was only when you were already on your way to Europe and Kate and I spoke again that things suddenly dawned on us."

"In other words, we didn't intentionally frame you on the mission!" Kate added.

"But you could have told me when you found out!" Daniel retorted.

"No, we couldn't have," Kate said firmly. "At least, not without taking other risks."

"What *other* risks?"

Lent laid his hands on Daniel's shoulder. "We couldn't tell you without compromising our safety too. Both your phones were bugged."

"Bugged? But I used Kate's secure cell phone. And how do you know anyway?"

"The second killer, Daniel. He could only have followed you because you made phone calls to Kate at the villa here. Each time, you gave away your location."

He felt stupid he hadn't thought of that. At the same time, he wasn't completely convinced.

"So protecting your villa was more important than my life?" he asked, not regretting the provocative tone.

Lent stood up slowly. "This is not my villa, Daniel. It belongs to an acquaintance of mine. He leads the geologic research into the tsunami that destroyed Geneva about one and a half millennium ago. That's the reason we were so lucky to have the submarine here. The good man also allows this villa to be used by an organization we are both members of. The location serves as our meeting point, so to speak. Now, the organization can exist only so long as its members respect its secrecy. Whether we did the right thing by protecting our location, I will let you judge by yourself tomorrow."

"Tomorrow? Why?"

"Firstly, because you deserve a good rest first, with a hot shower and a good meal. Secondly, because tomorrow will be a critical day. Not only because we'll witness the passing of the throne in Holland and see what the House of Orange has decided to do with the document we just sent them, but also because there will be a meeting here at the villa of the organization I just told you about. Some influential people will be attending, and I have the honor to announce that both you and Kate have been invited to be present, as a reward for your efforts and what you did for the world."

Daniel looked at Kate, who seemed as curious as he was.

Part VIII

94

Daniel opened the large curtains of the bedroom and admired the breathtaking view over Lake Geneva, glittering in the morning sun. He had slept very well, which was no surprise after the uninterrupted action of the preceding days and nights. After taking a shower, he put on the fresh clothes that were left for him and looked in the mirror. Although at Stiglitz & Arrowsmith he probably would have been refused entry in them, he descended the large stairway, already smelling the fresh coffee.

He found Lent and Kate sitting in the magnificent garden room, with chairs lined up in front of a large screen. On a side table stood a platter with fresh croissants, fruits, and coffee.

"Good morning, Daniel," Lent greeted him. "I was just about to wake you up. Sit down quickly; the ceremony's starting!"

Kate gave him a wink, and he took the seat next to her to watch the screen. On the top left corner he read "Amsterdam—Live," and the image showed a large crowd in front of a palace-like building.

"It's the Royal Palace on Amsterdam's Dam Square. That's where the ceremony's taking place. There they are!" Lent pointed to the screen excitedly. It showed the queen and her eldest son slowly treading to the pair of thrones placed in the center of the large marble hall.

Daniel was fully awake now.

The commentator explained some ceremonial details of the passing of the throne and provided names of some other royal guests. From time to time, shots of the city of Amsterdam appeared, all dominated by the Dutch red, white, and blue flag together with orange banners.

A short ceremony followed, through which the new king took power. Then the new king's wife joined him, and together they started climbing the marble stairway.

The outside cameras now all focused on the facade of the palace and the tiny balcony overlooking Dam Square. When the balcony doors opened, the public on the square below cheered excitedly. The royal couple appeared, and the applause of the crowds intensified even more.

Kate watched in mounting agony how the new king waved to his subjects with white-gloved hands. His wife held her large hat with one hand while smiling broadly. Kate immediately regretted not having included additional conditions in the list she'd given to Van Olden. Due to a recent change in the law the woman would even carry the title of *queen instead of princess*—the first sign of the couple's megalomania. She bet that the next symptom would be the institution of the king's own birthday as national holiday, a common thing among undemocratic rulers.

When the new king stopped waving and approached the microphone placed in front of him, Kate gave in to her tension and grabbed Daniel's hand. They looked at each other briefly, knowing it would be the moment of truth.

The crowds became silent, and the king started his speech with some general remarks on the history of the House of Orange and its decisive role in the history of the Dutch nation. Then he followed with a brief overview of his mother's contributions during her reign. A notable excitement erupted when the king announced that he wanted to express his views and intentions regarding the fulfillment of his job.

Lent, Kate, and Daniel were all sitting on the edge of their chairs. They noticed how the king shifted the paper in his hands and paused briefly. Then he cleared his throat.

"I believe in a modern form of royalty," the king began, "whereby the role of the king, in accordance with basic democratic principles, excludes any political influence. For that reason, I will ask both government and parliament to work together on a change of the Dutch constitution, transforming the role and position of the king into a purely ceremonial one."

"Yes!" Kate flew up from her chair and cheered loudly. She took Daniel's face in her hands and gave him a kiss.

"Congratulations to you both!" Lent added excitedly. "You did it!"

"Hush! He hasn't finished yet!"

The king looked up from the paper. "A modern interpretation of royalty also implies that all members of the royal family should be submitted to the same tax laws as citizens. In addition, palaces and other property belonging to the Dutch state should not be claimed for use by the royal family without justification. Therefore, I have decided to abstain from any future use of the magnificent building where we are today, and hand it over the city of Amsterdam again for full public use, in line with its origins."

An enthusiastic applause from the Amsterdam crowds followed, and after a short session of waving and greeting, the royal couple disappeared from the balcony.

On the shores of Lake Geneva the cheers were not less abundant. Kate hugged both Daniel and Lent, who had the villa staff serve drinks to celebrate their victory. They observed the ceremony some more while sipping from their glasses. When they watched in satisfaction as the royal family's convoy left Dam Square, the large wooden door of the villa's garden room opened again, and a servant entered.

"Sir," the servant addressed Lent, "I have been asked to accompany the three of you to the conference room. You are expected now."

95

Kate and Daniel followed Lent's footsteps through one of the corridors of the Swiss lakeshore mansion, excited about what was to come.

"What's that?" Daniel asked, surprised by a sudden roaring sound.

"A helicopter," Lent said. "It probably just brought in the last attendants."

Daniel looked out of a window but didn't see anything, apart from several limousines lined up on the parking lot. *Influential people*, Lent had said: Daniel was very curious now.

Kate and Daniel were guided to the basement floor. Their footsteps resonated on the stone floor of the long corridor. Dimmed lights illuminated large wall carpets on each side. A servant opened another wooden door, and a large, windowless conference room appeared in front of them. When Lent entered the room followed by Daniel and Kate, the thirty or so people seated around the large table stood up and applauded.

Daniel and Kate looked at each other in surprise, not knowing what to expect.

While they were guided around the table to the three remaining empty seats, Daniel recognized some of the faces and was stunned: a former British prime minister, the founder of a major software company, and several other faces of the world's economic and political elite.

Lent hadn't said a word too much, Daniel thought. He immediately understood why the villa had to be kept secret at all costs.

Once they were seated, an older gentleman stood up and welcomed everyone briefly. He mentioned point one on the agenda and asked Lent to report on what was mentioned as his project.

Lent stood up again and started a speech.

"Ladies and gentlemen, I'm very pleased to announce that my project has come to an end today. And a happy end at that, as the largest obstacle on our path has been removed. You will recall the dire position the world had been brought to by a group of individuals connected to the Dutch crown, all based on a centuries-old claim of Dutch ownership of the American territory comprising roughly the state of New York. The claim forced the United States to temper its ambition to promote republicanism in the world, and close its eyes to undemocratic developments in the Netherlands. As a result, both countries have relinquished their true history and the links that bind them, and they have aborted the historical mission on which they had once embarked: making the world a better place. It's a mission that also lies at the heart of our distinguished society reunited here today, and a mission that, as from today, can be continued by both countries where they left off.

"The history of the United States will have to be rewritten slightly. To this end, Mr. Van Wart, sitting next to me, has already contributed greatly. As far as the Netherlands is concerned, its citizens will have to decide how they wish to organize their state: as the famous republic that has made it a great country, or as the kingdom that it currently is. One thing is sure, however: the populations of both countries are well placed to contribute to our geopolitical goals. We now know their similarities are no coincidence, as America is merely the continuation of the Dutch Republic, with New Netherland as seedling.

"In the past, some courageous people, most notably President Franklin D. Roosevelt, have tried to remove the obstacle from the path named progress, but in vain. It is only today that both countries finally have their hands free to actively pass on the flame to the rest of the world. Thank you."

A brief applause followed, and Lent took his seat again while the society's chairman took over.

"Thank you, Mr. Lent. An excellent result. And as a sign of appreciation it was decided unanimously and exceptionally to grant both Mr. Van Wart and Miss Bates authorization to stay with us for the rest of this meeting. Now I would like to go to agenda item number two and ask the member concerned to report on his progress."

While another speaker rose, Lent took the meeting agenda lying in front of him and passed it to Kate and Daniel. It had no title, no logo, and was undated.

Kate and Daniel looked at the document for some seconds and then at each other in amazement. They were looking at a list of some of the largest problems the world was currently facing.

Was Lent's society trying to solve them all?

Daniel leaned backward and pulled both Lent and Kate toward him.

"Thank you, Mr. Lent, for having us here. And for all you did for us," he whispered.

Lent shook his head. "You should thank Kate. She was the one who negotiated with the House of Orange. And as we've seen, all of the conditions have been granted!"

Kate smiled at them and raised her finger in objection. "No, you're wrong. There's still one thing missing."

Both men looked at each other quizzically.

"What?" they asked at exactly the same time.

"Surprise!" Kate said with a big smile. "It's a gift for you, Mr. Lent. I'm sure we'll hear about it very soon."

96

After the White House press assistant had adjusted the microphone to the right height, the President took his place behind the world's most famous lectern—the one adorned with the Presidential seal and the eagle holding arrows firmly in its left claw. The President laid his notes in front of him and waited for the signal that sound and camera were ready.

"Ladies and gentlemen, good morning. Today is a memorable day for the United States of America, as I can announce a very special project, which pays tribute to the history of our nation and its people. More specifically, a tribute to the very founders of our country: the Dutch settlers and their colony New Netherland. Although our nation, through its famous melting pot, is the fruit of countless people of many origins and cultures, there is no country that has left such a fundamental imprint on American history and culture as the Netherlands.

"Unfortunately, that part of our history has remained relatively underexposed, and some recent developments have forced us to reconsider that situation. It is therefore with considerable pride that I can announce the development of the Dutch Heritage Monument and Theme Park, which will highlight the joint Dutch-American history and other aspects of the country that shaped America.

"Of course, there is only one place where such a center can be located: in New York City, the city previously known as New

Amsterdam. The federal government will work closely together with the mayor of New York, who has already pledged me his full cooperation in finding a suitable location, on or close to Lower Manhattan.

"For this symbolic project to materialize, we can largely rely on the largest private donation the United States ever received, made very recently by a donor who choose to remain anonymous.

"I firmly believe that the project will contribute to commemorating and reinforcing the principles of independence, democracy, and liberty that laid the foundation for both countries, and guaranteed their prosperity. And I sincerely hope it can function as a reminder and provide hope to all people who live in places in the world where these principles have not been established yet. In the words of the great Franklin Delano Roosevelt:

"In the truest sense, freedom cannot be bestowed; it must be achieved."

Epilogue

After Daniel Van Wart enjoyed a prolonged stay in Europe, a large part of which he spent visiting the Netherlands, he returned to the United States. The firm Stiglitz & Arrowsmith ousted Van Olden as a partner when his role in the plot and blackmail of the United States became clear. The firm rehabilitated Van Wart and asked him to resume his work, an offer he is still considering.

Kate Bates continued her practice as an attorney in Amsterdam, focusing on cases involving human rights issues. She was asked by the Dutch parliament to become a member of the drafting committee for the amendment of the Dutch constitution abolishing all royal powers, which she accepted. Due to her role in the disruption of the conspiracy, she was awarded a decoration by the Dutch state, the Order of Orange-Nassau, which she refused.

William Lent was named by the American President personally as a member of the committee overseeing the development of the Dutch Heritage Monument and Theme Park. In parallel, he continued his involvement in the secret society attacking the world's major obstacles for progress. He still lives in the Hudson Valley.

The Chin managed to escape from the chateau. When he learned of Smeenk's suicide during the preparations of his latest assignment, he gave up the mission. With the money earned on his missions for the Dutch crown, he decided to retire.

The Dutch king accepted his new role, limited to a purely ceremonial one, and exercised his reign in conformity with it. He was the last Dutch king to exercise royal influence on Dutch politics by putting his signature under the bill that changed the Dutch constitution to abolish all royal powers. The Orange capital that remained after the American donation was rendered public, submitted to taxes, and placed under custody of the Dutch state.

The American President set in motion the development of the Dutch Heritage Monument and Theme Park, triggering a nation-wide boost in interest in the country's history. He was reelected with a large majority.

About the Author

Zachary Finch is an international lawyer. He currently lives and works in Paris, France.

Sources & Further Reading

Campbell, Douglas—*The Puritan in Holland, England and America (Vol. I, II)*

Coenen Van Torchiana, Henry Albert Willem—*Holland, The Birthplace of American Political, Civil and Religious Liberty: An Historical Essay*

Goodfriend, Joyce D.—*Before the Melting Pot—Society and Culture in Colonial New York City*

Griffis, William Elliot—*Brave Little Holland, And What She Taught Us*

Griffis, William Elliot—*The Story of New Netherland*

Haring Fabend, Firth—*Zion on the Hudson—Dutch New York and New Jersey in the Age of Revivals*

Irving, Washington—*A History of New York*

Irving, Washington—*The Sketch Book of Geoffrey Crayon, Gent.* (contains *The Legend of Sleepy Hollow* and *Rip Van Winkle)*

Jardine, Lisa—*Going Dutch—How England Plundered Holland's Glory*

Jacobs, Jaap—*The Colony of New Netherland—A Dutch Settlement in Seventeenth-Century America*

Krabbendam, Hans; Van Minnen, Cornelis A.; Scott-Smith, Giles—*Four Centuries of Dutch-American Relations*

Panetta, Roger (ed.)—*Dutch New York, The Roots of Hudson Valley Culture*

Pirsson, John W.—*The Dutch Grants, Harlem Patents and Tidal Creeks*

Rose, Peter G.—*Food, Drink and Celebrations of the Hudson Valley Dutch*

Schama, Simon—*The Embarrassment of Riches—An Interpretation of Dutch Culture in the Golden Age*

Scheltema, Gajus; Westerhuijs, Heleen—*Exploring Historic Dutch New York*

Shorto, Russell—*The Island at the Center of the World—The Epic Story of Dutch Manhattan and the Forgotten Colony That Shaped America*

Stott, Annette—*Holland Mania—The Unknown Dutch Period in American Art and Culture*

Tuchman, Barbara W.—*The First Salute—A View of the American Revolution*

Van Der Sijs, Nicole—*Cookies, Coleslaw and Stoops—The Influence of Dutch on the North American Languages*

Veenendaal, Augustus J.—*Slow Train to Paradise—How Dutch Investment Helped Build American Railroads*

www.ingramcontent.com/pod-product-compliance
Lightning Source LLC
Chambersburg PA
CBHW022247020726
47496CB00004B/1108
9782955610206